Sea of Demons
Heidi Stark

Contents

INTRODUCTION

Sign up for exclusive content and her newsletter here.

You can also find out more about Heidi and her upcoming books on social media:

Facebook Page

Facebook Group

Instagram

TikTok

Important Note About this Book

This is a dark romance, which I'm guessing is why most of you are here.

But it does contain a number of triggers, including graphic violence and gore, graphic murder and torture, mentions of PTSD, depression and anxiety. It mentions sexual assault and other forms of abuse, as well as child abuse, child death and suicidal ideation. It also contains several graphic sex scenes for 18+ audiences including dubcon and somnophilia.

This is for everyone who needs a good vacation and something dark and smutty to read by the pool.

Chapter One

Skyler

"You can't kill me," he sneers, his thin-lipped mouth contorted in an ugly scowl. I don't know where Devon got her gorgeous full lips from, but it certainly wasn't from his side of the gene pool. "She'd never forgive you. She'd have nothing to do with you."

The tall, burly man has gone from having a strong posture and a calm demeanor to cowering and pale in a matter of minutes. I guess that's what happens when four bigger, younger, and stronger guys come to kill you.

We're inside an industrial warehouse abandoned partway through construction. The man sits in a basic metal chair to one side of the large space, shackled to an old metal radiator, with a large chain wrapped firmly around both his wrists.

Stacks of lumber and bags of cement line the room, and coils of hose and electrical wire protrude from the walls. Luckily for us, there's no shortage of places like this around here when we need to take someone somewhere to teach them a lesson.

Despite the man's visible fear, he won't stop talking and trying to convince us to change our minds. He seems deluded and full of bravado, despite the helplessness of his situation and the fact that what he's saying couldn't be further from the truth.

"Who?" Dom growls, his mouth clenched and his eyes narrowed.

We all know who the man is referring to, but we want to hear him say it.

"You know who I'm talking about!" he sputters, spittle flying from one corner of his down-turned mouth and landing on the floor about a foot away from Dom.

"Say her name," Dom demands again, his eyes flashing as he kicks at a nearby sawhorse as if to punctuate his point.

"Devon, you idiot!" The man's flinty eyes narrow into tiny slits as he glares back at Dom, but his derision doesn't hide his fear. His loud voice is just noise, at odds with his ashen face and the pulse straining through his corded neck. "My daughter. Who else would I be talking about?"

"Oh, she's quite aware of what we're here to do, and she's actually fine with it." Zeke's voice is calm and level like usual, despite the reason we're here.

"You can't be serious. I'm her father! She'd be devastated if I wasn't around."

His gaze betrays him, his eyes dropping to the floor as he realizes there's no way his daughter is coming to his rescue after everything he's done. His skin is developing a nervous sheen, similar to the dusty sheets of plastic and tarps that have been placed over tins of paint and the other construction supplies scattered across the room.

"You're deluded, buddy," Rake shakes his head, causing his dark curls to bounce against his shoulders. An eerie calmness replaces his normally jovial tone. "You can call us whatever you want, but I can assure you she knows why we're here and she's given us her blessing. In fact, she's going to be here soon to tell you herself."

"You can't be serious." The man's tone and posture both slump with resignation, but he's still trying to act surprised by this turn of events. He attempts to readjust his wrists and winces as the large chain pinches against them.

"Oh, we're dead serious," I growl, impatient at having to listen to this guy's voice as he continues to pretend he's deserving of any form of leniency. "You almost let her one evil man sell her to some other morally corrupt people. Your own *daughter. Sold. By you.* To pay off some debt that you couldn't afford." Bile rises in my throat and blood rushes to my temples as I say the words out loud. "The worst part is, you didn't even really try to stop it from happening. You just ran away and fled the island, leaving her here to suffer because inside you're just a sad little man who can't keep your shit together." He's despicable and I've never felt more okay about killing someone. Not that I usually give it much thought these days.

Despite the futility of his situation, I guess my last comments must have crossed some line in his mind, and he leaps from his chair and lunges toward me. The radiator groans, the large chain clanking against it and holding him in place.

I snicker as Rake extends one of his long, muscular arms and plunks him back into the chair with ease.

Devon's dad is no weakling, and judging by his scars, he's been in plenty of fights over the years, but he's no match for the four of us or the chain that restrains him. We're not only younger and stronger than he is, but we also have something else going for us. All four of us are completely in love with his daughter.

"See, here's the thing, you pitiful fuck," I growl, my rage beginning to take over at the thought of what he did to her. At what almost happened to her because of him. "Where we differ is that we'd do absolutely anything for Devon. She means absolutely everything to us. And that includes going after anyone who has ever hurt her." I drop my voice even lower, my gaze locked on his. "And you hurt her more deeply than anybody else really ever could. You damn near destroyed her, you vile fuck."

The man lowers his eyes as if he's ashamed, but only for a second. I'm sure he's justified his actions in his mind, and we're about to hear his deluded rationale.

"Look, I knew she'd get out of it, okay? She always manages her way out of tough situations." He shrugs, but the motion is almost as weak as his pathetic excuses. "She's a strong girl. And she's clearly fine now."

My fists clench involuntarily and I barely resist the urge to rock him right in the face. I know I'm going to get my chance soon and I have to be patient. I hope the other guys keep their cool for now as well. We need to make this despicable creature hurt before we let him slip away into the comfortable blanket of eternal darkness. And we need to give Devon the opportunity to say goodbye.

"Do you know what it took to get her set free, you dumb fuck?" Zeke's eyes are cold as ice, and I can tell that even though it takes a lot to get past his even-keeled shell, we're riding on the edge of that line. There's a fire burning inside him just like there is in the rest of us, and it's getting ready to detonate.

"The financial cost, not to mention the impact this has had on our business? All four of us would do it again in a second for Devon. We'd do absolutely anything for her. But no, she couldn't get out of the situation by herself, and you didn't even know we existed when you made your selfish, unforgivable choice to put her at risk. And the toll it's taken on her has been devastating. No, you don't get to take some type of warped credit here. She got into it because of you, and out of it *despite* you."

He pauses and takes a deep breath, running a hand through his closely cropped dark hair. I can tell he's really trying not to lose it, which is usually not a problem for Zeke. Unless, like now, it involves someone trying to hurt someone he loves.

"So don't say you knew she would get out of it herself. Because she nearly didn't. And that would have been on you." He pauses, collecting himself once again, and his tone grows as cold as his gaze. "And now you're going to pay."

Devon's pitiful use for a father can see his plea for freedom still hasn't succeeded, and he grows paler still. An almost imperceptible tremble takes over his body, as if he's finally realizing we aren't just there to scare him. That we're about to end his sad excuse for a life.

Good. I want him to feel every part of this, including the anticipation of what's about to happen.

He deserves for this to be more slow and painful than we're going to make it.

But we don't have forever.

So this will have to do.

Chapter Two

Devon

"But I love you, Devon," he pleads. "You're my one and only daughter." His voice rasps and wavers as he tries to convince me he deserves a best dad award.

I roll my eyes.

"I looked after you while you were growing up. I provided a roof over your head and made sure you had food on the table."

Despite his imposing stature, he looks oddly small, surrounded by my four muscular men in this large industrial space. It's like I can see right through his outer husk, and he's found wanting.

"Well, congratulations for going above and beyond," I sneer. "Let me order that number one dad trophy you so deserve." But my voice, although bitter, also reflects sadness as I realize he's never going to make up for what he did to me. And that his life has to end today. It's the only way forward.

"I think part of you cared about me," I say, my voice low. "You did what you thought you needed to do, which wasn't much. But what's obvious, Father, is that you view me as dispensable. I was less important to you than paying off a debt to a truly evil man. You had hate in your heart for my mother, and you treated her so poorly, until the day she died. I've struggled with watching how you acted toward her my entire life."

He fidgets at my words, a darkness passing over his face showing that they ring true.

"And I think somehow your hatred of her extended to me," I continue. "To all women, possibly. I can never forgive you for what you did. It was the ultimate betrayal. You put yourself and your wellbeing before me, and almost ended my life because of your own choices and actions. And then you just ran away and left me to die, or worse. Death would have been preferable to what else could have happened to me if these guys didn't step in."

He clenches his eyes shut, and I realize for one of the few times in his life he's close to tears. I've only seen him cry once before, and that's when his own father died. I'm nowhere close to tears myself, although I'm sad about what's happening in some ways, and the irony is palpable.

When he reopens his eyes, although it's difficult, I force myself to meet his pleading gaze. And I may be imagining it, but there could be a hint of remorse hidden away somewhere deep within his pupils. Then again, it could just as easily be self-pity and regret for not doing a better job of hiding from me and my guys. The ease with which the guys enticed him back to the island, promising a mysterious opportunity, was pathetic. Clearly, he believed that enough time had elapsed for us to overlook his return.

"Please, Devon. You're going to regret this. You only have one father."

"My deepest regret is continuing to believe you would turn your life around. That one day you would surprise me by being a slightly better person."

I frown as I remember the futile hope I clung to for decades. "I forced myself to go on vacations with you year after year. And it was never about this trust fund that somehow I still don't have access to, even though I'm in my mid-thirties. I was still trying to seek your approval, despite everything you did. Despite the pain you caused me, and despite the sadness and the darkness that you caused to grow deep within me, part of me still wanted you to be proud of me."

Deep sadness suddenly grips hold of me, in combination with my anger, and my eyes sting as my own tears finally threaten to spring forth.

"People would tell me not to go and they'd ask me how I could suck it up and actually spend time with you. And you know what? I justified it. I said you weren't as bad as everyone made you out to be. That you had improved as you'd gotten older. And the sad thing is, that was a lie I was telling myself and everyone else. Because you are way worse than anyone ever said you were. They didn't know the half of it."

His face flushes, and he's momentarily speechless. "We had some wonderful times together, Devon," he eventually says. "You must remember."

Flashbacks flood my mind. The beach picnics where we'd prepare sandwiches and set out a big blanket and tell stories until the sun went down. Drives around our neighborhood where he'd have me close my eyes and guess where we were, and he'd turn this way and that to get me all discombobulated. The board games where I'd catch him cheating, but he'd inevitably concede and he'd just laugh and laugh when I figured it out. The way we'd dance in the living room, my feet standing on his as he led me around. He had me thinking I was the greatest ballroom dancer ever, while the fireplace crackled in the background. He's right. It had its bright moments, although these memories were rare. They're just little cruel punctuations of joy amidst the far more frequent incidents of mental and physical abuse he dished out to my mother and me.

A solitary tear rolls down my cheek. I ball my hands into fists, and my nails dig into my palms. They're jagged from my gnawing at them earlier today, knowing this was going to take place.

I hate that I'm crying, because I know he thinks tears make you weak. I don't want him to see me like this, but I have no choice. Now isn't the time to deny my emotions. I have to speak my truth one last time.

Noticing the tear, my father's expression hardens once again the way it does when he believes he has the upper hand. "Oh, you're crying because you want pity from me? Even though you're doing this to me?" He sneers, his lip curling in contempt. "You weren't the perfect child, Devon. Let's be real." Condescension drips from his tone.

The audacity of this man, in his final hours, having one last jab at me. To gaslight me. To justify trying to sell me to an evil man, because I mildly misbehaved the way most children do.

My flow of tears abruptly stops as quickly as it began. "Because I acted up as a teenager and I took money out of your drawer to buy snacks? Because I smoked at school and stole your alcohol and cigars now and then? That hardly stacks up to anything that you did. To how you treated my mother. To how you treated me."

"She cheated on me, you know?!" More spit flies out of his mouth and I flinch as a drop lands on my bare shoulder. His eyes glint cruelly under the warehouse's industrial lighting. "I didn't even know if you were mine for the longest time."

I quirk an eyebrow, my own eyes narrowing. "This is really what you choose to tell me right before you die? This is your astonishing deathbed revelation?" I snarl, my teeth bared. Invoking my mother's memory like this feels like just another betrayal in a line of shitty betrayals.

"Also, you should know that I'm dying," he lowers his voice. "I'm riddled with cancer, Devon." He's back to the pleading, sniveling coward he was earlier. Throwing out anything that might constitute a last minute Hail Mary.

"That makes it even worse that you sold me off, *father*! If I can even believe anything you say." Blood pounds in my temples at his sheer audacity as he tries to earn my pity. "Wouldn't you just have let Tane's men kill you if you're already dying? Instead of dragging me into your mess?"

Even up to death, my dad plays the victim.

Everything that ever happened to him, in his mind, has been because of a woman. Whether it be his own mother, his wife, his only daughter. All of us are to blame in his eyes. From his vantage point, each of his many poor choices reflects on us and never him.

I sigh. It's obvious to me at this point that he's far from redeemable, and he'll go to his grave blaming everyone but himself. And I've had enough.

I look over at the guys, noticing for the first time they're all wearing black and their clothing is a little more formal than their signature casual style. Like they've dressed for a special occasion, which I guess this is in some ways. "It's time," I say, and my voice is steady now.

They each gaze back at me with concern.

"Do you want to be here while we take care of it?" asks Zeke, placing a powerful hand on my upper arm and squeezing it gently. His touch makes me feel warm inside despite the circumstances.

"No. I can't be here for this. But it needs to happen." I've thought about this long and hard, but I can't bring myself to watch my father's murder. This conversation with him has given me all the closure I think I'm going to get, and now I need to get out of here.

Another lone tear rolls down my face as I turn back to the sad creature whose facial features are now sagging, his head hanging down.

"Goodbye, Father," I say, my final words to an unfit parent. "See you in hell."

He opens his mouth to reply, but for once in his life he seems to think better of it and shuts it again.

His eyes dull with the resignation of a man about to meet his fate, and he gives a slight nod.

It took him his whole life to learn to shut the fuck up.

At least he learned one lesson, even if it's not the one I was hoping for.

CHAPTER THREE

Dom

I'm going to enjoy every moment of this.

Not just because I very much enjoy hurting people, which I do.

Not that I ever thought I would delight in killing my girlfriend's father, because that sounds like a deal-breaker for most relationships.

You're supposed to seek your father-in-law's approval in normal circumstances, after all. But there's nothing normal about this predicament.

I want to make this hurt more. For it to take days, to take weeks. But I know that even though her father deserves every ounce of pain I could dish out, it would only hurt Devon to prolong this. She'd be waiting, wondering. And I know that she just wants it to be over. Done. A distant nightmare.

"Your daughter deserved much better," I snarl at the man I've grown to hate. "But don't worry. We'll take excellent care of her. Unlike you."

I crack my knuckles in anticipation of what's about to happen. The other guys are letting me take the lead on ending his life, and will only step in if they're needed. Which they won't be. But first, we're all going to take pleasure in causing this man untold pain.

I gather a tarp from across the room and drag it over closer to the man.

"We may as well try to minimize the mess so there's less to clean up afterward. There's going to be a lot of blood." I explain, and the other men nod.

The man gulps.

"Get up," I growl at the man.

He remains sitting in the metal chair, his feet planted on the ground.

He scowls at me and spits in my direction.

"Get the fuck up, I said." He winces as I kick him hard in the shin with my steel-toed boot.

He sighs and gets to his feet. I pick the chair up and lift it high in the air, and bring it down over his shoulder. The force violently knocks him to the side, and the chain clanks again, but keeps him tightly secured to the radiator.

Rake picks up a cylindrical red air compressor with a hose attached and carries it over to the tarp. He also retrieves a pair of pliers from a table in the corner. The man gulps as Zeke and Skyler carry over a table saw. I gather a nail gun and steel rods and bring those over as well. We may as well make use of all the items strewn about the warehouse.

He gulps, his eyes bulging as the four of us descend on him with our equipment.

Then we get to work.

By the time we're done, Devon's father is unrecognizable and very dead.

His mouth is gaping open, his jaw dislocated and shattered. He no longer has teeth, as we yanked each out one-by-one with the pliers while he howled in pain. His gums are bloody sockets, and we sliced his tongue out to punish him for the vitriol he spewed at his daughter.

The compressor shot air into his nasal cavity at hundreds of feet per minute. It ruptured one if not both of his lungs, damaging his sinuses and leaving his breathing labored and painful until the end.

We ruptured eardrums his eardrums by the inserting the long steel rods found resting under one a sheet of plastic. He will never hear her beautiful voice again.

We peppered his body with nails that were shot into his flesh at close range, leaving him looking like a cross between a human pincushion and a voodoo doll.

We cleanly sawed off his fingers and toes after we sanded down the pads, and the resulting nubs are now bloody and ragged. Because he doesn't deserve to touch her, but he deserved to be punished for the way he used to.

We streaked his face with his own blood. We plucked his eyes out with a box cutter knife while he was still conscious, unworthy of laying eyes on his gorgeous daughter ever again.

I've killed many men and tortured many more, and I enjoy toying with my prey, but this was the next level. He shrieked and made noises like I've never heard before while he floated in and out of consciousness. I'll enjoy recalling his guttural howls and whimpers in my dreams.

"Are we done?" I eventually ask the other guys.

"He can't get any more dead at this point," replies Rake, spitting on the rapidly cooling corpse and kicking at it with his foot.

We methodically break down the body, rolling up the pieces in the tarps and plastic sheets. We work in silence, our faces grim, until finally the warehouse looks like it did when we found it. Except for the tarps and plastic sheeting that nobody will miss, it's impossible to tell anyone has been here since construction stopped. Let alone that we tortured and killed a man and dismembered his body in this room.

By the time we're done, hours have passed, and it's pitch black outside.

Zeke and Skyler head back to the house to check on Devon, leaving Rake and me to finish what we started.

We take the pieces of the body and place them in our truck and head up into the mountains and into the jungle. Old jazz tunes play on the radio while Rake navigates the winding terrain. It's not what we normally listen to when we're driving, but today is no ordinary day.

To be on the safe side, we bury the body parts in three separate locations. Not that anyone will be looking for the sad excuse for a man.

As we drive back down the mountain, I reflect on what we just did. It was satisfying inflicting so much pain on someone who hurt Devon so badly, but now that it's over, I can't say I feel truly fulfilled.

We never used to be like this, but sometimes love changes you, and it's not always for the better. Sometimes it brings out your inner darkness. Sometimes it teaches you what you're truly capable of, and that's not always pretty.

Drenched in her father's blood, we head back to the house.

One less monster free to roam around.

Time to focus on the next.

Chapter Four

Devon

As the minutes tick by, I second-guess myself. Should I have stayed and watched my father die? This is hell. Purgatory. Waiting here in my room in silence while I know what's happening back in the dusty warehouse. I don't know how long it will take, or when they'll be back. It doesn't feel right to open a book or turn on the TV, and there's no way I could concentrate on anything, anyway. This leaves me alone with my thoughts, which is always a dangerous place for me to be.

My room is cool from the gentle breeze circulated by the air conditioning, but my body is warm and itchy all over. I can't stop fidgeting, and I keep catching myself biting the inside of my cheek and rubbing at my brow.

At some point, I feel a strong, warm hand on my shoulder and I open my eyes and roll onto my back. It's dark outside. I must have dozed off. My head is thumping, my mouth is dry and my nerves feel frayed. It takes a moment before reality hits and I realize why I've been waiting here alone. No wonder I feel like shit, like I have the worst hangover in history.

"Is—is it done?" I ask, squinting up at the dark figure above me. It's Skyler and, despite him still being one of the most attractive men I've ever seen, he looks tired with a tightness around his eyes and his mouth set in a firm line.

"Yes, Devon. It's done. Dom and Rake are off making arrangements with the, uh—." He can't seem to bring himself to say body, even though he and the others deal with them regularly these days. I know his hesitation is out of respect for me and the peculiarity of this situation.

"Did you make him pay, or was it quick?" I don't know if I truly want to hear the answer, or if I can even process it right now. But there's also an element of morbid curiosity that drives me to ask.

"We did what we thought was best for you, and to make things right." Another voice comes out of the darkness to my right, and I glance over as Zeke's face comes into focus. I hadn't noticed him there at first, apparently only able to focus on one thing at a time right now.

I nod, not entirely sure what his answer means. Of course, I assume they didn't let him die without pain. They didn't hide their animosity toward him. Beyond their love for me and their hatred of what he did to me, his actions had a devastating impact on their business. Besides losing significant money because of him, they've had to compromise their moral code that used to define who they were, and their boundaries have been shattered. I've seen the change in them, a new darkness, and it's taken a crushing toll. In a way, he fucked them over almost as much as me.

Still, it's hard to believe he's really gone.

"I can't imagine how hard this is for you, Devon," Skyler says softly. His large hand rests on my upper arm, and it feels comforting and supportive.

I clench my jaw and take a deep breath, willing myself not to be consumed by the swirling grey mist that threatens to suffocate me from the edges of my brain. I blink hard, because I know I must not cry. At least not yet. Or I might never stop.

"I'm okay," I say, my voice as unsteady as my thoughts.

Zeke looks worried, and he moves to the other side of the bed. He kneels beside me and places a hand on my arm. "It's okay if you're not okay, you know," he says.

I take another deep breath. "I really am fine," I say, not sure if I believe it. But to say anything else would feel like I was second-guessing what took place. I can't be weak at this moment, even though I'm wondering how life got me to this point. And I can't ever let the guys think I don't support their actions. They did what needed to be done.

Zeke and Skyler glance at each other but say nothing. Maybe they're not sure of the right words. But who would be in a situation like this?

The men both get to their feet and move toward the door, stopping to turn and look at me on their way out. They're unusually awkward, as if they don't want to leave, but also think staying might only make things worse.

I look up at them, and their facial features blur. My body feels weighed down by thick cement even though it's only covered by a thin sheet. All I can picture is my father weighed down with cement now, being thrown into a river of acid, his face contorted in a cruel scowl while his gaze locks on me. In my mind, his face turns into an abstract swirl, but his eyes remain intact and fixed on me while his body dissolves and melts away into nothingness. My own eyelids grow heavier and heavier until finally everything fades to black.

Chapter Five
Rake

"How's she doing? Can I see her?" I feel panicked, not having been able to see Devon's face since she left for the house. The other guys are sitting around the kitchen table, but I can't sit still. I'm jumping from one foot to the other, my nerves still humming with adrenalin.

Dom and I just got back to the house after taking care of the cleanup. The entire process took a couple of hours, but the gravity of what we did today made it feel like years. It's strange to think back to a year ago. Back then, something firmly rooted us in our belief that we could have power on this island without stooping to too much torture, let alone murder. But I guess life has a way of challenging and changing who you are. Once you reach a certain point, you can justify just about anything.

Skyler shakes his head. "She's sleeping. We should let her get as much rest as possible. She'll need all the mental and physical strength possible to get through this."

As much as I'm craving her presence, I nod. This isn't about me or what I need. As hard as today was, Devon is the one who is suffering the most.

There's food on the table that Skyler or Zeke must have whipped up earlier, but it remains uneaten. I guess the events of today have given none of us much of an appetite. My stomach is churning and my mouth feels like I've been chewing on sandpaper, and I have a sudden craving for water. I take a glass from the counter and fill it with the tap. I take a deep breath and, even though I have the urge to gulp it down, I sip slowly, trying to still the acid that's rising in my throat.

"Do you think she'll hate us? Me?" Dom furrows his brow. I know he feels the most responsibility for killing her father. While we were all complicit and each of us took part in the torture, he's the one who inflicted the most pain and ultimately took his life. But he also made it clear ahead of time that he wanted to do it. He despised that man just as much as we all did, maybe even more. Devon's tales of her father's neglect over the years seemed to spark something particularly heavy within Dom, and he insisted he wanted to be the one to make him pay.

"No," says Skyler, his tone genuine as he shakes his head again. "There's no way she hates you or any of us or what we did today. Nobody is to blame here but him. He got what he deserved."

"He's right," nods Zeke. "But that was fucking brutal. This one was very personal, unlike the other men we've killed in the course of business." He glances at me and Dom, his jaw clenched. "Thanks guys for taking the cleanup. I know it wasn't easy."

"Of course," I reply. "It's the least we could do for Devon."

The air hangs heavy as each of us contemplates the day and what happens next.

Dom glances at Skyler. "How—how do we help her get through this?" He clears his throat. "How did you cope when you lost your dad?"

Skyler swallows and shifts in his chair, not giving an immediate answer. I know his father's death caused him immense pain, and it's not something we talk about. He balls and un-balls his fists and his eyes flash. For a moment, I think he's going to take a swing at Dom, but then he takes a deep breath.

For the first time in what feels like forever, it seems like Skyler is going to share his feelings.

Maybe today has changed us more than we realized.

Chapter Six
Skyler

Dom's question takes me by surprise. It's been a while since I've heard my father mentioned, and it unsettles me. My scalp prickles and I feel a slight shiver down my spine, adding to my unease.

My father's death almost completely broke me. It undeniably left a permanent scar.

Being told I was a constant disappointment by the man I looked up to most. Being compared to my brother and to Zeke. My father never understood me and considered me weak because I was unwilling to go to the criminal lengths he did. Because I strived to live by a moral code that, ironically, has now gone out the window because of what Devon's father did to her.

My father's passing wasn't the major even, just the last seal on layer after layer of pain and confusion that a lifetime of therapy could never fix.

But it's these men, my chosen family, who helped to pull me through the darkness when I was incapable of finding light myself. To quiet my own inner critic and my overwhelming fear of failure.

I was able to overcome my resentment toward my father's adoration of Zeke by focusing on how selfless he is, and how he prioritizes chosen family and loyalty over all else. He taught me to believe in my ability to lead, regardless of what my father said about me.

Dom, after losing so much in his own life, was able to remain a gentle giant until we needed him to be something else to get jobs done.

Rake, so upbeat, hiding his trauma which he keeps buried so deep underneath.

They're the ones who helped get me through. The reasons I didn't descend into my own dark nightmare. They saved my life over and over again, just by being there. By maintaining their unquestioning loyalty and brotherhood.

So, as hard as it feels to answer Dom's question, I feel like I owe them all a response.

My chest tingles as I formulate my reply. I hate feeling this vulnerable. "Well, I don't think the death of a parent is something you ever get over, especially when there are so many deep, underlying issues. I imagine it's more difficult than if you had a positive relationship. It's probably still very challenging to lose a parent in better circumstances, but at least you'd have wonderful memories and some sort of closure. But when it's like this, with countless layers of hurt and pain, there are so many things left unsaid."

"So, how did you do it? Get to where life was manageable again?" Dom is pressing me, but I know he's not trying to needle me. It's driven by his anxiousness to make things right for Devon.

I take a deep breath. This is uncomfortable for me, because it nicks at old wounds that I thought were mostly healed. I feel like they're raw around the edges again now, like they've been picked at and are now threatening to open back up and spill their bloody, infected contents. But I owe Devon this much, if by sharing my experience it helps them to help her.

"Your support, really," I shrug. "Having you as my family. Knowing I could count on you. That it didn't matter what each day would bring. And when I acted insane or just didn't want to talk, you wouldn't judge me. That you didn't pretend to know what was best for me. You allowed me to breathe, and I also knew you weren't going anywhere."

"So we'll do the same for her," says Zeke, and the others nod.

"Whatever she needs, whenever she needs it, we will be there," adds Rake.

"And we'll follow her to the ends of the earth and beyond if that's what it takes," says Dom. He was loyal to her already. However, curiously, killing her father seems to have made him feel even closer to her than ever.

Despite the craziness of the day, one thing is clear.

Whatever happens, Devon has four men who would put their lives on the line for her without hesitation.

Men who would give up their very souls if it made her happy.

Men who would torture for her.

Men who would kill for her. And who would seek revenge on anybody who ever hurt her.

And we're going to spend every day, every moment, of the rest of our lives showing her how much she is loved.

Chapter Seven

Devon

The Next Day

"How are you feeling, baby?" Skyler's voice is brimming with concern as he and Dom gaze down at me. I've made it from my bed to the couch in the living room. When I woke up, I felt claustrophobic from lying within the same four walls where I waited to hear the news that my father was finally dead. It's less suffocating to be in another room.

I think about his question for a moment, not sure how to describe my emotions. "Numb, I guess." I shrug and chew on my lower lip, caressing the arm of the couch. "I thought I'd feel something more. Satisfaction, sadness, I'm not sure. But I just feel empty. It needed to be done, though. We all know that."

"What can we do to make it better for you?" Skyler places his large hand on the small of my back, bringing instant warmth that chips away at the icy wall around my body.

I look up at him, soaking in his strong features and tattooed body, and something stirs within me. Glancing over at Dom's broad shoulders and muscular physique only serves to intensify the feeling.

"Distract me. I just want to feel loved." I lock eyes with Skyler, and he can tell I mean what I say.

Without question, Skyler pulls me to him and kisses me. I can feel his emotion. He needs me as much as I need him. With every touch of his lips against mine, I can tell that he wants and needs to heal and be healed.

Dom wraps his powerful arms around me from behind, like a warm cloak that could both comfort me and crush me. He pulls me into him, while Skyler cradles my chin with care in both of his hands. His kiss is hungry as his tongue explores mine. He presses in closer. I'm trapped between them, but there's no place I would rather be.

There's a strange comfort in knowing that Dom just killed my father, and now he's here with his body pressed into mine. And also that Skyler coordinated the hit to take place yesterday after months of planning. There's no question that these men would do anything for me. And it's mutual. I would follow them to the end of the earth and beyond. Our souls are intertwined and there's no going back.

Skyler's kiss intensifies, and I reciprocate, my tongue exploring his. I realize I'm not just hungry, I'm starving for both of them. I need them to feast on me, to devour me. Only then can I heal.

Dom runs his hands up my hips and waist and underneath my shirt. He slides his massive palms up my chest until they cup each of my breasts. I moan as his rough thumbs and forefingers massage my nipples, and they pebble at his touch.

Skyler's hands leave my chin and roam downward until they cup my ass, pulling me even closer to him.

My own hands lift backward until they cradle Dom behind his neck. He dips his head forward and kisses me softly on my neck, and I almost burst into tears at the tender touch of this giant man.

Skyler's hunger intensifies, and he bites down on my lip. I taste copper as Skyler mashes his lips against mine and I don't know if it's my blood or his. Maybe it's both, and the thought of our blood mixing like our souls makes my pussy and heart throb.

Dom's hardness presses into my lower back as Skyler's does to my abdomen and I grind myself between them. I'm enjoying the feeling of being jostled and unable to pull myself away. Not that I would want to.

My core is heating, fueled by the desire I have for these men and the anticipation of what's coming. I need them both more than ever.

"You're so strong, baby," Dom growls into my ear. "Your spirit is relentless and unstoppable. You won't let this break you. And neither will we." I tilt my head back, for a moment breaking my kiss with Skyler to make eye contact with Dom. His gaze locks with mine, and it's like he's seeing into my soul.

"He's right, Devon. We believe in you," rasps Skyler. I turn back to him and wrap my hands around his neck, pulling his lips to mine once again. If only I believed their words as much as they clearly do.

My heart races as I slide my hands down Skyler's muscular chest and to his hard length. I rub him through his pants, and he groans at my touch. I grind my hips back against Dom as well, enjoying the feeling of his own hardness as it continues to press against my lower back.

I need them both inside me right now. I can't wait any longer and my pussy throbs with primal need.

"Please. Now," I rasp, unable to get any more words out.

It's not that I want to numb myself further or to block my feelings out. It's the opposite. I need to feel pleasure and pain, and need to feel alive. I need to work through my feelings by feeling their desire and their love.

Dom reaches forward to unbutton my shorts and lowers them, followed by my panties. At the same time, Skyler reaches down and pulls my shirt up and over my head. I stand naked, still sandwiched between them.

Dom reaches around my waist and slides his large hand down my stomach. Little butterflies erupt across my skin as his fingers approach my pussy. I moan as he slides a rough finger across my clit and down my folds, sliding it inside me. It glides right in, slick with my arousal.

Skyler dips his head and takes a nipple into his mouth. I moan again as he sucks and swirls his tongue around it. Little zaps of electricity hurtle from my nipple to my core as Dom continues to finger me.

"Yes, this," I gasp. I need this and more. I never want it to stop.

Still sucking on my nipple, Skyler lowers his pants and I reach down to run my hand along his hardness. Behind me, I feel Dom lowering his own pants and I moan as his bare erection presses hard against my flesh.

"Is this what you want?" Dom growls.

"Yes, more. Please," I pant, still incapable of complete sentences. My heart is racing, and my pussy is pounding. These men are not my distraction. They're my salvation. If only Rake and Zele were here as well. But for now, these two are all I need.

I yank Skyler's shirt off, revealing his bronzed pecs and rippling abs. I dot his chest with kisses and he grabs at my breasts, squeezing my nipples between his strong, rough hands.

Dom adds another finger, and I cry out as it enters my pussy. "She's soaking," he growls, and Skyler groans with desire. "See for yourself," he rasps, removing his fingers.

Skyler wastes no time, preferring to check with his cock instead of his fingers. He lines himself up with my entrance and slams himself into me until he's deep inside. I cry out with pleasure at the way his girth stretches my walls as he fills me up with his hardness. I clench around his hard cock, hungry for him to be as far inside me as possible. Like I want his whole being to be inside of me, consuming me.

Dom holds me still as Skyler thrusts into me. "We're here for you," he growls into my ear. "We'll always be here for you."

"I know," I pant as Skyler rails himself into me while Dom wraps his burly arms around my chest, caressing my breasts with his massive hands.

I reach back and take hold of Dom's thick cock and he groans as I stroke at it, desperate for it to be inside me, too. I feel him bending, lowering himself behind me until his cock lines up with my ass, his pre-cum leaving a trail down my ass that drips its way down to my back entrance.

"Are you sure you want this?" he rasps, his voice thick with want.

"Yes, I need it," I moan. I can't wait any longer. Skyler is usually more than enough on his own. Any of the four men are. But today, right now, I need more. I need both Dom and Skyler inside me.

I'm slick with desire as Dom slides his cock into my ass. I feel it stretch as he works his way in, careful not to hurt me despite his impressive girth. "Good job, baby girl," he grits out as he slides his way in further, his thickness creating a stinging sensation that crosses the line between pleasure and pain that leaves me crying out for more.

"You're so good at this, taking both of us at once," rasps Skyler as he continues to fuck my pussy while his brother works his way further into my back hole.

"How does it feel having our two big cocks inside you? Me in your pussy and Dom in your gorgeous little ass?"

"So... good..." I pant, the feeling of fullness consuming me and tickling my nerve endings.

"You're doing so well," rasps Dom. "I can't wait to be balls deep inside your ass." And soon he is. His torso pressing into my back while embeds his cock in my ass as far as it can go.

He thrusts now, too, in time with Skyler, their hips rolling in sync. They both cling to me, Dom's massive hands around my hips and Skyler's around my waist, their large fingers pressing into my soft flesh.

Blood races around my body, leaving me lightheaded as it darts through and from my extremities. Shivers of pleasure take over every inch of me, little sparks igniting with every thrust.

"God, you feel so good, baby," grunts Dom. "I've never felt anything like it. And you're doing such a great job." His words make me melt even further. I'm dripping all over Skyler's cock, which he continues to plow into me while his brother fucks my ass.

With every thrust, the coil within me tightens, and I feel full. Both in my body and my soul. These two men who would do anything for me, who would give their lives for me without question, both inside me at once. Showing me they love me. Helping me to feel. To process what just happened. Proving how much they want me, and how much they need me.

"Fuck. Skyler. Dom," I let out a loud moan as my orgasm crashes over me. I cry out, louder this time, as wave after wave of pleasure slams over and through me, every nerve ending in my body radiating electricity. My hips buck try to buck with abandon, but they have nowhere to go, still sandwiched between these two large men with their cocks impaled deep inside me. My pussy spasms, clenching around Skyler, and my ass squeezes around Dom's rock hard cock as it continues to slam into me.

"Oh god, Devon," Dom cries out as my ass clenching around him takes him over the edge and he releases into my ass. I feel his cock pulsing within me and he pulls himself into me as far as he can go while he rides his own orgasm.

As his orgasm subsides, he gently pulls himself out of me. I moan as the tip of his cock releases from my ass, craving its presence again straight away.

Skyler also pulls out, but only for a moment. Dom helps him lower me to the ground with care, and with the same urgency I feel for his cock, he slides himself back into me. He props himself up on his forearms and pounds into me, letting his lengthy cock almost slide out all the way before slamming back in again, filling my pussy. I rake my nails against his back, crying out each time he slams in to his hilt.

Dom sits down near my head and looks on as Skyler slams into me, watching his brother fuck me. Knowing he just had my ass as well, he can't look away. My pussy clenches even tighter around Skyler's cock as I meet Dom's gaze, his eyes dark with lust. "Good girl," he growls. "You took my cock in your ass so well. And now look at you, the way you're letting Skyler fill your pussy up with his gigantic cock. Being such a good little slut for us. Our little whore. Do you like it?"

"Fuck yes! I love it!" I pant. "You both feel perfect. So good."

"Such a good girl," groans Skyler. "You feel so fucking good."

I moan as his pace intensifies, and it somehow feels like he's inside me, even deeper than before, with every thrust. Based on the sensations deep within me, I swear he's slamming into my cervix, and it feels like he's rearranging my insides every time he bottoms out in me. I cry out every time he plows his impressive length into my pussy. He angles his hips so that his thrusts grind against my clit and I moan as the coil deep inside my core tightens again, winding itself close to the point of no return. "You like that?" he rasps in my ear.

"Mmmhmm," I moan. He leans down and bites my lip, teasing me, pretending to silence me.

"I'm going to come for you, baby girl," he rasps, and his body tenses as he continues to thrust. "Jesus, fuck!" My pussy clenches around his cock as it pulsates, and he releases his load deep inside me. He's holding onto my hips so hard I know I'm going to have bruises later as he presses himself as far into me as he can go without snapping me in two. His last thrusts continue to rub against my clit and send me over the edge right after him. My back arches, my head tilts back and my legs tremble like they never have before. Sparks of bright white light explode in my periphery like someone is setting off fireworks in my brain. Electricity crackles throughout my body as I come all over his cock, his seed and my arousal mixing deep within me.

I lie there, panting, as Dom looks on, absorbed by the sight before him. I close my eyes, just for a moment, while I regain my breath. Skyler leans down and places a gentle kiss on each of my eyelids and then my lips. I kiss his tender lips back as my heartbeat makes its way back to normal.

I feel more than satisfied after the way they fucked me. A deep feeling of being wanted, and of having a home with these men where I belong, has replaced the numbness of what happened yesterday.

Skyler takes care as he slides out of me and I feel his and Dom's absence acutely, even though they're both still here in the room with me. He pushes himself up and nods to Dom, who leaves the room for a moment and soon returns with a soft, damp cloth that he hands to Skyler. Despite his strength, he uses a soft touch to wipe me clean and then pulls me to my feet.

Dom approaches me and wraps his giant arms around me, encapsulating me in a warm hug that makes me feel like I'm in a strong but soft cocoon.

Skyler trails kisses me along the back of my head and down to my neck.

With a massive hand, Dom tilts my chin upward and his gaze locks with mine. He dips his head forward and his lips meet mine in a tender kiss. My strong and gentle giant, who would never hurt me in a way I didn't want.

"See? We've got you, baby girl," he says, his voice gentle. "We'll always be here for you. No matter what you need."

Chapter Eight

Aidan

We're once again assembled around the kitchen table in our compound on the outskirts of the industrial neighborhood. But this time, it's all eight of us. The Brixtons and the snakes. There's a proper boardroom in the adjacent office wing of this building. However, the kitchen has become our de facto space for meetings with people we consider close.

It still feels a little weird, being in partnership with these guys. But we're coming to terms with the value of strength in numbers and what these four men can bring to the table. We've acknowledged it's the only way we're going to have a chance against Tane Brown, and even with their help, I'm nervous it might not be enough.

Zeke is the first to speak up. "What if we sent the girls on a recon mission? Like, send them to a hotel out that way. They can get a bit of rest and relaxation and also see what they can find out about Tane and his setup. Besides, it wouldn't hurt to get Devon away from everything, given she just lost her dad."

I frown and run my fingers through my hair as I think of all the scenarios that could play out if we sent them to another island by themselves. "I don't like it at all," I sigh. "If he catches them nosing around, they'll be sitting ducks. Easy pickings, and we won't be there to save them."

The thought of Devon and Angel being on another island where Tane's stronghold is located, without us there to protect them, terrifies me. We've had a few close run-ins already with some of his stronger men on this island, and from what I've heard, he keeps his best men close by his side. They're evil and ruthless, just like him. And they've proven they will kill women without hesitation. I have no doubt they'd take great pleasure in harming ours.

"Yeah, man," nods Slade, his brow furrowed and his arms crossed tightly across his chest. He's the dictionary definition of resting bitch face, or in his case resting chef face, and today is no exception. "How many times has Angel been kidnapped since she got here?"

"Including by us?" Brick asks, his eyes twinkling and a little smile playing across his lips. He's no doubt mentally reliving the memory of the time we took Angel captive. And how that ultimately resulted in her becoming our life partner. Although it could have ended in disaster, I know Brick gets a kick out of our relationship with Angel's origin story.

Despite the seriousness of my concerns, I smirk. Angel hasn't had an easy run of it since crossing our path. Between us, her psycho stalker, and Zero and Swarenski's guys, she's been held against her will four times since being on the island, and she hasn't even been here that long. The odds are against her for kidnappings.

Surprisingly, she hasn't run as far away as she can get, and instead she's stayed with us. She really must care about us. That said, a fifth kidnapping might be the tipping point for even the most patient person.

A shiver runs down my spine, and my smirk reverts to a frown. While Angel has survived being a captive so far, I have a feeling anyone kidnapped by Tane himself has a very slim chance of making it out alive. He takes people crossing him very personally, and it ends in torture and death. There's no way I can put her at that kind of risk. It's our job to protect her. I could never live with myself if she ended up in a trap of our own making. And I'm sure the other guys feel the same way about Devon.

"We can have them use fake names and they could wear disguises." Brick grins, always the one to put an elaborate touch on any scheme. The weirder the better, from his perspective.

"This isn't the time for jokes," says Zeke, pressing his lips together in a firm line. "I don't think a fake mustache and a floppy hat are going to be sufficient here, and that's not what I had in mind at all." He narrows his eyes. "We have to be serious about this. Their lives could be at stake. And so could our business."

"Fake mustache? What are you even talking about? This whole thing is stupid." Dom rolls his eyes and glares at Zeke and then Brick. "If we do this, and I understand Aidan's hesitation, we'd trying to draw attention away from them, not to them, you idiots."

"Who are you calling an idiot?" Brick growls and narrows his eyes at Dom, clenching his angular jaw. I notice his fists balling by his sides, which is never a good sign. Brick is always ready to use them, and he enjoys inflicting pain. And he and Dom have some kind of weird rivalry. We consider both the unofficial enforcers of their respective brotherhoods, and they naturally seem to detest each other.

"Listen, that's enough guys." My voice is firm as I look each of them in the eye, one by one. "We're over the petty back-and-forth bullshit between us, remember? It's not productive, and it takes us away from focusing on what matters. We need to stay focused and work together."

Brick and Dom both look down, sheepish, like children being reprimanded in the classroom for immature behavior.

I continue. "But yes, no fake mustaches. However, we definitely couldn't let them visit Tane's island without proper disguises. Let's be serious about this. No bright red and pink hair for Devon, and no vibrant purple hair for Angel. They'll need to change their clothing style to upscale resort wear as well. Essentially, they need to blend in and look like bougie tourists."

"But not too bougie or they'll attract all sorts of attention then, too," nods Skyler. "They can't go around dripping in diamonds and whatnot."

"So what I'm hearing you're suggesting is that the girls need to get makeovers?" Rake arches an eyebrow and smirks, letting out a low whistle. "I don't think they're going to like that."

I sigh. He's right. They will not be thrilled, but if this plan is going to work, it has to be done. "Look, they'll only be temporary makeovers, and it's for their own safety and to advance our cause." I glance at the others. "Who wants to do the honors of telling them?"

"Hell no! Not me." Dom crosses his burly arms over his broad chest, fear in his eyes at the thought of sharing this information with the two very assertive women.

"Or me." Rake puts his hands up as if to physically deflect responsibility.

"Or me." Slade pretends to turn and run away.

"Haha, don't all volunteer at once," I sigh, figuring I'm going to end up having to do it by the way everyone else is acting.

Knowing how Devon and Angel behave when they feel like they're being told what to do, I understand the trepidation these men have about breaking the news. They're really not going to enjoy being told they need to change their appearances. I guess I'll take one for the team.

"I'll do it!" Brick blurts suddenly before I have time to take responsibility, a funny expression on his face that I can't quite pinpoint.

"You will?" I quirk an eyebrow and clench my jaw. The man has me suspicious. "Why are you so quick to take one for the team when everyone else is running away, Brick? What's your angle?"

Brick always has an angle. Most of the time, it's because whatever he's scheming is likely to bring him some form of amusement. To spark his almost childlike joy that's triggered by the most random, and often warped, things. But it also tends to center around what might give him some kind of 'points' with Angel. I wonder how he's intending to play this.

Brick tries to conceal the grin that's beginning to spread across his face, and ends up looking like he's wincing in pain. "I have no idea what you're talking about. There's no angle. Someone just needs to tell them and I'm merely volunteering. Teamwork and all that."

"Okay, yeah right," Slade rolls his eyes, and I can't help but smirk. Roman laughs and shakes his head. The snakes haven't quite figured out our dynamic, and they all look on with confusion.

I'll figure out Brick's angle later.

But for now, it's time to get our plan in motion.

CHAPTER NINE

Devon

I narrow my eyes. "The guys are up to something. I can feel it."

Angel glances up from her phone, arching a flawlessly manicured eyebrow. She's been scrolling through it for the last half hour or so, checking on all her apps and researching things as usual. "Oh yeah? Like what?"

"They keep glancing over here and they're talking in low tones again." We're sitting on the overstuffed couch in the living room, which is right near the kitchen where they're having a meeting. The TV plays music videos at a low volume in the background, its screen casting shapes and patterns across the back wall. We're both enjoying glasses of a crisp Sauvignon Blanc that Angel picked up at the local grocery store on the way over.

Normally, we'd be involved in most business meetings with our respective guys, but we're trying to get them to bond and we don't want to get in the middle of it. They're a stubborn bunch, and they need to figure out how to get along without us needing to supervise them. Still, we're staying close by in case things get out of hand like they have in the past. Basically, we're babysitting eight grown men from a close distance.

"Ugh, I hate it when they do that." She rolls her eyes and puts her phone down, giving me her full attention. She picks up her glass of wine and takes a slow sip. "Do they think we aren't aware we know when they're scheming something?"

I smirk. "Yeah, you'd think they'd have figured it out by now. I think they're talking about us, though. I think I overheard both of our names. We might be part of whatever this scheme is."

"Oh god." She rubs her forehead with her fingers and rolls her eyes, and then glances toward the kitchen area at the sound of approaching footsteps. "Well, it looks like Brick is heading over this way, so I guess we're about to find out."

Brick ambles over, a mischievous look on his face. But given that's his typical facial expression, even sometimes when he's torturing people, I'm not sure what it means.

"Hi ladies," he says, beaming at us with his straight white teeth. I can see why Angel is attracted to him with his muscular frame, his manly beard, and his overall quirky lumberjack surfer vibe. And the fact he has a reputation for taking great pleasure in torturing evil men doesn't hurt, either. "We have something to tell you! Well, *I* have something to tell you."

"Oh dear. You were right, Devon. Spill it, Brick," smirks Angel. She quirks her eyebrow in his direction. "Is it good or bad news?"

"Only good for you two," grins Brick.

I was right. This sounds far too positive to be true. Something *is* up.

"We're sending you on a vacation. All expenses paid. To a resort up the coast on the island to the east of us." Brick's eyes are sparkling as he delivers this ostensibly excellent news.

"Really?" Angel's eyebrow arch seems painted on as her head tilts further to the side. It's like she's trying to read inside Brick's brain, which I imagine is quite a scary but exciting place to be. "We're planning to overthrow control of the islands and you're sending us on an all-inclusive vacation? Do you just want us out of your hair or something? Are we getting in the way?"

"No, Angel," says Brick, a shadow passing over his face as if he's truly disappointed by our lack of immediate excitement.

"Don't look at me like that," she says, frowning at Brick. "It makes me feel like I've taken a balloon from a toddler and popped it in front of his face."

I feel a gnawing sensation in my gut, and my scalp crawls. "This isn't some sort of pity party for me, is it? Because of my father?" I frown at Brick.

His face falls further, and he pouts, making him look like a sad puppy dog. "No, no. Both of you, please stop thinking the worst. I'm trying to tell you this is a good thing. Will you please listen?"

We glance at each other and then back to Brick, and we both nod.

"Thank you." He looks relieved by our compliance. "First, it's not an all-inclusive resort, but it's still a very nice one." He shrugs. "And we want you to go and enjoy it, and to spend some much-deserved time relaxing. We just also want you to scope things out while you're there. Think of it as a combination of business and pleasure."

"Oh, like check on what Tane and his guys are up to? Like a recon mission?" I'm picking up what he's putting down. Tane's primary stronghold, and his largest army, is on the largest of the islands. It can't be a coincidence that this is where they want to send us. "Won't he recognize us, though? And are you guys coming, too? It seems like it would be hard to find anything out if all ten of us rolled up as a group. We're hardly a team that's easy to float under the radar when we're all together."

"Nope, just a girl's trip," he explains, grinning. "That's the whole point, so you can get intel before the rest of us show up to execute the last parts of the plan."

Angel and I glance at each other again and shrug. It seems like a reasonable idea.

"And there's one more thing." Brick pauses and breaks eye contact, and suddenly appears flustered. He tucks a stray lock of hair behind his ear and clears his throat. "Speaking of being invisible," he blurts, "you're both getting makeovers before you go. You'll need to dye your hair and get new wardrobes and everything."

Angel and I look at each other and back to Brick.

"Um, excuse me?" Mention of hair dye is a surefire way to get Angel's attention. One, because she's a hairdresser. Two, because she has this shockingly vibrant purple hair that's her signature, and Brick just mentioned dyeing it. My red hair with pink highlights is hardly subtle, either, but it's not a key feature of my business in the same way it is for her.

"Yeah," he nods. "But it's just temporary. You'll need to blend in a little more with the other hotel guests." He shrugs. "Tane will be on the lookout because he's a pretty paranoid individual, and he'd get word the moment you set foot on the island looking the way you both normally do. But we think if we get you looking more... normal, I guess you could call it... you'll just seem like two regular friends on vacation. And then you'll be able to get much closer than we ever could without drawing undue attention."

"Do you know how long it took me to get my hair like this?" Angel frowns and holds up a lock of her purple hair, and narrows her eyes at Brick. "Copious amounts of bleach and toner. The dye. The balayage technique? And it's part of my brand, and part of why clients come to me. If I dye it some normal color, I'm going to lose money on color services until it gets back to normal. People literally come into the salon and say, 'Oh wow, your hair is so cool. How do I get something like that?' and voilà, that's hundreds of dollars right there."

"Angel, I know how important your business is to you. And you know how much I love your regular style. But think of the big picture, baby," pleads Brick. "Like I said, this is only temporary. You'll be able to go back to your regular fantastic self as soon as we get back. And besides, you need a vacation. It's so well-deserved. You'll have actual time to relax, enjoy some sunshine and maybe get like a massage at the spa or something. Dyeing your hair is a small price to pay for getting key info on Tane, and you'll be able to dye it back in no time."

Angel eyes Brick with skepticism. "What information are you expecting us to get on Tane?"

"Yeah, I have the same question." I narrow my eyes and chew on my lip. "It's not like we can roll up to his compound and just start nosing around, disguises and hair dye or not."

"We want you to figure out who he's connected with over there, and how things operate. He has a ton of business interests, just like we do, but we're missing some key information that will help us take him out. Like, who are his most trusted guys on the ground? Does he have any enemies locally, specifically people we could ally ourselves with, who know the area well? Can you get any insight into how we can access his compound? That kind of thing." He shrugs, his palms open at his sides.

"I guess that would mean getting out of the hotel and heading to a few venues... like restaurants and bars, maybe? And seeing what we can overhear without being too obvious?" I arch an eyebrow and glance at Angel. This gig doesn't sound too bad, as long as we don't tip anyone off and give ourselves away. That could be deadly, especially without the guys there as our backup.

I hate thinking I require men around to protect me, but they've proven themselves to be loyal protectors that we sometimes do end up needing. So it's scary thinking about doing something like this without them. My guys basically haven't left my side since we first met, and I've gotten used to them constantly being around.

Brick nods and beams at me. "Precisely."

"Brick..." Angel gazes intently at her man, her eyebrows drawn together and her lips pursed.

"Yes, darling?" he says, his voice as smooth as honey. "You know you can ask me anything. What's on your mind?"

She takes a deep breath. "As you know, I've been kidnapped a bunch of times since I've met you guys...".

"Four times! We were just discussing that," he nods and smiles, without missing a beat. As if it's a totally normal thing to have happened.

"Jesus, you've been kidnapped *four* times?" I can't help but blurt, my voice raising in shock. "Wow, I thought once was bad enough." I knew Angel had been through some things since she got here, but wow.

Angel smirks. "Well, to be fair, your father tried to sell you to Tane Brown, so I think that's worth at least three kidnappings, maybe more."

"Hey, no need to rub in that my father was a loser and an asshole who would sell his own daughter to pay off a debt." I say it with humor, but it still hurts to hear the words. Who would do that to their own flesh and blood, to a daughter they proclaimed to love above all else? Oh yeah, that's right. My father. The one who was just killed by the guys. This still feels very raw and my eyelids suddenly feel gummy. I blink hard.

"Oh fuck, I'm sorry Devon. I didn't mean—." Angel's voice trails off.

"No, you're fine. Sometimes I forget, too. He was a forgettable man in life, so it makes sense for him to be in death as well."

Angel purses her lips in skepticism, but she lets it go for now. "How can you guarantee I won't be kidnapped again, Brick? I don't think I could deal with it another time." She frowns. "Especially by someone like Tane. He might end up trying to sell both of us like he tried with Devon."

An icy shiver crawls up my spine as I remember how it felt. Knowing Tane was going to auction me off to the highest bidder because my father couldn't stump up the cash to pay off his debt. My guys helped me to escape his clutches, ironically with the help of the Brixton men who were enemies back then. But I doubt we'd be so lucky a second time. "Tane's so sick and depraved he'd probably conjure up some type of two for one, buy one, get one free, special for the two of us. The buyers would go wild at that." I shiver again. Gross. The buyers... of humans. With their sick plans. "Nope. I don't think we'd get out of this one in one piece if things were to go wrong."

"That's why you need effective disguises," shrugs Brick. "And you'll have to just be really careful about the questions you're asking and who you're surrounding yourselves with. It's really important to the plan, but most importantly to your safety, that you remain undetected."

"And you won't be there to save us if we need you. Which is kind of terrifying as much as I hate to admit it," I say, frowning. "Will you be staying here on this island while we're over there?"

"We're still figuring it out. We just know we can't all roll in there together and that there's value in the two of you going over there ahead of the larger group. But we wanted to let you know about the general plan as quickly as possible. Start planning your disguises, and we'll let you know when we have more details on exactly how everything's going to go down."

"Oh no, no, no," I say quickly, before he has an opportunity to escape the living room. "Not so fast, big guy."

Angel smirks at the accurate descriptor.

"If you're going to get us to do this, we're going to be intimately involved in planning the finest details," I insist. "We have to be on board with everything. Nothing can slip through the cracks here. We can't leave anything to chance."

"She's right," nods Angel. "You need our help, and we'll be safer if we make sure everything's being well thought through."

"Okay then," shrugs Brick. "I have no problem with you being involved in the planning, especially seeing you're going to be the two people largely carrying out the mission. Besides, we could use some feminine energy." He gazes at us with large, almost cartoonish eyes.

I glance at Angel, and we both roll our eyes.

"Feminine... energy... did you really just say that, Brick?" I smirk.

"What?" He shrugs. "It's true."

"Just..." Angel looks exasperated. "Why..."

"Why what?" Brick furrows his brow.

She puts a hand on her forehead. "Nevermind. I just... it's fine."

I stifle a laugh, which Brick notices, making him even more confused.

"Well, it's sorted then," I say. "We'll meet you in the kitchen shortly with our bras and our periods and lipstick and everything."

Now it's Angel's turn to smirk.

"Bring your vaginas too, please," grins Brick. "I think we will have uses for them, too."

Angel and I both groan. "Oh my fucking god," we say, in chorus.

The guys clearly still need some work, especially Brick. But at least now, with Angel, I have a partner in crime to help me work things through.

What started off as a mutually strong dislike has blossomed into a strong emerging friendship. And now the guys are going to have to deal with much more than they bargained for.

This sounds like it's going to be fun.

And dangerous.

I just hope we make it out alive.

Chapter Ten
Angel

As we walk into the kitchen, Brick rolls a whiteboard to the table and starts drawing a diagram.

"The girls are up to speed, so let's make sure we're all on the same page. I'm a visual person, so I'm going to map this all out." He nods at the other guys and then at Devon and me. "So, as I was saying, we're going to set you up in a hotel." He draws a circle and marks it with an 'H', and adds two stick figures who I assume are meant to represent us. He adds boobs to each of the figures, confirming my assumption is correct. I know which one is meant to be me, because he takes the time to add nipple bars.

Devon glances at me and smirks.

I roll my eyes but then smirk, too. As well as being hot and weird, this guy is pretty fucking hilarious.

Brick continues. "You'll get to know the local area and gather information for us. We want to know the names of people closest to Tane, as well as intel on anyone who might be in conflict with him. Any information on weak links would be especially helpful. And then, of course, we need to know more about his compound and any other real estate interests. His business dealings. Any information on Tane at all could be valuable to us." He bullet points each of our targets, and also adds little arrows from the stick figures that lead to little boxes on the whiteboard which I'm guessing are meant to represent restaurants, bars and the like. Beside each, he crudely draws additional stick figures.

"And when do you guys become involved in all of this?" I quirk an eyebrow.

Brick draws eight additional stick figures and a plane with an arrow pointing to the island.

"Enough with the stick figures, Brick," Aidan rolls his eyes and Brick frowns, clearly offended by the lack of appreciation for his artistic endeavors. "We get the point. And as soon as we have enough information to actually take him down, we'll all rush over," he explains. "We'll need to act quickly because our presence is going to be very obvious when we all roll up. We'll have to get there fast and move even faster when we're on the ground."

"That's exactly what I was trying to show visually," says Brick. He glances at me and Devon. "What do you think about the plan? Did my diagram help?"

Devon shrugs. "I guess if you want a job done right..."

"What? You send in the fairer sex?" Slade narrows his eyes and twists his mouth in a mock scowl, but then he gives it away with a smirk.

"Not this feminine bullshit again. Brick already tried to pull that card, although I think he gives off more feminine energy than both of us combined." I gesture toward his loud floral shirt that's peeking out underneath his signature vegan leather jacket. Meanwhile, Devon and I are wearing monochrome tank tops, shorts and combat boots, looking like we're about to kick some ass. Sometimes I don't think Brick understands how he comes across, like a giant excitable puppy who is always authentically himself, which, similar to Rake, sometimes involves flowers and unicorns and sequins.

"What if you two decide you like each other better and turn out to be giant lesbians? Decide you don't need or want us after all?" Rake grins and nudges Brick with his elbow, and he also laughs. Despite their ages, they're like a pair of schoolchildren when they get together.

I glare at them. "What if you all decide to cross swords while we're off on the other island? Decide you're an octuplet of gay lovers who can't stop sticking your dicks in each other?"

The guys all shift uncomfortably in their seats, avoiding making eye contact with each other. Zeke clears his throat.

Devon stifles a laugh. "Now that's a mental image. We're off gathering intel to bring down Tane and the guys are staying back here playing hide the sausage. Now we know why they're really trying to get rid of us."

"Enough!" Zeke blurts, his face turning red. "This is serious. It could be life or death."

"Are you having second thoughts?" Skyler quirks a brow at Zeke. "This was your idea, you know."

Zeke's mouth presses into a thin line. "I'm aware of that. I just don't know what other option we have. Does anyone have a better idea?" He glances around the table, but everyone remains silent. A few of the guys shake their heads. "Okay, no takers. So, are we all in?"

I glance at Devon, and we both nod. "We're in," I say.

"Then so are we," says Aidan. "I just hope we don't end up regretting this."

Chapter Eleven

Devon

"You're actually quite good at this, you know?" I wrap a lock of hair around my finger and admire it in the well-lit mirror at Angel's upscale hair salon. It's brown with blonde highlights, which is definitely not something I'd ordinarily choose, but I have to admit it looks kind of cute.

"Hair? Yeah, it's the one thing that keeps me sane. Kind of." Angel pulls a face and swishes her own hair around. Instead of her signature vibrant purple, it's an ash blonde. She's also toned down her makeup, trying out subtle neutral tones instead of her usual winged black eyeliner. She looks very different from her usual self, but it also works on her somehow.

"Did you ever think you'd be coloring people's hair to make them *less* interesting?"

"Well, no," she laughs. "But I guess the guys are right. We do need to blend in over there. And it could be worse. I'm not the kind of person who usually plays things safe, but in this case, I think they know what they're talking about. The last thing we need is to attract Tane's attention before we're ready and the guys are all there, too."

"Do you think we'll actually be able to pull this off?" I quirk a brow. "Get the info that we need to take him down once and for all?"

She crinkles her nose and shakes her head. "I have no idea. But I guess we're either going to succeed or dye trying. Like D-Y-E. See what I did there?"

I snort. There's nothing like a good pun, and she knows it.

She picks her purse up off the sleek and immaculate marble countertop. "Time to go shopping for some unmemorable resort wear?"

I roll my eyes and grab my keys and wallet. "Let's get this over with."

I begrudgingly exit the fitting room and twirl around in front of Angel. "I look like something out of a Macy's catalog."

"I never thought I'd see the day you'd wear Vineyard Vines anything," giggles Angel. "But I have to say, those shorts are cute on you."

The shorts are a departure from my usual black and gray wardrobe. Not by much. I mean, they're still a dark navy blue, as close to my usual as I could get while still technically introducing some color. But I've matched them with a top that's khaki with a floral print. Yep, you got it. Khaki. The stuff I associate with beige neighborhoods. One where the apex of the social calendar on any given month is Brenda's potluck or Sharon's Tupperware party. The type of town where the men sit around talking about upcoming IPOs to keep an eye out for and alluding to their net worth. And where the women sit in the other room gossiping about Georgina from the PTA having an affair with Todd, the local barber.

I'm not saying that's what small town life, or otherwise 'regular' life, is like for everyone. But I've constructed that version of it in my head and I'm sticking with it for the purpose of rebelling against these silly outfits. If I have one pet peeve, it's being told what to wear. Especially by a man.

"Do you ever wonder what it would be like if we were more... normal?" I ask, twisting a lock of my dyed brown hair around my finger, still feeling like it looks so foreign compared to the usual red and pink that I'm so used to.

"What do you mean?" Angel quirks an eyebrow and tilts her head to one side.

"Well, when I was growing up, people would always talk about living in a cul-de-sac with a white picket fence and 2.5 children. Maybe a dog and a cat. Having dinner parties with friends and building up a solid 401(k). You know, that type of thing. Where the major conflict is whether the length of your lawn meets the homeowner's association guidelines. Or whether Jenny returned the casserole dish after the last dinner party at her place. I just wonder sometimes what it would be like if I'd chosen that life."

She smirks. "I think it's a perfectly pleasant life for some. But I think you, my dear, would be completely miserable. As would I. We'd be bored out of our brains and probably catatonic on Valiums and vodkas just to get through the day."

I laugh. "Yeah, I guess you're right. And there's no way I could go back to being in a relationship with just one guy. I don't think our type of relationships flies with the typical homeowner's association."

She laughs as well. "Yep, that would be a deal-breaker for sure."

We finish picking out a selection of outfits in neutral tones, and I reluctantly admit to finding some of them quite cute. Not that I intend on wearing any of them after this assignment of ours is over. We check out and head back to the house, enormous shopping bags in tow.

This is starting out to be more fun than I expected.

I just hope we're still alive by the end of the trip.

Chapter Twelve

Aidan

"Show me how much you're going to miss me." Angel glances at each of us and bites her bottom lip, her twinkling eyes giving her a bewitching look that makes me melt inside. She's such a seductive vixen when she's not even trying.

"What do you mean?" I ask, trying to sound innocent, even though I have an inkling of what she has in mind.

Standing in front of us, she yanks off her top, revealing her gorgeous breasts with her sexy pierced nipples. Her skin glows under the gentle golden light emitted by the overhead lamp. She releases her ponytail and her hair cascades around her shoulders in soft, bouncy waves.

My cock immediately hardens in my pants, and I'm sure the other guys are having the same reaction. She's gorgeous, irresistible. And she's all ours.

Roman approaches her first, wasting no time to dip his head down and take one of her nipples into his mouth. He tugs at the piercing with his teeth, and she moans as the rest of us look on.

I move forward, transfixed by her plump lips that are softly parted, her chest rising and falling as Roman continues to suck on her tit. Reaching my hands behind her neck and tilting her head back, I dip my own head down so that my lips and tongue meet hers in a deep, hungry kiss. I bite her bottom lip and our teeth clash momentarily before our tongues find each other again, exploring with longing. She tastes spicy and sweet, and in the back of my head I realize this is the last opportunity we're going to have to do this for a while. Not wanting to cloud this moment by thoughts of being away from her, or the danger of what we're about to do, I push the thought out of my head and continue to kiss her.

Slade approaches her from behind, running his hands down her back and cupping her ass. I feel her arch her hips back and grind against his palms.

Brick is the last to join the rest of us, and he goes straight for the prize, dropping to his knees and crawling to her like an excited puppy. I look down, briefly stopping our kiss. He pulls a knife from his pocket and slices her panties off. Ripping them from her body, he briefly holds them to his nose and inhales. He grins up at her. "You're fucking intoxicating," he groans. While Slade holds her still, Brick takes one of her legs and places it over her shoulder, spreading her wide open and giving him access to her glistening pussy.

She moans as he rubs her, and she grinds eagerly against his hand.

Her eyes darken with lust and her breath quickens as Brick slides two large fingers inside her, and she lets out another soft moan as he slides them in and out.

"Oh god, you're so fucking wet," he growls, his fingers immediately slick with her arousal.

Roman continues to swirl his tongue around her nipple, tugging at the silver bar with his teeth until she cries out.

Brick dips his head forward. "Oh, fuck!" she cries out at the first touch of his tongue.

He laps at her pussy from her entrance up to her clit and back, soaking up every drop as he devours her like a starving man at his last meal. "Jesus fuck, you taste amazing. I can't get enough of you," he pulls away to growl, and abruptly sinks his head back between her thighs.

I'm mesmerized, unable to pull my eyes away as I watch him licking and sucking on her soaking cunt while his fingers continue to work her tight pink hole.

I lean forward and growl in her ear. "You love it when we all fuck you together, don't you?"

"Yes," she pants.

"Good girl," Slade growls in her other ear while he continues to hold her still for Brick. "That's what we like to hear. You're our good girl."

She moans at his words, and at the sensations caused by Roman's mouth on her breast and Brick's tongue and fingers on and inside of her.

I quiet her by leaning forward again and kissing her deeply. She gasps in my mouth, her breathing hot and raspy, as if she might float away at any moment.

She tilts her chest toward Roman, who reaches up and plays with her other nipple while he continues to suck on her tit. She grinds her hips against Brick's palm and tongue while Slade continues to caress her gorgeous ass, one arm now firmly wrapped around her waist to hold her in place for the rest of us.

I can hear Brick's tongue lapping at her pussy and sucking on her clit, and the wetness of her arousal as his fingers slide in and out of her. Hearing another man eating her out only serves to bring me joy, as long as it's one of these three men. And I know I'll get my turn soon enough.

The fact we all know how to please her, and know exactly what she wants, makes me feel giddy as she continues to moan into my mouth.

She pants into my mouth as our tongues lash against each other, and I know this means she's getting close.

She reaches down and pulls Brick's head hard into her.

As if we read each other's minds, which sometimes I honestly think we do, we all suddenly pull away, moving toward the edge of the room and leaving her standing there naked.

Her eyes flash and she glares at each of us in turn, her mouth dropping open.

"What the fuck? Fuck you!" She places her hands on her hips in defiance.

"Just kidding," I say, and we all laugh. "We would never leave you hanging. We're just going to switch things up."

She rolls her eyes. "You assholes. That was so mean! You'd better make it up to me right away."

"Oh, we will," growls Slade. "We're going to make you come over and over again. We'll make sure you're really going to miss us."

This time, it's my turn to plunge my fingers deep inside her wetness. I start with two and quickly add a third, and she moans as I stretch her walls with my large hand.

Slade eats her out this time, flattening his tongue against her slit as she cries out, the coil within her tightening again as she rapidly approaches her peak. He focuses on her clit now, lapping at it, devouring her.

Her body tenses, and she cries out, her voice echoing around the room. Her legs tremble and luckily Roman is there to hold her up or she surely would have collapsed. Her hips buck wildly and she pulls my face into her pussy. I continue to lap at her as she shudders against me, licking up every drop of her wetness.

After what seems like forever, her orgasm subsides.

She smiles at us. "Fuck me," she says. "I need one of you inside me."

Roman eagerly volunteers, pulling her into a deep kiss.

She looks down at his large, erect cock and licks her lips. "Actually, let me fuck you."

He lays down on his back, his erection pointing straight up.

As we all look on, she crouches over him and lowers her soaking wet pussy onto his hardness and slides it all the way down his length. He lets out a groan. "Fuck, you're so tight, Angel."

"Whose cock is this?" she asks, smiling down at him with a contented expression.

"It's all yours," he rasps as she slides up and down on his shaft. She presses her hands into his forearms on either side of his head, holding him in place and giving herself leverage as she gyrates on top of him.

"And whose pussy is this?" she asks.

"Ours," we all reply at the same time. There's no question we all want to be where Roman's cock is right now, but we all know we'll get the chance.

"That's right," she rasps. "This pussy is all yours."

That's the beauty of this arrangement. For whatever reason, between the four of us, there's no jealousy. We know what we have in Angel, and we're all prepared to share her. And she seems quite happy with the arrangement.

Angel continues to roll her hips on top of Roman, the sound of her arousal echoing around the room alongside her soft moans as she bounces her pussy on his cock. She angles her hips, and I can tell she's adjusting her position, so her clit rubs against his body with every thrust. The woman knows her best angles, that's for sure.

Sure enough, her breath grows faster, and I recognize she's getting closer. So does Roman, because he thrusts into her from below, drilling her with his cock. They move faster now, and I stroke my own cock as I watch their crescendo build. I notice the others doing the same in the background, also eagerly watching as she writhes on top of him, the overhead golden light casting a glow on her delicious ass. Her breasts bounce and her piercings sparkle in the light.

She's spectacular. The biggest turn-on I could ever imagine. And she's ours. I'm not sure if I'll ever get used to it. I'll certainly never take it for granted. My own strokes go faster in pace with theirs.

She tilts her head back and yells, "Oh fuck!" as her hips buck wildly. Her cries ring out around the room as her orgasm hits her full force. Roman's face contorts with pleasure as he releases into her, his own orgasm fueled by the clenching of her pussy as she continues to ride him. "Fuck yeah," he groans.

Seeing her enjoyment is enough to take me over the edge as well. I release, my cock pulsing as I spill my seed onto the floor. I'll worry about that later.

Glancing around, I can see I'm not the only one who can't control themselves in Angel's presence.

She sees it too, and a cheeky smirk plays across her face. "Did you enjoy the show, boys?" she asks as she climbs off Roman.

I approach her and pull her to her feet. "You should take a nap, sweetheart," I say, tipping her chin and meeting her lips with mine. "But make it a quick one. We're just getting started. It's going to be a long night."

CHAPTER THIRTEEN
Devon

After an uneventful flight, we grab our luggage and exit the airport.

Much like the island we call home, this one is also covered with lush palm trees, ferns, and banana trees, as well as vibrant flowers that attract colorful bird life. As we twist through the curving highway, we pass sandy beach after sandy beach, all of them unique. The water is a deep sapphire dotted with frothy white waves that crash and spray over black reefs.

Volcanic rock is the major difference between this place and our home island. The dark channels of black rock make the surroundings feel desolate. Different vegetation grows in microclimates along the way. Large volcanoes rise out of the water, creating an impressive landscape.

Reaching a lusher area, we drive past bungalows and hotel complexes, occasionally driving by a tourist bus. Billboards advertise adventure activities and restaurants catered toward the tourist crowd. Fishing and parasailing boats are anchored off the coast, and an occasional jet ski speeds by. An occasional group of seagulls flies overhead, and the air hangs thick with the smell of briny ocean water and seaweed.

Eventually, we arrive at the hotel. We drive into the paved entryway lined with palm trees and colorful birds of paradise and hibiscus planted in brightly patterned ceramic urns. Based on the driveway alone, I can tell the resort sprawls over multiple acres and is insanely gorgeous. Uniformed employees grab luggage from rental cars and ride shares, ferrying them back and forth from the valet podium. I hop out of our rental and a lizard scurries by into a nearby bush. We selected a red convertible, which sounds like it might stand out, but actually seems to represent about eighty percent of rental cars on the island.

The lobby is open, and a gentle breeze flows through from the front entrance to the beach side. Stairs cascade above and below us, leading to amenity spaces I can't wait to check out. The lobby is bustling with new arrivals, and the efficient staff discreetly take care of their luggage and direct them around the sprawling complex. We take our place in the check-in line, which is long but seems to move fairly quickly. Usually lines like this make me antsy, but I try to remind myself this is more like a Trader Joe's line than the queue at, let's say, the DMV. Hopefully, everyone is eager to get their check-in completed as quickly as possible so they can get their vacations started.

A couple in front of us lingers at the check-in desk. They look to be in their late fifties or early sixties. The woman wears a garish oversized tropical print dress with comfort sandals. She also wears a bright sun visor that her layered shoulder-length brown hair cascades over. The man wears a matching tropical print shirt with baggy shorts and socks under his sandals.

"Harold, what's the name of that place that Betsy told us about again?" Her voice is shrill and very loud. "Betsy is our neighbor, you see," she explains to the front desk agent. "She's very well-traveled. She goes to the Hamptons at least four times a year. And she's been here before, too. Stayed on this very property. She's the one who recommended it to us for our anniversary trip."

The man next to her, Harold, I guess, nods enthusiastically. "The queen something... or maybe it was princess. Something to do with royalty."

"What was it?" asks the check-in agent, patiently. "A restaurant, a hotel, or a store, maybe?"

"I'll look it up and check," says Harold, putting on his glasses and pulling out his phone. He stabs at the keys with his pointy index finger. "Oh, what's my password again, dear?"

"Oh Harold, you're always forgetting your passwords! It's our wedding anniversary, you silly goose!" She turns to the check-in agent. "He's always forgetting his passwords." The check-in agent nods politely.

"Oh yes, of course," says Harold, looking more confused than ever. He's getting flustered now.

I groan inwardly. I have a feeling it's going to take Harold a while to pull up this information, if it even exists.

"While he's looking that up, I wanted to inquire about an upgrade," says Harold's wife. If her name turns out to be Karen, I don't think I'll be able to keep in a laugh.

"An upgrade?" asks the check-in agent.

I bet he gets asked about this at least five times a day.

"Yes, you see we're gold members. We're special guests, being part of your loyalty program, and I was hoping you'd be able to offer us something less basic than the garden view room with two beds. We're hoping for more of an ocean view, maybe with a king bed. And a spacious balcony would be nice too. Maybe a hot tub."

The check-in agent smiles benignly. "I'm afraid the hotel is fully booked, ma'am. We're not in a position to do upgrades for the duration of your stay. But just to confirm, you booked and paid for the garden view room with two beds, correct?"

"Well, uh yes," says Harold's wife, a thin-lipped frown forming on her face. "But I didn't expect that we'd end up actually having to stay in... that."

"I can assure you it's a very nice room, ma'am," the agent explains. "It's one of our most popular choices."

"Don't call me ma'am," the woman snaps, her face twisting into a scowl. "It makes me feel old, like my mother. And we don't come here for *very nice*, we came here for *out of this world*."

"Ma-.. what would you prefer that I call you? May I recommend that you select the room that best meets your needs the next time you book?"

"Cheryl," she snaps again. "And I demand to speak with your manager. This isn't the type of service I expect at this caliber of hotel. There are so many options for places to stay around here, and I expect to be treated well for selecting this venue."

Haha, Cheryl. I was so close with the Karen guess. A Cheryl seems like a close cousin to a Karen. Maybe they're even sisters.

"Bingo!" exclaims Harold. "I'm in!" He holds up his phone in victory as the screen illuminates to show it's been unlocked.

Yep, Harold has successfully remembered his wedding anniversary and gained access to the inner workings of his phone. From his excitement, you'd think that he'd hacked into a billionaire's secret bank account and wired himself all the funds. "Now to find where I put that note." He pores through his phone, holding it a couple of inches from his face.

Angel glances at me and rolls her eyes.

I smirk in response. She turns to face the front desk, and I glance at her side profile.

She really does look different without the bright purple hair. She's still gorgeous, of course. Maybe that's even more obvious now. The hair is almost a distraction, the thing your eyes are immediately drawn to because it's just so bright. She's smart to do it like that, given her line of work. But I also wonder if deep down there's another reason that she's purposely drawing people's gaze away from the real her. That she's using her hair as a deflection so they don't see her beyond it.

I know that's one reason I dye mine all sorts of wild colors. Sometimes it's easier to guide people to see what you want them to, rather than letting them try to figure you out all on their own. To avoid them honing in on some imperfection, some flaw that's outside of your control. I'd rather be a bit ridiculous most of the time and have people fixate on that, than have them come to the conclusion that I'm 'less than' in some way.

Okay, maybe I'm projecting.

Or maybe my brain is just trying to think about something other than Harold and Cheryl and how annoying they both are, and how they're taking so long with this front desk agent that we literally might never ever get to check in. We could just fade away right here, the welcome cookie we were handed on arrival the only thing keeping us from starving and becoming skeletal remains, dying of starvation in the check-in line because Harold couldn't remember his wedding anniversary and Cheryl wanted an upgrade for having 'gold' status, the status everyone gets just for signing up with the hotel's free loyalty program. Fuck me.

"Ah yes, it's the Queen... how do I say this...". Harold attempts to pronounce a lengthy word and I wouldn't even know how to spell it because he butchered it so badly. Beneath his extremely professional facade, the check-in agent winces. It's almost imperceptible, but I see it. I'm not an expert in pronunciation, but Jesus. Do better, Harold.

"Uh," says the check-in agent. I can tell he's trying to decide whether to gently correct Harold, but I think he's beyond help. After a brief assessment, the check-in agent must agree, because he seems to think better of it and merely says, "That's on another island, sir."

"Oh, I could have sworn Betsy said it was here." He looks at Cheryl, who is still scowling. "Didn't Betsy say it was here for sure, Cheryl, love?"

"Harold, I don't care about the Queen whatever-it-is. I want to speak to this rude young man's manager." Cheryl's face is growing red, and Harold reddens in response to her snapping at him.

"I'm sorry about this," he says to the check-in agent. "This visit isn't going quite as expected. It's not off to the best start."

"I'll be placing a review on TripAdvisor *and* Yelp. Everybody will know about our experience. We review every place we go, you see," Cheryl snips. "And we will make sure everyone who is anyone hears about this!"

With the patience of a saint, the check-in guest maintains his professional, although not entirely authentic, smile. "Certainly," he says. "I would be delighted to page my manager for you." He picks up the phone and dials an extension. The phone is quickly answered, and the check-in agent speaks in low tones, asking someone, presumably his manager, to meet Harold and Cheryl at the check-in desk.

Angel continues to tap away at her phone while I keep watching the Harold-Cheryl shenanigans unfold. I wish I had popcorn. A suited man approaches the check-in desk from an office in the back. He smiles, and I see his eyes try to read the couple. He must deal with special people like this all day. I wonder how he makes it through. If he drowns his sorrows every evening or has some other way of dealing with all the entitlement that oozes from the pores of people like this. I'd say I hope they pay him well for his trouble, but I can almost guarantee that they don't. What a life. One I'm glad I didn't choose.

The man nods politely while Cheryl proceeds to give him the run-down of her interaction with the check-in agent, highlighting how inconvenienced she's been by not being given something she never intended to pay for.

While at first he appeared supportive, Harold now looks mortified, but he still timidly nods in support of his wife. What a cuck.

I smirk when the manager politely shakes his head, denying her request for an upgrade and reinforcing his employee's assertion that the hotel is indeed sold out for the next few days. But then he leaves and returns with an expensive-looking wine bottle and two champagne flutes. He hands them to the irritating woman who clasps them greedily in her scrawny hands, her fingers decorated with ugly nail art.

"See, Harold? It always pays to be the squeaky wheel," she says, loud enough for everyone in the check-in line to hear. "This is *real* champagne, even. Like from the Champagne region of France. Not that bubbly wine from the grocery store." She pours him a glass of the pale golden liquid. "You can tell by the speed of the bubbles in the glass. Do you see those bubbles, Harold? Aren't they just divine?"

"Yes, dear." Harold looks at Cheryl like she's an alien and drains his glass.

Chapter Fourteen

Devon

After it finally being our turn to check in, we follow the directions to our adjoining rooms. While we each definitely want our own space, we decided it would be both fun and practical to open up the connecting doors as needed.

"I could get used to this," says Angel, checking out my room after she gets done exploring her own.

"Me too," I say, taking a peek into her room and seeing it's a mirror image of mine.

The rooms are both spacious and clean, with neatly made beds that look super comfortable.

Fluffy white towels have been carefully folded and placed on chrome shelving above deep bathtubs. The closets contain fluffy white robes bearing the hotel's logo along with wall safes. Mini kitchenettes boast espresso machines and basic kitchen and bar equipment for preparing simple meals and beverages. Each room has a small couch facing a large TV. Both have balconies that overlook the ocean, and over the hum of the air conditioning unit, the sound of the ocean can be heard as waves roll onto shore.

"Well, let's unpack and get started," I say. "No sense in wasting any time."

"I'm down," says Angel. "I'm sure we'll find some time to relax. But I'm keen to get started as well."

If I'm going to follow someone around and learn all his secrets, I feel like I need to be inside his head. And I feel like I'm currently missing some important pieces.

"So, what does Tane do anyway, to make all his money? It feels like we're following a bit of a ghost. But he's like a ghost that everyone knows exists."

Angel quirks an eyebrow and purses her lips. "What do you think he does, Dev? He traffics weapons and drugs and women, obviously."

I roll my eyes. "I mean, I know that. But does he have a front like your guys? How does he get by on the island, on the face of it all? People seem to know who he is. I feel like he has a familiar face, where the guys try to avoid that back home, except for Roman, maybe."

"In a similar way, I suppose. But yeah, he is more visible. He has a bunch of restaurants all over this island and beyond. I think Slade even worked for one briefly."

"How did that come about? Is he a chef by trade or something?"

"Tane? No, I don't think so. From what I can tell, he's just someone who came into money and figured that the restaurant industry sounded glamorous. That, and it gave him access to do his back door drug deals and funnel illegal revenue through them fairly easily. It seems like it's less trouble than a casino or clubs in some ways, but he has those too. People just don't know as much about those parts of his business unless they're in them. I only know because of the guys."

"Where do you think we should start?" I'm curious to see what Angel has found out with all her phone research. Sometimes I think she should just get the thing permanently attached to her hand because she's on it so much. I guess it would get in the way when she's cutting hair, though, which she seems to be pretty good at.

"I think we need to get out of this resort complex," says Angel, gesturing at the sprawling cascade of buildings around us. "We're surrounded by the most gorgeous yet curated scenery on the island. We can snorkel, yoga, swim, paddle board, spa, tennis, hike, sunbathe, golf, read, eat and drink to our heart's content without ever stepping off the property. There's even aqua Zumba and in-water cycling, for fuck's sake. A literal bicycle that you pedal on while sitting in the pool. But we're also surrounded by tourists, and they're hardly going to have the scoop on what Tane and his people are up to. We could fluke it and come across an employee who knows something, but that would be a huge coincidence."

I nod. "Yep, I hear you." I'm not a fan of relying on coincidences, although sometimes the universe throws me a serendipitous bone and I'm totally okay with that. It's just not something I want to hedge all my bets on. "So you're saying we need to get out and explore, find some places where actual locals spend their time? Anything particular in mind?"

"Well, there's a strip of restaurants and bars not too far from here. I don't think we should go to one of Tane's because that would be too obvious and his employees would almost certainly report back if we started asking around. But somewhere... adjacent, I guess. Maybe somewhere his employees might go for pre- or post-shift drinks or a meal. We'll need to take a car, but that area sounds like a decent spot where people who live on the island hang out on their days off. I think we should get our bearings there and figure out the top spots. We can visit a few times during our stay if we need to, but let's get oriented and figure out where people seem to be more in the know."

"Sounds like a plan."

As if on cue, Angel's phone jingles.

She glances at it and smirks. "It's Aidan. He can smell a plan a mile away, even when it's in early formation. Let me get this."

I nod as she picks up the call and puts him on speaker.

"Hey babe. It's both of us. How'd you know we just figured out our next moves?"

He laughs. "I'm here with Zeke. We knew the two of you wouldn't take long to figure out where to go. So we're just checking in."

"Hi Zeke, baby!" I call out.

"Hey Dev," he replies in his deep voice, which almost makes me melt. God, that is one hot man.

We explain our idea of visiting a local place where we might overhear something.

"That seems smart." Aidan pauses. "Can you do something for us while you're out that way?"

"Of course! Anything for you," says Angel. "What do you need?"

"The chicken wings at Fritz's are meant to be dope. Can you have some for us?"

I glance at Angel and she grins. "I'm sure we can fit that into our tightly packed schedule," she says. "Just don't expect us to get the vegan ones on Brick's behalf. He can try those himself when he gets here. Whenever that will be."

Chapter Fifteen

Roman

"We didn't think this through, sending them away like this. I'm still very concerned and getting increasingly more worried." Aidan frowns and runs his hands through his hair.

"Agh, I know! A whole week without sex." I cross my arms over my chest and clench my jaw. I don't like being away from Angel. She's usually here within touching distance, and I like to touch her a lot. Based on her typical reaction, she reciprocates my feelings.

"I guess we can still do stuff... the long distance way." Brick wiggles his eyebrows and grins.

"What do you mean?" I ask.

"Like video sex."

I quirk a brow. "You've tried that, man?"

He shrugs. "I mean, once or twice. It was a long time ago, though."

"Wait, so like we'd all sit there in a room jerking off to our woman?" I wince. "That sounds... weird." I don't mind sharing Angel with my brothers, but this seems like new territory.

He shakes his head. "Well, no. I imagine one of us would go and talk to her in a separate room. I didn't mean the entire group of us would sit there with our dicks out. Besides, I thought we'd already established a no sword-crossing rule before the ladies left."

Slade walks in, clearly catching the last part of the conversation. He shakes his head and palms his face. "Sword-crossing? Jesus, you guys are a mess."

"Oh, so you're fine with not getting any while she's away?" I'm skeptical. Once he broke out of his shell and became intimate with Angel, he seems to not be able to get enough. Not that I can blame him. She's the best.

"I don't want anything from any of you, if that's what you're implying." He frowns. "And I'm a loyal man."

"No, no, that's not what I meant. It's just—ugh, nevermind. You don't need to be so ornery all the time, Slade. I was just saying I'm going to miss Angel in all sorts of ways, that's all."

"Whatever. Shut up," he growls. "I don't want to hear about your sexual deprivation. I'll manage mine in my own way."

"Easy now," I smirk. "I don't want to hear about your jerking off plans."

Slade storms off, even grumpier than usual.

Chapter Sixteen

Angel

The main part of town is essentially one main road lined with buildings featuring ornate wooden balconies that give it character from a bygone era. I guess that's why they call it Old Town, even though the restaurants and stores that line the streets are all very modern. It's clear that the locals take pride in the streets, which are frequently swept to keep everything pristine for the tourists that meander along the sidewalks.

There are restaurants and bars and souvenir shops, and the odd convenience store sprinkled along the way. Little side streets take passersby down to the nearby beach. There's an occasional bridge where ducks and other native birds wander and squawk below in little creeks that trickle down from the inland mountains.

The road doesn't see much traffic, but the odd truck passes by here and there carrying multiple surfboards in the back. We also see the occasional telltale rental car—usually a Mustang or a Wrangler—as it makes its way to find parking at one of the metered spots bordering the town.

"This is adorable! I can't believe I hadn't made my way over here already," says Devon, swooning as we pass by a row of palm trees next to an art studio festooned with large metal canvases and sea glass collages. "Oh, I know! Me too. I came once, but it was only for an overnight trip on my way somewhere else. Someone described it to me as being something like a college town, but it's so much more than that. Or maybe I just went to the wrong college!"

"We're not on the mainland anymore, Devon," I laugh.

"You can say that again," she grins. "It's like we're in a different world here, living on these islands. I never want to go back."

"The good thing is that we don't have to."

"The good thing is that we don't have to."

CHAPTER SEVENTEEN

Devon

The first place we go to is an indoor-outdoor restaurant surrounded by lush vegetation. A brightly colored sandwich board outside the front door highlights their daily specials.

We take a seat at one of the cute umbrella-covered outdoor tables with a view of both the inside of the restaurant and the bustling sidewalk. It's the perfect place for people-watching and getting our bearings.

"This place is cute, but there seem to be a lot of tourists here and not so many locals," I say, noticing the high ratio of socks-and-sandals combos, generic tropical shirts and around-the-neck cameras.

"Yeah," nods Angel. "Glancing at the prices, I think we've walked right into a tourist trap. I'm sure not many locals come here. But the food is meant to be good and I'm hungry. Plus, we have a good view here of where we might want to go next."

She's right. Looking around from our table, we can see at least five other establishments, two restaurants and three bars, and get a sense of the vibe of each.

"That sports bar looks promising," I say, pointing at an upstairs venue. There are posters outside advertising weekly trivia and open mic nights as well as daily happy hour specials. There's also some kind of VIP discount card aimed at locals.

Angel nods. "Let's check that place out next, and then maybe that one next door to it, too." She gestures at the adjacent venue, which looks to be a diner with an attached bar. "We can sit at the bar and maybe grab a snack if we're still hungry. Not that we need to visit them all today."

Our server appears at our table. She's cute with a wide smile and big green eyes, wearing the uniform of a floral dress and a hibiscus in her shoulder-length blonde hair. "Hi! I'm Rachel. I'll be your server today. I'm going to grab you some waters and will be right back for your orders."

Normally I'd roll my eyes at her over-the-top perkiness, and the way her voice rises excitedly at the end of every sentence, but she's being nice, and her personality suits the upbeat venue, and so I decide not to be a bitch for no reason.

After perusing the menu, Angel decides on a house slushy cocktail, and I pick a double shot of whiskey.

"Really?" I arch an eyebrow. "You like that fruity shit?"

"When in Rome..." she shrugs. "I'm trying to blend in." She gestures around, and sure enough, at least half the tables have the drink which, based on the menu description, looks like the one she just ordered. She narrows her eyes at me. "Besides, you're the one blowing our cover by ordering shots of whiskey neat on a tropical island. Everyone back home knows that's your signature. You really should be mixing things up."

She has a point. I shudder at the thought of ordering one of the nasty concoctions that the islands are known for. But I might have to suck it up, unless we can find a true local spot where people don't raise their eyebrows at a beer and shot combo. Dyeing my hair was one thing. Wearing khakis was another. But those are manageable. Drinking a fucking lava flow? No, thank you. A girl has boundaries.

Rachel the perky server returns and takes our drink orders. "What can I get you for food?" she asks. "I recommend the Alaskan king crab legs."

Of course you do, love. They're the most expensive thing on the menu. I'd usually say that out loud, but over here I'm trying my hardest to be on my best behavior. The guys would be so proud of me, holding back like this. Maybe I'm turning over a new leaf. Nah, I'm just being a bitch with my inside voice.

"I think I'm going to go with something local," I say, smiling sweetly at our server. "But thank you for the recommendation. I'll have the sesame crusted ahi steak, but can you do that with a side salad instead of the rice?" I ask.

Rachel nods and enters the order on her tablet. "It comes with vegetables already. You okay with that?"

"Yeah, I'm good with double veggies." I wink at Angel. "Trying to get in that five plus a day where I can. The guys like to tease me about it, calling themselves my four plus a day."

Angel laughs.

Rachel shoots us a weird look but then quickly recovers. "Okay then, great," she says, scribbling my request down on her order pad. "And for you?" She gestures at Angel.

"I'll do the goat cheese salad, and can I add some grilled fish to that? And give us some macadamia nut hummus to share as well."

"Great. Do you want this all at once, or how it comes out?"

"Whatever order it comes out is fine," Angel replies.

"Great, I'll get your drinks going and your food should be out shortly as well." Rachel beams at us and walks away.

"You have to be fucking kidding me," Angel groans.

I glance up at her to see where she's looking, and follow her gaze to the table next to us where a familiar-looking couple is being seated by a host. "Oh my fucking god, what are the chances? Out of all the places to go on the island, *they* end up here?"

"Must have a good score on yelp."

"Well, yeah, I guess. To be fair, that's how I found it."

"Why, hello there, neighbors! You were in line with us at the hotel!" It's Harold's unmistakable drawl. We've been spotted. I didn't know they'd even noticed us in the check-in line. I'm surprised he's not mortified after Cheryl's performance, and the way she treated the lovely check-in agent. Maybe he's just so used to her by now that he doesn't realize how vile and obnoxious her behavior is. Or maybe he's just as bad, but does a better job of concealing it.

"Oh… yes, you look familiar," I murmur, trying not to engage. I can tell from the way Harold is beaming at us with excitement, and the way Cheryl has tilted her chair in our direction, that an escape isn't going to be easy.

Angel clears her throat and nudges my leg under the table.

"Is this your first time on the island?" he asks. "I'm Harold, by the way. And this is my lovely wife, Cheryl!"

"Hi there!" Cheryl says excitedly. "Are you enjoying your stay?"

Angel stuffs her straw into her mouth and takes a giant sip of her blue, fruity concoction.

I down my shot of whiskey in one go. "I'm Devon," I say, "And this is my wife, Angel. Yes, this is our first time on the island, and we're here on our honeymoon. We're having an…" I conspiratorially wiggle my eyebrows at Harold and then Cheryl, "…amazing time."

Angel almost spits out her cocktail.

If there's one thing I know how to do, it's finding out the way to make people feel awkward. And if there's something that's likely to make Harold and Cheryl feel awkward, it's the thought of two lesbians scissoring in the room next door.

"Oh, uh.. I see," says Harold.

Angel excuses herself to go and use the restroom and I turn my attention to my phone, scrolling through the ebook app to find my next read.

Harold and Cheryl glance nervously at me and start speaking in hushed tones, which for them is still clearly audible by everyone at the surrounding tables. "I knew some lesbians once, at school," Cheryl says, clearly completely oblivious to the fact I can hear every word she's saying. Why are American tourists so fucking loud as a general rule? It's obnoxious. "They were—."

I drown her out. I don't need to hear her uninformed opinions on human sexuality, and I guess we technically did start it.

But at least my cover story worked, and they've stopped talking to us. Their loudness could only attract unwanted attention, and the last thing we need is them inviting themselves along on our recon mission.

Angel returns to the table right as our food is served by Rachel the perky server and a couple of food runners.

The meal is surprisingly decent for such a touristy location. One perk of being right by the ocean being the mouth-watering, high-quality, fresh seafood that's hard to mess up.

As we're wrapping up our meal, Cheryl leans over conspiratorially and begins to talk to us again.

"I've heard that the thread count at our hotel isn't as high as they claim it is on their website, would you believe it? Outrageous. Outrageous! And then they expect us to tip the room attendants. The audacity!"

I can't deal with her nonsense any further, so I blurt out the first thing that comes to mind. "It was lovely chatting with you both. But we need to leave now. Angel wants to scissor!"

"Yep, I sure do! Nothing like some good quality scissoring action to celebrate being a newly married lesbian couple!"

Cheryl and Harold cheeks grow red, and Harold clears his throat but doesn't seem quite sure what to say. Cheryl doesn't even try to respond, and just stares awkwardly at her plate. Excellent. I've finally gotten them both to shut the fuck up. The other patrons should be sending me a celebratory lava cake for my troubles.

After finishing our meal, we return to the hotel.

We have other places to check out, but have decided they can wait until the next day when local hospitality workers are more likely to have the day off.

Besides, I miss the guys, and I'm ready for some virtual quality time.

Even when they're miles away, I can't get them out of my head or my heart. And I don't want to.

Chapter Eighteen

Angel

"You really told them you had to go scissor?" Brick and at least three of the other guys erupt into raucous laughter on the other end of the phone. We've got all eight of them on speaker, and we're regaling them with our tales of Harold and Cheryl. They might be annoying as fuck, but they make for entertaining but cringeworthy stories.

"Sure did," laughs Devon.

"But did you actually follow through?" asks Rake.

"What? And scissor? Of course we did." I roll my eyes and Devon smirks.

"Wait what? You did? I knew it! See, I knew you were going to do that while you were there!" Rake exclaims. "I knew you wouldn't be able to keep your hands off each other!"

"Oh, shut the fuck up, Rake." I growl. "Did you cross swords with Zeke yet?"

"What? No!" He blurts, clearly flustered.

I hear Zeke almost choke through the phone.

Aidan jumps in. "Okay, okay. Nobody is crossing swords or scissoring, not that there would be anything wrong with that if everyone involved was into it. But this isn't why we're calling." I don't need to see the video to know that he's back in business mode, and is probably running his hand through his hair with a serious look on his face. So predictable, but he keeps the entire group on track, even more than Zeke or Skyler. Devon's guys have begrudgingly accepted Aidan's leadership role within the overall group, even though it took them a while and it was a fairly painful process. "On a more serious note, what were you able to find out?"

"We have to go back to a few places nearby. A couple of them seem fairly promising, but I guess we'll have to see and it might depend on the day. They have reputations for being popular local hangouts, and the regulars could well be associates of Tane's. I'm not sure how far up the chain they'd be, but we have to start somewhere."

"Excellent," says Zeke. "Sounds like a great start."

We wrap up the call, but before I end it on our side, I hear Slade's voice on the line. "Hey, Angel. Can you stay on for a little while longer? There's something I need to speak with you about. Alone."

"Of course," I reply, excited to get some alone time with him. I wonder what he has in mind, and I can't wait to find out.

Chapter Nineteen

Slade

"You're wearing the outfit I got you." I can't help but smile as I realize Angel did it on purpose. I enjoy picking out clothing for her. It might sound weird, but I can picture what her perfect body will look like when I look at things on the rack. How the curves of her gorgeous breasts will fill out a top. The way a strap or a sleeve will accentuate the angles of her shoulders or the muscular contours of her upper arms. How a pair of shorts will caress the curves of her butt cheeks or highlight the angles of her waist and show off her cute belly button.

It's a bit like when I'm cooking a meal and I can see the ingredients coming together on the plate hours before I've begun preparing them. And Angel isn't just a snack, she's a fifteen course degustation menu at a three Michelin star restaurant. She's my food and sex muse.

And now, here she is, on camera, showing off the most recent outfit I selected for her. A sheer black fishnet crop top, with a lacy black pushup bra underneath that's allowing her cleavage to peek out just enough to give me a glimpse of hopefully what's coming soon. She normally wears shorts, but for this outfit I selected a skirt. "Easier access." I'd winked at her when she looked up at me after pulling it out of the shopping bag. She'd arched an eyebrow at me, questioning the departure from her usual wardrobe of shorts and a tank top. She'd returned my gaze with eyes that darkened with desire, knowing I fully intended on teasing her, sliding my fingers up inside her, hiking the skirt up over her hips and having her sit down on my cock in a discreet public location. By her gaze, I could tell she was picking up exactly what I was putting down, and she didn't mind in the slightest. I love her so much. She's a devious dirty sex kitten and I can't get enough of her. The fact she brought it with her and wore it today makes my frosty heart melt just a little. Only she can have that effect on me.

A strip of her delicate, milky flesh separates her crop top from her skirt. I wish I could burst through the phone and touch it. It's so smooth, and I love running my hands over that part of her, feeling the soft curve of her belly. I long to kiss her belly button the way I do when we're in person, an intimate gesture between us that makes her crave my cock.

"I love this outfit you picked out for me, baby," she purrs.

"But you're supposed to wear that skirt for me in person so I can do things to you when nobody else is watching," I growl. "And maybe sometimes when people *are* watching."

"Soon, baby, I promise," she winks at me through the phone. "And for now, I get to tease you. I'm going to go and shut the door."

I watch as she gets up, sneaking a peek at her perky ass as she places her phone down and gets up off her bed to close the door interconnecting her room with Angel's. She returns and lies down on the bed on top of crisp white sheets, her head and shoulders propped up on a collection of fluffy pillows with a tropical print. Her headboard is ornate and metal, and my cock twitches as I think about tying her to it with rope, and maybe even handcuffing her.

"I can see you eyeing the headboard, you deviant," she says, winking at me.

"Mmm yeah, I was just thinking of all the opportunities it provides," I growl. "I might order you one as soon as we've finished here, if you're a good girl, that is."

Her eyes get a little dreamy when I call her a good girl. I know she loves it, that it does things to her. And it has the same effect on me. I like it even more when she says, 'Yes, Chef'.

"Well, I'm going to have to be a good girl then, aren't I? Because that sounds like a lot of fun."

She lets the camera trail over her body, and every part of me wants to reach through the screen and run my hands all over her. She's so fucking gorgeous. All of us guys really are very lucky. It's not just the way she looks, it's everything about her. Funny, whip-smart, witty, a little mean when she wants to be. But always loving, caring, thinking about what's best for us. Our lives have all changed for the better since having met her. The fact she's incredibly hot and makes me want to bust my nut every time I lay eyes on her is just a bonus.

My cock twitches as she lets the camera zoom in on her chest and teases me with a view from above, highlighting the curvature of the top of her breasts. It feels kind of artistic, seeing her body from the angles that she's choosing through her phone. She laughs softly, probably also thinking that this is a bit different from how we usually do things.

She places the phone down, propping it against something that enables her to be hands free, and she turns around and gets on all fours. It's the perfect angle to show off her curvy, ample ass. Her skirt rides up over her hips of its own accord, her lacy black thong teasing the outline of her plush pussy lips. Jesus. I let out a groan as I imagine tracing the outline of her pussy with my fingers. My cock strains against my pants. I want nothing more than to grab her roughly by her hips and plow myself deep inside her. I'd find it hard to choose between her pussy or her ass. Maybe I just want to start with my tongue inside her from behind. Any of it, all of it. I want all of her and to do all the things all the time.

Not being able to reach out and touch her right now is torture, but it's also kind of exciting. Maybe I need this. Not that we need to spice up our relationship or anything, because we're very much fine in that department. And I could never, ever grow complacent or take her for granted, because I know what I have and I'll do anything to keep it. But the inability to access her body in the flesh, yet still being able to see every inch of her, is doing things to me. It's completely on her terms, too. She gets to decide what I get to see, and she can whip the camera away at any time. This is torture of the best kind.

"You like this view, baby?" she asks, reaching around and trailing her fingers along the line of her panties, exactly the way I just imagined doing myself.

"Oh fucking hell yeah, I like this view. It's a million dollar view, baby. I could watch you like this forever. Although at some point, I'm going to need you to peel those panties off."

"Be patient, lover," she moans, teasing me by sliding one finger inside her panties.

"Oh my god, yes. Tell me how wet you are," I growl. "I need to know everything."

"Oh baby, I'm starting to get very wet." She pulls her finger back out of her panties and I can see that it's slick with her juices. God, I want to suck on her finger so badly right now. I love the way she tastes. She's the most delicious thing in the world as far as I'm concerned.

"Am I making you hard, baby?" she asks, looking up at me through her full, dark eyelashes.

"Like a fucking rock," I growl. "Want to see?"

"Yes, I want to see," she says, turning around to face the camera.

I angle my phone downward so she can see my cock in my hand.

"Oh baby," she moans. "I want you inside me so bad. I want to see you stroke it."

I'm happy to comply with her directions and I stroke myself on camera.

"Take your panties off, baby," I growl. "Actually, take off everything. I want to see you completely naked."

She grins at me and peels her clothing off item by item, starting with her top. "I love this bra you picked out for me, baby," she says, rubbing her nipples through the sheer, lacy fabric. "It makes me feel sexy."

"You should always feel sexy," I growl, continuing to stroke my swollen cock. "You're the sexiest woman I've ever seen in my life. But I'm glad this makes you feel extra good. You deserve it."

She slides the straps down and lowers the material underneath her breasts, revealing her milky flesh to me. Her nipples are puffy, pushed forward by the silver bars that run through each. My cock twitches aggressively at the sight. I couldn't believe it when she came home with pierced nipples. I almost came in my pants when I first saw them like that. It was so unexpected and so, so very hot. She did it for herself, too, not knowing me or any of the other guys had a thing for the way they look, which made it even better.

Angel lets the camera focus in on her pussy and I can see it's glistening with arousal. She wants this as much as I do.

I groan at the sight of her. "Jesus, you're soaking. I can imagine the way you feel, and your scent. You're so close, but yet so far. I need you back here with me."

"Well, baby, this is the best we can do for now. You still get to see me up close. This is kind of fun, no?" Her voice is husky, and she gently teases herself, dipping her finger into her arousal and using it to rub her clit.

"Yeah baby, play with your clit," I rasp, mesmerized by this view.

I stroke my cock in rhythm with her fingers. "Mm, I like this close-up view of your pussy. And I want to taste you so fucking bad," I groan, imagining my tongue swirling around her clit, and slipping it inside her. I want to devour her and leave no part of her untouched. I'm not used to wanting something and not being able to have it. This is tough, even though I know it's only for a few more days.

"Slide a finger inside," I growl. "Two fingers."

She does exactly what I ask, inserting her second and middle fingers inside her glistening pussy and gliding them in and out of herself. Jesus, I wish that her fingers were any part of me right now. Literally any part. Don't care which. As long as it gets to be inside her.

"Just think about all the dirty things you want to do with me when you get here, Slade," she says, moaning softly at her own touch as she continues to finger herself. "Make a list, and we'll check off every single one, one by one, and go back and do the ones we like the best all over again."

I groan at the thought. Jesus, she's so incredibly sexy, I could never get sick of her. And I fully intend to take her up on her offer.

"Want to see if we can come at the same time?" she asks, tilting the camera back up and smiling at me, her eyes half-lidded as she continues to rub herself just the way she likes.

"Ladies first," I growl. "You come first for me, baby."

"Such a gentleman," she giggles.

"I want to see all of you, though," I say. "I love the close-up of your pussy, but I want to watch the pleasure on your face when you come. The way your body arches in ecstasy, the angle as you tilt your throat back. I can almost see the stars that you've described in the back of your head. That's my favorite part of being with you. It's what I live for."

She places the camera back on something that affords me a view of her entire body in all its gorgeousness. "Like this, baby?" she whispers. "Is this how you want me?"

"Yes, my sexy girl. You're just perfect, exactly how I want you. How I need you." My voice is husky, the pace of my strokes intensifying as I watch her fingers focusing in on her clit and then sliding into her as far as they can go. I love the way she touches herself. I might have to make her do it more when she gets back. Watching her through the camera, and at these angles, I'm learning a thing or two about how she likes it. I need to take some mental notes so I can give it to her better than ever when I get to have her in person.

I angle the camera back down so she can see me beating my cock. "Look what you're doing to me, Angel."

"Mm," she moans. "That's so fucking hot."

"Come for me, baby," I growl. My breath is raspy and ragged, and I can tell my own orgasm isn't far away.

She rubs herself in sync with my strokes, letting out soft moans.

"I can tell by those sounds that you're getting close, baby," I grit out, stroking myself harder to keep pace. "Use your other hand to fuck yourself with your fingers."

She's giving herself the full treatment now. One hand focuses solely on her clit, the other's fingers pumping into herself. Her chest rises and falls rapidly, her nipple piercings glinting in the light as her breasts bounce gently, squeezed between her two upper arms. Her skin is covered in a slight sheen, her cheeks and chest pink with excitement.

"Oh god, I'm coming, Slade," she moans. "I'm about to come for you."

Her hips buck into the air and her back arches, her stomach tightening, and she continues to finger herself and twirl her other hand against her clit as the orgasm takes hold of her. Her head flies back, exposing her delicate throat, and her eyes stay locked on the screen.

Her pleasure and her angles are too much for me to keep contained, and why would I not want to come at the same time as this insanely gorgeous woman? My body tenses up and I release all over my bare torso.

She moans at the sight of my seed splashing over me. "I can't wait for you to come inside me, baby."

"Me neither," I groan as my orgasm slowly subsides. "I fucking can't wait to spill deep inside you."

We both lie there for a moment in each of our rooms, silent except for the sounds of our heavy breathing that we both fight to regain control of. I can hear and feel my heart beating in my chest, and know I'd be able to see and feel hers too if we were next to each other. My imagination will have to suffice for now.

"Wow," she says, still a little breathless.

"You can say that again," I pant. "Just wait until I'm there in person."

"Mm," she moans. "I've never wanted anything more."

Chapter Twenty

Devon

The next afternoon

After some poolside relaxation and a quick lunch, we're ready to do some recon on the next spot on our list, which opens mid-afternoon.

"This place is *much* more my speed." I glance around in appreciation at the dimly lit venue. The walls and bar-top are covered in peeling black paint, and the barstools are upholstered in tattered vinyl and look like they've seen some things. There are a few holes in the wall, probably the result of overzealous patrons punching their way through in a fit of excitement or anger. A pool table with ripped felt sits off in the corner, and a couple of pool cues that have seen better days lay discarded nearby.

"I find it's funny when I see a pool table like this in a dive bar," Angel smirks. "Like, I get it. Pool is fun, especially when you're drinking. But what possessed someone to say let's give people a bunch of alcohol, and then arm them with these long wooden sticks that can be used as spears, and give them a bunch of balls, and ask them to do competitive shit that requires coordination? It sounds like a recipe for disaster."

"Right?" I laugh. "I think the only thing that can be worse in a drinking venue is darts. Like, here are literal stabby little things that you are supposed to throw to *stick into other things.*

"Oh yeah, totally," Angel laughs. " I've seen many a dart game in a dive bar change focus from the target to a person's flesh. And I'm here for it."

After getting our bearings, we select a couple of barstools right in the center of the length of the bar. Somewhere where we're well-positioned to hear maximum conversations around us and to observe as many patrons as possible. The center of the action.

We're both dressed relatively demurely. No khaki for either of us today, settling instead on blacks and grays. It won't behoove us to dress like complete tourists here, but we also don't want to come across as 'new locals' that people take an interest in. We want to listen, absorb, and then get the fuck out of here without raising any eyebrows. Our cover story, if needed, is that we're industry folk visiting from another island. Not entirely a lie. But if we get too many questions, our plan is to duck and divert. The last thing we need is word getting back to Tane that two women bearing our descriptions are on the island asking questions about him. We need people to feel like they're volunteering us information rather than us seeking it out.

The bartender, a burly stubbled man in his mid-fifties, seems like a seasoned pro. The bar is about half full to begin with, and he mixes basic drinks effortlessly, like it's only taking one tiny fragment of his attention even when he's mixing several at the same time. He's a little gruff in his approach, but he's getting people what they need, and seems to lighten up a bit when people talk to him about baseball. Richard, he says his name is. I get the sense Richard knows a lot about what's going on in this town by the way he interacts with people who are obvious regulars. As they drink more, they talk more, like most folks do.

There are patrons to our left and right, and as they sip their drinks, they share stories about their families, their work life and local scandals. Someone named Griffin seems to create a bit of mischief, because his name comes up several times in several conversations we overhear. He has a reputation for being a troublemaker, involved in graffiti and other vandalism, theft, and joyriding.. But from what I can tell, he seems to focus his shenanigans solely to the detriment of tourists, and doesn't seem violent, so the locals who are recounting his latest exploits don't seem to mind. I have a feeling Griffin isn't a person of interest in terms of our research, but it's kind of fun to hear about what he's getting up to. I've formed a picture of him in my mind where he looks like a cross between Pete Davidson and Machine Gun Kelly.

And then, as if a gift is bestowed on us by the universe, we get our first real tip of any benefit.

The infamous Griffin enters the bar. He needs no introduction because he's loud and tipsy and looks just how I pictured. He even has the audacity to be wearing a t-shirt that says his name on the front *and* back. Obnoxious, but also helpful for identification.

"Evening, ladies!" He slurs as he clumsily makes his way past, his eyes slightly glassy, and he props himself up on a barstool at a high-top right next to us. He has dirty blonde hair streaked with pink, and his eyes, when they are able to focus, are intense. From a distance, I could swear one is blue and one is brown, although I'm not quite close enough to tell. He's tall and somewhat muscular and covered in tattoos, and if he wasn't teetering and tottering around, he'd probably be quite attractive.

"Hey Griff," calls a man seated near us at the bar. "Thought you'd never arrive." A couple of others raise their glasses in his direction. "We've just been talking about you."

"You know you can count on me," he drawls, clearly liking the attention. "I wouldn't miss it for the world."

"Oh my god, what the fuck?" I mouth at Angel, worried they're just going to be yelling over us for the rest of the evening.

She grins back at me. "Just let it play out. He's a loud talker. We might hear something useful."

Sure enough, she's correct.

"I heard Jonas was going to do some work for Denzo," Griffin calls out to the man at the bar.

"Oh yeah? Must be mean getting that close to Tane. I can't even imagine."

Angel's eyes flick to mine but quickly return to the menu in front of us. Our ears prick at the sound of Tane's name. Please let this be the same Tane we're looking for. Although, I'm pretty sure that's a safe bet. I think anyone else bearing that name would change it if they lived here. From what we can tell, nobody wants to risk upsetting this scary man, and he doesn't seem to be okay with sharing anything, his name included.

"That's the one. He's pretty close to him," nods an excited Griffin.

"Good for Jonas," says the man at the bar. "It sounds like he's moving up the ranks with that crowd."

"Yeah, I'm a bit surprised, to be honest," yells Griffin. "He's never struck me as being very smart. But he's clearly impressing someone."

We listen for a while longer, but the conversation becomes generic sports talk. Eventually, Griffin and the man at the bar go play pool in the corner.. But that's fine with us. We've been here for just over twenty-four hours and we already have what sounds like a decent lead. It seems Griffin was more useful to our research than we initially gave him credit for.

Chapter Twenty-One

Devon

We head out to the pool area and find two sun loungers in the first row, closest to the water. We place our two striped pool towels on the loungers and kick off our flip-flops, taking a seat and reclining. The sun has barely risen, casting a mesmerizing mixture of pinks and oranges and purples over the ocean, and the air is crisp and cool.

The pool attendant team is out and about setting up, preparing for a busy day ahead. A few early birds have gotten up first thing and placed towels in prime positions around the pool. I wonder how long it will take most of them to come back and actually use the space they claimed, or if some of them will even come back at all. Like Harold and Cheryl, it seems like some folks think the entire hotel—hell, the entire island—revolves around them.

Angel frowns. "You'd think if someone just wanted to come down for a quick swim, they'd take their stuff with them when they left. Then other people could use the space when they didn't need it."

"You're giving humans too much credit, Angel."

"Ugh. I guess. At least we're early enough to get some decent seats, and we're actually planning to spend the whole day here. When I came down to scope things out yesterday, the entire pool area was just covered in towels. Every single sun lounger was taken. But there were almost no people here. It was like an abandoned towel city, where all the sad beach towels go to die."

She's right. And I would have found it tempting to run around picking up everyone's towels and throwing them in a big pile. It seems like it would be satisfying.

"Good for them. It would be a pretty scenic place to die." A shiver tickles my spine as I remember while we're here. I hope this doesn't become my gravesite, as attractive as it is. "Let's not, though, okay?" I add quickly. "My plan is to get out of here in one piece, and I hope you want that as well." I don't even want to think about what might happen if Tane gets wind that we're here.

"Yeah, let's worry about that later," she says. "The guys were right. We *do* deserve a proper nice day by the pool. We've been through a lot these last few months, and there's more big stuff about to happen. It makes sense for us to reset a bit, and recharge our energy. We're going to need it."

I lean back in my sun lounger, enjoying the feeling of the very mild morning sun and the gentle breeze coming off the ocean and softly tickling my skin.

By now, a few other early birds who actually intend to enjoy the pool have trickled in. They're the organized types, bags filled with extra towels and waters, pool toys and snacks at the ready. These folks mean business. I'm sure they'd never put a towel down on a lounger they didn't intend to use. These are my kind of people.

The pool area is now properly set up for the day. The gentle notes of island music pipe through the speaker system, peppered with the murmurs and occasional squeals of vacation conversations. Poolside breakfast service has kicked off and servers are making their way around taking orders.

As the morning goes on, I realize I still like the idea of relaxing more than actually doing it. The concept of sitting back and letting the day go by while my mind totally just lets go of everything troubling, everything requiring concentration or logical thought, is appealing. But I find it impossible in practice. The only way I can tune out what's happening every day is by immersing myself in an engaging book or podcast. Even then, I occasionally still find little thoughts knocking around in the back of my mind. Sometimes it's not about anything particularly important... maybe just reminding myself of an errand I need to run, or reflecting on a past conversation with someone. But today, my wheels are turning. We need to take this opportunity to find something that will help lead us to Tane. Of course, I want to impress the guys, so that's part of it. But

I also hate the idea that if we don't find out anything useful, this would just become some kind of wasted trip.

The further the morning rolls on, the more people come flooding into this part of the hotel. And it's almost like the later it gets, the obnoxious meter also intensifies. Several guests are speaking at a cacophonous volume that makes me want to take out a universal remote and mute them all. I'm not sure if it's because they're giddy because they're on vacation, if they've consumed too many tropical drinks, or if they just want to feel important. Nobody trying to relax on vacation needs to hear about who stole the church prize at home, Margaret. Or how your coworker takes too much PTO, Nancy. Or how your best friend is really such a backstabbing bitch, Betsy. Okay, if I'm honest, hearing Betsy's story was kind of amusing.

As lunchtime approaches, and the golden sun makes its way around the resort grounds, people dressed in casual attire stream into the pool area. Everyone is eager to score an early check-in, but the resort is near capacity. To avoid an additional wait for bellhops to take their bags while the team readies their rooms, people wheel their large suitcases around the pool.

Feeling hungry, we navigate our way to the crowded bar, trying to avoid being jostled by exuberant tourists or tripping over their clunky luggage.

"This has to be a health and safety issue," I frown, and Angel nods in agreement.

"Yeah, it's like having to jump hurdles in order to get to the bar. Who would bring their suitcases to the bar, for goodness' sake?"

"I'd normally make more of a scene, but I'm trying to blend in." I frown, resisting the urge to give everyone around me the evil eye. After what seems like way too long, we zigzag our way across the treacherous route and hop onto tall stools flanking the octagonal countertop.

"Ladies, what can I get for you?" A gregarious bartender greets us in his uniform of a tropical shirt featuring a nametag identifying him as Barney. He flings coasters down in front of us, bearing the name of the upscale resort that people are currently desecrating with their selfish luggage choices.

After perusing the menu, I order fish tacos and Angel orders a flatbread pizza. We opt for vodka sodas. "Make mine a double," says Angel. "This is a shit show." She gestures to the chaos around us and Barney laughs.

"Oh, just wait until everyone's a few drinks in. Now that's a real shit show."

Noticing our agitation and perhaps sensing we're not typical hotel guests, Barney prioritizes our drinks and brings them over quickly. While waiting for our food, we see he's right. People around us glug down sugary cocktail after sugary cocktail, and their voices grow louder and more animated.

In a brief lull in orders, Barney heads over to chat with us while he polishes glassware and chops some lemons and limes into uniform wedges. "So what brings you ladies to the island?"

"Oh, we're just perusing." I smile back.

"First time here?"

"Yes. Have always wanted to visit but haven't had the opportunity."

"Nice," he nods. "What are your initial thoughts?"

"Oh, it's gorgeous! And don't get me wrong, I think this resort is just amazing except for the sea of suitcases here," I say, gesturing to the surrounding calamity. "But we're looking to explore something a little more... local, you might say."

"Oh yeah? I know a few places," he nods and grins. "Lived here all my life, born and raised. What kind of vibe are you going for?"

"Somewhere the locals like to go," says Angel. "We really want to experience the culture."

"Well, I recommend Jolene's, which is about a twenty-minute drive from here. That's usually good for people-watching, if that's what you're into. And it's a fun place. You'll see what I mean if you go."

Angel looks at me and grins. "Oh, that's absolutely what we're into!"

Chapter Twenty-Two

Angel

"Are those saloon doors?" I eye the swinging wooden double doors with fascination, only having seen them in movies and on TV.

"OMG," Devon laughs. "I believe they are."

"Well, howdy," I giggle, putting on my best drawl. "Didn't expect to see them around these here parts."

Devon shrugs. "I think we've both already seen a lot of things we didn't expect to on these islands. Nothing surprises me anymore."

My mind flashes to everything that's happened in my time here. The dead man in my hair salon. The inside of the multiple compounds where I've been held captive. My stalker getting his comeuppance. And the fact I live with four smoking hot men who would do anything for me. "Okay, you're right. You've got me there."

The saloon doors weren't just for show. Inside, the bar is like something out of a spaghetti western. The decor is heavy on the wood, with a long bar stretching down one side and prominently featuring a wide range of whiskies. The floor is peppered with regular tables and chairs as well as high-tops.

"What can I get for you ladies?" The bartender looks like he walked in out of the past. He sports a mustache that's twirled at either end, and he's wearing an embroidered vest over the top of a crisp white shirt and a long white apron. He even has a black bow tie and matching arm bands.

We order two double shots of a rye that's hard to find on the islands.

"Interesting choice. It's not one that we get a lot around here. I like it." I'm surprised to hear he has a distinct New York accent that, thanks to popular TV shows and movies, I'd normally associate with organized crime. Nothing about this place makes much sense and I like it.

We finish our first drink while making small-talk with the bartender, who tells us his name is Frank and that he's been on-island for about ten years. We keep to our loose cover story, that we're visiting for the first time and just want to get a sense of local culture.

I order a second round. "What can you tell us about how this island operates?" I ask.

Devon shoots me a look. My question was probably more direct than it could have been.

"There's a decent visitor's center here, you know. They have all the pamphlets and things that explain everything about where to visit and what to do and see here on the island." My question has sailed right over his head, and I can't stop myself from digging further. "Oh, we're more interested in the real information about what goes on here. The secret sauce and what makes things tick. The dynamics about how this place really runs."

The man eyes us suspiciously. "Are you reporters or something?"

"No. Definitely not reporters," I say quickly.

"Then why all the questions? You haven't even finished your second round of drinks and it feels like you're poking around in the island's business." He narrows his eyes. "You don't seem like typical tourists."

Shit. I was too aggressive with my question. I'm just anxious to find out anything that could help us.

"Okay, Frank," Devon says suddenly and unexpectedly. "Let us be straight with you. We're both fairly new to one of the other islands. In the past, however long we've both been here, I've been kidnapped to pay off a debt my father owed, and barely escaped death or worse. My friend here has been taken hostage no less than four times and evaded a deranged stalker who obsessed over her for decades and followed her from the mainland after a long stint in prison. We believe recent fucked up things that have happened on our island stem from whatever is happening here. So, apologies for the bluntness of our questions, but we intend to find out what the hell is going on and put an end to it for once and for all."

I resist the urge for my jaw to drop open. And I thought my question was too forward.

The man considers us for a moment as he presses his mouth into a thin line. After what feels like an eternity, he nods with conviction.

"Listen, ladies." The man eyes us both. "I don't think it's smart for you to be snooping around asking questions about Tane fucking Brown. Because that's what it sounds like you're doing." His eyes grow large. He glances around the bar as if to confirm we're the only other patrons in there. We still are, except for one quiet couple who sits in the opposite corner out of earshot, despite Frank's naturally loud tone. He leans forward conspiratorially. "You have to know he's the most powerful man on this island. On any of the islands. And he has plenty of connections back on the mainland and further afield that should terrify the living fuck out of you." The man pauses. "But you seem to be coming from a good place."

"Oh, we are. I can promise you that."

The man sighs and runs his fingers through his hair. "Look, this is really putting my neck on the line. But all I can tell you is there's a guy that seems to be on the outs with Tane and his second-in-charge, Denzo." There's that name again. "He and Denzo in particular used to be super tight. I'm not sure what happened, but I heard they're not currently on speaking terms. Usually, that'd mean that this guy should no longer be alive, but for whatever reason, they're letting him continue on. But he seems to being kept out of their business dealings, at least for now. If you do go and talk to him, I suggest you do it real soon, because knowing those guys, their temperament could change any day now."

"What's this guy's name?"

"Diego. Alvarez is his last name."

"And where can we find this Diego character?"

"He's easy to find. He's the best butcher on the island. Which is why maybe they've decided to keep him around for now, just at arm's distance. He comes in handy for them from time to time, from what I understand. He has a... special skill set, you might say. Plus, he provides all the meat for Tane's restaurants."

I can't help but shiver at the implication. Devon's glance flicks to me almost imperceptibly as well. The implication of Diego's skill set is not lost on her, either.

Her eyes narrow. "Why are you deciding to help us anyway, if it's so dangerous for you? What if this is a trap? Sending us into a butcher's shop to ask around. For all we know, this Diego guy is a dangerous lunatic with sharp blades and a relationship—although you say it's former—with Tane's second-in-charge?"

The man narrows his eyes right back at Devon, but then he shrugs. "Eh, you know... I'm getting old. I'm getting kind of tired of this island's bullshit. I never would have volunteered it without you asking, and it was pretty ballsy of you to walk in here and start poking your noses around so boldly." He gestures around the saloon. "Look at this place. It's never been able to get off the ground and live up to near its full potential with all the protection money I've been forced to pay Tane and his men over the years." He gestures at some shabbily repaired tables and booths and a pool table with ripped felt and splintered pool cues. This place definitely has seen better days. "And to add insult to injury, his goons are always coming around and disrupting my other patrons, getting into fights and damaging the place. They never pay for repairs."

His tone is bitter, his mouth pinched into a sour expression and a tightness developing in his otherwise kind eyes. "And when you go through a personal crisis, they never come around. They're not there when you need them." He shrugs. "So, I'm thinking maybe it wouldn't be so terrible if someone came around and shook things up. Which I get the sense you and whoever you're working with might just have the potential to do. I take it you're not just working alone," he says, looking us both up and down. His voice lowers further. "And besides, you kind of remind me of my daughters that I lost a while ago. You exhibit a certain tenacity from what I can tell, and I respect that. Reminds me of back on the East Coast." His eyes become watery, reflecting the bar's soft light, but no tears fall. "Just make sure you don't befall the same fate that my daughters did from nosing into things that shouldn't concern them. Look after yourselves, ladies. Be safe. You're really lucky it was me you came and asked those questions, or today might have been your last." His tone grows urgent as the saloon doors swing open and four more patrons enter the near-empty bar. "One more thing. If Tane gets wind of what you're up to, you'd better get the fuck off the island, and fast."

"Thank you so much," says Devon, her eyes now watering too. I wonder if the man notices, but he says nothing. There's no doubt that the man's words about his daughters got to her a little. I reach over and give her arm what I hope is a reassuring squeeze. "We'd better get out of here. Let us close up and pay our tab and we'll leave you alone."

The man waves his hand in dismissal. "Eh, forget about it. This one's on the house."

Thanking him, we head out, almost getting hit by the swinging saloon doors as more patrons make their way inside.

"Well, then," I say as we make our way to the rental car. "I didn't think that was going to be particularly useful. It was a fucking empty saloon! But I believe we just received a little golden nugget of information about this Diego guy. And that guy Denzo's name came back up. He sounds scary. Well, they both do, actually. His second-in-charge and a violent butcher who probably hacks people up as a side hustle. But I think we just got one step closer to Tane."

"Yep, you're right," nods Devon. "I believe we just found our next target."

Chapter Twenty-Three

Angel

A bell on the door jingles as we enter the butcher shop. The store is empty, except for a dark-haired man with a tanned complexion who is vigorously cleaning behind the counter. Heavy metal music blares from an overhead speaker as he puts on an impressive demonstration of elbow grease. He either can't be bothered to look up when we enter or he just doesn't hear us over the loud drums, guitar and lead vocals that shriek about death and violence and gore. His forearms are ink-covered masterpieces, and he has a distinctive spider tattoo on his right hand.

The glass display cases and stainless-steel countertops are spotless. It's clear the store owner takes pride in his shop and service to the community. At least on the face of it. On the way in, I noticed a couple of stickers proclaiming the spot had won the neighborhood store of the year three years running.

Rows of uniformly sized sausages stack neatly next to fresh ground meats and cured charcuterie. One side of the store has shelves filled with condiments, some of which are made on-island and support a children's charity. Quite the community spot, by the look of it. Clearly a crowd favorite.

Slade would have an orgasm just looking at the quality and variety of meats in this place. Although, despite the cleanliness of the store, it still bears the unmistakable scent of raw meat, which is uncooked flesh and sinew when you think about it. Brick, unlike Slade, would not be impressed at all. He only salivates over chopping up human flesh and bone. Which it sounds like this guy just might, too.

I peek into the back, and it's like night and day between the front and the back of the store. While the back area still looks clean, massive carcasses hang on large industrial hooks. I notice the linoleum floor is peeling back there and the windows are grimy. I glimpse a rust-stained sink next to a variety of industrial-looking equipment meant for slicing large quantities of meat.

I shiver as I remember it's not just animal carcasses he's known for slicing and dicing expertly with his scary-looking tools. To think, all the customers who come in here for their weekly protein shopping list never have a clue that this man has possibly carved into countless bodies, disposing of them for Tane over the years. This aspect is what would impress Brick. As welcoming as this place looks, this man has a darkness that he's clearly hiding. The back room of his butcher's shop is likely a more accurate representation than the facade he puts up front. We need to tread carefully here.

"Um, hello," I call out over the heavy metal music. "Are you Diego?"

The man glances up briefly, just for a second, before looking back down at the counter he's furiously scrubbing. Even at a quick glance, his eyes are a dark, chocolate brown with a peculiar intensity that makes me feel like he's seeing right through me.

"Who's asking?" His voice is gruff, and he continues to avoid eye contact.

"We heard you might be able to tell us something about what's going on over here. About Tane and... Denzo, I believe it was." Wow. Devon is not beating around the busy today.

The butcher brandishes a cleaver and I do my best not to flinch as he raises it above him. For a second, I think it's meant for us and I almost flinch. But he hacks at a sizeable chunk of meat on one of the chopping blocks in front of him. Blood splatters on the back of the glass display case and his apron.

The man scowls. "Who told you that?"

"I don't know his name." There's no way I'd throw Frank under the bus.

He lifts his gaze to meet mine and glares at me. "Well, whoever it was, they were mistaken. And you have no business nosing around here. I recommend for your own good that you stop right now."

"Sorry," I frown. "They just said you might be able to help us. That it might be useful for you."

My eyes flit to a large meat grinder in the back. It glints menacingly under the light, and all I can think about is whether this man has used it to slice up any of his and Tane's victims.

"Well, I can't," he growls. "And I suggest you don't come back here. The questions you're asking are dangerous. To me, to my family. And to you. So, take your prying, nosy faces and get the fuck out of my store. And don't come back. Consider this a warning." The cleaver in his hand reinforces his point as it gleams intimidatingly underneath the overhead light.

I put my hands up as if in defense. "Okay, well, we're sorry to bother you."

"You'll be more than sorry if you bother me again. Get the fuck out of here."

"Well, wasn't he just a box of sunshine and rainbows?" Devon states rhetorically.

I snort and shake my head. "He was clearly annoyed we were there. But did you maybe detect some fear there, too? Implying his family might be in danger just for talking to us?"

"It was a little hard to tell over all the scowling and the hacking of giant pieces of meat with massive cleavers. That was all very distracting. But yeah," she shrugs, "I think you might be right. Fuck, I hope he's not going to run off to Tane or whoever and tell him we were nosing around. If he's tipped off, we're fucked. Maybe we should have thought this through a little longer before rushing in there and showing our hand."

"Well, I was a little surprised by your directness. But we can't just sit around and wait until we find someone who we're certain isn't going to tip Tane off. We'd be sitting there a year from now, none the wiser. With a massive hotel bill. And Tane would only have gotten stronger."

"True," she sighs. "I just wish it felt like we were making more progress. We've been pushing the boundaries for the sake of speed, and it could backfire big time."

"We'll get there," I nod, attempting to convince myself of my own words as much as Devon. "I'm sure of it. We've already got two names that seem like pretty solid leads."

She nods again. "Yeah, we've just got to be persistent. Relentless."

"Relentless," I repeat, rolling the word around in my mouth. "I like that."

Chapter Twenty-Four

Angel

"Are you sure you unpacked your suitcase properly?" Aidan asks through the phone.

"That's a weird question!" I reply. I'm used to unexpected questions from these men, so it shouldn't surprise me. "But I know you can be very particular about how you arrange your things, Aidan. You'd probably have had everything folded, hung up, ironed and even steamed within five minutes of walking through the door."

"Hey, I'm not that bad!"

I smirk, knowing full well that's exactly what he would have done. He's predictably organized in just about every aspect of his life.

"Don't smirk at me through the phone! I can't *see* you, but I know you're doing it!"

I laugh at being caught. He knows me too well.

"Okay, let me see what I've missed. Because so far I have found nothing that I haven't packed myself."

To be fair, my suitcase would probably terrify Aidan if he saw it right now. As hard as I've tried to keep it organized, things have come unfolded and there is a trail of clothing between my luggage and the nearby dresser. I've made a half-assed attempt at trying to organize things but haven't followed through. Cleaning my salon? No problem. It's always speckless, a testament to my commitment to providing a safe and healthy environment for my clients. Keeping my own living areas tidy? That's another story. Not that I'm unclean... I'm just oblivious to clutter when it's my own and in my own space.

I root around in the suitcase and sure enough realize I haven't taken stock of all its contents. At the very bottom, to one side, is an immaculately wrapped package that I haven't seen before. Soft tissue in my favorite color, teal, encapsulates a rectangular shape, and a black satin bow adorns the outside.

"Well, the packaging is beautiful, for one," I squeal, turning the box over in my hands. "And in my favorite color."

"Only the best for our Angel," he replies. From the tone in his voice, I can tell he's pleased I noticed the effort he made with the wrapping. "Open it."

I carefully untie the soft bow and rip open the wrapping.

Inside is a box containing what appears to be some kind of state-of-the-art vibrator. It's bright pink, and the packaging—while discreet—also advertises a plethora of vibrating, oscillating and suctioning functions.

"Aidan!" I feel myself blushing, but at the same time, I feel a twinge in my core. This looks interesting and fun.

"We were trying to be thoughtful. We knew you'd be missing us. It's supposed to be top of the line."

I laugh. "Okay, well, thank you. This *is* very thoughtful. And I'll definitely be putting it to use. I miss you guys so much, and can't wait until we're all in the same place again."

"Well, that's going to have to do for now. Because if anyone else ever touched you..."

"That would never happen," I say, and I mean it. "You four are all I want and all I need, and I'm so lucky to have each of you in my life. I don't need anyone else. That said, I appreciate this thoughtful gift to get me through the hard times."

"We're going to expect video footage of this, you know." Slade's voice booms down the line.

I laugh. "That sounds fair enough to me for the trouble you've gone to."

"I want to see too!" Brick calls out.

"Me as well!" yells Roman, who sounds like he must be over on the other side of the room.

"Okay, okay," I reply. "It's a date."

I take the vibrator out of its clear packaging and examine it more closely.

It's a dazzling blue color with silver accents. As I turn it over in my hands, I hear Brick let out a low whistle. "Jesus, that thing is even fancier than I remember when we picked it out!"

"You all picked it out together?"

"Yeah, we all wanted to be involved in this important choice," laughs Aidan.

"They say it's a triple threat," adds Brick.

"Like the 'caress of a lover's fingers'," adds Roman.

"And it's waterproof and made from body-safe silicon," adds Slade.

"Just like your favorite cooking utensils," I laugh. These guys are hilarious. And they deserve for me to show them my appreciation and to know just how much I can't wait for them to be here.

Here goes nothing.

I press the power button, and it begins to whir. It seems to be fully charged. Of course it is. Aidan thinks of everything.

Pressing a few more buttons, I test out some other settings and settle on one that seems to be medium pressure.

I'm turned on by the thought of putting on this show for the guys, even if it makes me feel a little awkward because I'm not used to it. So I start with something I'm more familiar with, dipping my finger into my arousal and use it to rub my clit.

I pull the vibrator to my entrance and slowly slide it inside me as far as it will go. It's length and girth remind me almost exactly of Aidan's cock—I have no doubt he did that on purpose and am quite frankly surprised I didn't end up with four vibrators in my suitcase, each precisely matching each of my guys' dimensions—and the little vibrations add a different feeling than I'm used to from using my finger alone. The little nozzle at the end snuggles into my clit, creating a slight suction that causes me to moan.

I try to look directly into the camera, but it's hard to keep my eyes open as little zaps of pleasure rush throughout my body in response to the vibrations. I don't think I'm going to last long with this thing, especially as I think about the four men watching me. I have no doubt they're all going to jerk off to this video, and the thought of them all stroking their big, hard cocks while they watch me play with myself is enough to send me into overdrive.

I roll my hips as I thrust the vibrator in and out of my soaking pussy. Part of it rubs against my G spot in a beckoning motion. Little ripples of pleasure course through me, like this thing was designed to touch all of my most sensitive parts at once. Whoever made this thing is a genius.

The coil in my core is tingling and tightening, my orgasm building with every second.

I increase the intensity setting by one level, and it's almost too much. It sends me crashing over the edge. My back arches and my hips thrash around and I continue to fuck myself with the large vibrator as my pussy spasms wildly around it while I come.

Eventually, my body stops clenching around the vibrator and I slowly slide it out.

"Taste yourself," groans Roman.

I obey, licking my cum off the shaft of the vibrator, and I hear Brick let out a groan.

"That was so incredible. Watching you do that was so fucking hot," grits out Aidan. "I want to put it on repeat."

I can't stop. Already, I want to do it again. "I'm not finished yet, guys."

"Oh, our Angel wants more," rasps Brick.

Giving myself a minute for the extreme sensitivity to subside, I adjust the setting once again and caress my pussy with the vibrator, running it from my ass all the way up to my clit. I moan at the vibrations that course through my core. A girl could get used to this thing. Not that it's anything to compare to my four guys, although maybe we should consider incorporating it into some of our intimate activities. This thing is fun.

I slide the vibrator into my pussy and moan as the second arm of it vibrates against my clit and again creates a light suction. It's like having four tongues on me at once, somehow, and it makes me miss my men even more. I increase the setting once again and it's like I'm having an out-of-body experience. "Oh god, I'm about to come again," I moan, and my body stiffens in anticipation as the vibrations continue to radiate throughout my core.

This time, I feel a surge of something within me and I try to resist but the sensation overtakes me. A warm gush flows from my body as a euphoric feeling zaps through my brain, leaving me lightheaded. "Oh, fuck!" I cry out. "Totally wasn't expecting that to happen!" I keep the vibrator inside me as my pussy continues to pulsate around it, and then slowly slide it back out.

"Wait, what just happened?" Brick asks. "I couldn't see!"

"I haven't done that in a really long time," I say, still a little shocked at the warm puddle I've created on the bed.

"You squirted?" Roman gasps.

"Oh man! We never make you squirt. I'm jealous of that thing!" Brick juts out his bottom lip like the vibrator just did him a personal injustice.

"Well, what was it like?" asks Aidan. "Tell us more, at least!"

I think about it for a moment. "It felt... different, but good. Like a ton of pressure being released all at once. And it was super warm, which I wasn't expecting."

"I wish I was there to see it in person," says Slade, dreamily. "That's so hot."

I smile. "Oh, I'm confident we can make it happen again."

"We? As in you and the vibrator?" Brick's jealousy is palpable.

"No, we, as in the five of us, silly!" I laugh. "No need to be jealous of this thing. Although, if you wanted to add this as a sixth to our relationship, I'd be okay with that too." There's a brief silence. "I'm only joking, guys. But I thought it might be fun to use with you when we're all together."

We all laugh, including Brick, although his is a tad shallow. I'm going to have to watch him closely or I'm pretty sure I'm going to find this thing smashed to smithereens in his torture basement. A warning to all other vibrators to never cross my path.

"I'll reserve my judgement," laughs Aidan. "I don't want you deciding you don't need us anymore and running off with that thing instead."

"That, I can promise you, will never ever happen."

Chapter Twenty-Five

Zeke

"To be frank, I'm still really concerned about how we sent them off on their own." I frown. I can't stop worrying that we've already put them in way too much danger. It sounds like they already may have shared too much with characters who sound more than shady. A butcher who cuts up humans, for goodness' sake. And this Denzo character sounds like a really dangerous guy, almost as bad as Tane himself.

If Tane gets wind that they're there and we're not around to protect them, I couldn't live with myself. Which is why I haven't been able to sleep since they left, and have stayed up all night ruminating on how to fix this without blowing their cover. "But I have an idea."

"What's that?" Dom raises an eyebrow.

"Well, as we know, it'll be too obvious if we all go over there at once. At least before we're fully ready to launch our assault on Tane. But I think if a couple of us go over there now, they can follow the girls around from a distance. Just to make sure they're safe."

"Like you want some of us to go and stalk the girls around the island?" Aidan looks doubtful and runs his fingers through his hair the way I've learned he does when he's feeling antsy.

"Well, think of it more like a bodyguard duty," I shrug. "But just one where they don't know we're doing it. A confidential bodyguard service, if you will."

"This sounds prime stalker to me," says Brick. "And I would know."

We all turn to look at Brick. He's known for making the most random comments, but now and then he outdoes himself.

"Well, do you want them to be safe or not?" I ask the group, glancing at them one by one.

"Of course we do," says Slade, his face getting red. He rubs at the back of his neck. "That's a stupid question. They're obviously the most important things in our lives. But why can't we just tell them the plan?"

"Well, do you think they'd have the willpower to stay away from us if they knew we were there?" I ask. "I'm trying to be practical here. If the two of them were seen with two of us, I just think it's too risky. It wouldn't be as bad as all ten of us being there, but it still raises the risk far more than I'm comfortable with. It feels like they're already in danger, and we have to be discreet."

"Well, who do you propose goes?" Dom arches an eyebrow and folds his burly arms over his massive chest. "Is this your excuse to see Devon before the rest of us?"

I've thought about this all night. "As much as I'd love to see them, we need to keep our operations running back here. I have things to do on this island which can't be done remotely. So I need to stay here. Same goes for Skyler and you, Dom. Rake, I think you're best placed to go on our end. What about on your side of things?" I eye Aidan, acutely aware of his natural leadership role among the Brixton men. And more recently, his de facto leadership over all eight of us, which I'm still not super comfortable about. But now's not the time to worry about that.

"Well, the same goes for me," he says, running his hand through his hair. "Roman needs to keep the clubs operational. They quickly fall into disarray without him keeping a firm eye on them, so we need to have his window away from this island as short as possible. Slade, you need to help him with that."

Slade eyes him with suspicion. "Why me? There's nothing I need to be keeping a close eye on right at the moment."

"Well, we also need someone to cook, and you're the best." Aidan grins at him, his eyes sparkling with amusement.

Slade rolls his eyes. "God forbid you idiots learn how to open a can or heat some noodles and prevent yourselves from starving yourselves to death if I need to go somewhere for a day or two."

Aidan shrugs. "It is what it is. Take the compliment, man. So that leaves you, Brick. As much as we need your muscle here, I think you're best placed to surveil the girls. And, surprisingly, you have much more restraint than Roman to stay away from Angel until we get the green light. But, Brick, you can't go creeping into her room to steal her undies or anything like that... this time."

Brick grins sheepishly and shrugs. "That was just the one time," he says, grinning. "And now she gives them to me voluntarily.". He glances at Rake. "So it sounds like it's the two of us, then?"

Rake nods with enthusiasm. "Vacation! We get to see our girls! And maybe participate in some violence!"

"Great. I'll make the reservation tomorrow," I explain. "I've also got some IDs and credit cards being made that you can use when you check in for the hotel reservation."

"Sounds like a plan. Really good idea, Zeke," nods Skyler, and the rest of the group nods along.

It really gives me a sense of relief knowing that at least some of the guys will be there in person just in case shit goes down.

I just hope we're not too late.

Chapter Twenty-Six
Devon

A tall man in a suit stands in front of me. Even though I've never seen him before, I know without question that it's Tane Brown. He's flanked by burly men armed with guns. Just some of his faithful goons with their undivided loyalty toward a complete madman. An evil lunatic. Someone who will stop at nothing to find me and take what he believes is his.

He has me tied up, defenseless. Naked, I'm unable to move. I tug against my restraints, but they're firm and unflinching. I wince as they scrape across my sensitive flesh.

He comes closer, and I see behind him stands another row of men. They all believe I'm theirs, too. They're the bidders that want to purchase me from Tane. Some are carrying sharp blades and others have brutal-looking whips. They all have their eyes on me, a mixture of scorn and lust and hatred in their eyes.

My father is in the back, and he charges toward me, his eyes dark with rage. His face is mottled and spittle builds up in the corners of his mouth as he screams insults at me. He berates me for everything he believes I've ever done wrong, and the other men laugh with scorn. He smirks as he tells them how much I deserve what they're about to do to me.

My pulse races, blood speeding to my temples and leaving me light-headed as I gasp for breath.

He points in my direction and lets out a guttural roar that causes my spine to tingle and makes my scalp crawl. Tane simply nods and gestures for the men to follow my father's instructions to harm me.

The other men do not hesitate and descend on me, wielding their weapons. They beat me, slicing at my flesh as I thrash around in an attempt to get away. I feel the welts forming and the blood that trails its way in messy smears across my body.

My chest is tight, and my lungs don't seem to work. It's getting harder and harder to breathe. My throat feels like I've swallowed glass, and I taste blood. My vision is blurry, and the periphery clouds with black spots that keep getting larger.

I hear screaming, the terrified cries of someone afflicted with the most brutal pain and suffering. But the beating doesn't stop. I feel my life force fading as my breaths take in less and less air and the blood drains out of me. My father continues to look on, his mouth twisting up in a sick, pointy-toothed smile. His face transforms, and soon he looks like Tane, and Tane looks like my father. They both just stare and smile as they watch the other men do their bidding.

The screams continue, rattling my brain. I realize they're coming from me. I'm barely breathing, but I'm shrieking at the top of my lungs.

I wake with a start, and reality comes flooding back. My breath is ragged and my throat feels raspy. My head pounds, and my body is covered in a thick sheen of sweat.

I hear knocking from the adjoining room. "Dev, are you okay in there? I heard you screaming." Angel opens the door a crack and pokes her head through."

Thank god that was just another night terror. But they're happening more frequently than usual, and they're becoming harder and harder to bear. "Yeah, I'm fine. Just a nightmare."

"Okay, well I'm next door so just let me know if you need me."

"Thanks. I just think this whole thing with my dad has me a bit rattled. My brain seems to be processing it in my sleep."

It's been about a week since my father ceased to exist. I knew it was going to happen, and I knew who was going to do it. I'm trying not to remember the exact date because anniversaries can be so triggering, and I don't need to add another one to my sad life calendar.

"It's a lot to take in. Anyone would find the whole situation traumatic."

"It's weird, though. You'd think I'd have a problem with my four boyfriends killing my father, but the whole thing just made me feel numb. It had to happen after what he did."

"I can only imagine. But you're right. It did need to happen."

It's been a long time since I've been able to refer to him as Dad. It feels more clinical to name him my father, but sometimes even that descriptor feels a little too close for comfort. Like we're inextricably linked, and I'm unable to disconnect myself from his being. He did nothing to earn it, and he's given me a lot of reasons to want absolutely no connection to him.

"If it weren't for my guys, and if it wasn't for the Brixtons, I'd be dead because of him. Or being sex trafficked or tortured by some sadistic fucks. Who knows when he'd have tried to weasel his way back into my life again and trade me for another debt? The risk would always be hanging over my head."

"Right. That would be even worse. At least now you will hopefully have some closure or know he can't come back."

I know that for many people, family is meant to come above everything else. And the same is true for me now, when it comes to my chosen family. I'd do anything for them, few or no questions asked. But when it comes to that asshole who happened to be part of the reason I'm born, he doesn't get that same level of respect.

Because he never afforded me that himself. I was something to check off his list, a thing he figured he was meant to do in his life, and that was it. Have a child just to say he did. And when it came down to it, my life was worth nothing more than a gambling debt to him.

"Exactly. So it seems fitting in a weird, poetic way, that his own life would end at the hands of the men who were given responsibility to hold me captive while he had one final opportunity to make things right. When he had one last opportunity to save me."

But he didn't save me, and now they've come for him.

And he's paid the ultimate price.

Chapter Twenty-Seven

Skyler

"Sometimes I worry that she's going to bear resentment for what we did." I frown at the thought of Devon having anything but love for us. But if I was in her shoes, I'm not sure how I'd be able to work through my emotions about this.

We're gathered around our kitchen table again, having a brief lunch while we get Rake's stuff ready for his trip with Brick. I have to admit I'm jealous I'm not the one who gets to go be there with Devon, even though I understand why Rake is best-placed to go. Being apart from her is harder than I expected, and it's making me worried about how she's feeling about things.

"I hear you," says Zeke. "But we had to do it. He may be responsible for her life, but he was almost responsible for her death as well. There's no way we could let him live."

"Zeke's right, Sky," says Dom. "I've been giving this a lot of thought. And the added pressure of Tane ordering the hit on him was the final straw. It's the only way he would allow us to fully pay off the debt from our perspective. If we hadn't, he would have just kept coming back again, over and over. But it doesn't mean it was easy to do. I've never been as conflicted about taking another man's life."

He frowns and I suddenly feel guilty, having forgotten that he is the one who technically put an end to things, even though we all took part in his brutal torture. "Do you think we went about it the right way, though?" My mouth involuntarily contorts into a scowl. "We really went in on him and made it hurt. Maybe we should have been a bit more... understated in our approach. And this isn't just about you at all, Dom. It's a collective thing. We all tortured the man and showed no mercy."

"Yeah," he shrugs. "Technically, we could have made it painless, and a surprise that he never saw coming. But that would have been too easy of an escape for him. He deserved to suffer, to feel the excruciating physical pain, to mirror the emotional pain he caused for Devon through his inexcusable actions. What kind of monster is willing to risk his daughter's life to pay off his debt to one of the most evil men around? And besides, we can't go back now."

"You're right," I sigh. "He deserves everything we gave him. I just hope it's something that Devon agrees with. Because I'd never want this to come between us. We all care about her far too much for that."

CHAPTER TWENTY-EIGHT
Aria

"*You do understand that you're ours, right? That we own you completely? That you were made for us, for our pleasure and ours alone?*"

My pussy clenches at his words. If someone had told me even a month ago that I'd be turned on by a man claiming me as his, let alone three men saying the same thing, I would have told them they were insane. That I'm an independent woman who would never let myself be controlled by any man. But there's something about the way this group of men treats me that makes me want them to exert complete control over me. They make me feel like I want to be submissive, to bend to their will compliantly, to take what they want to give me. Nothing more, nothing less.

"Show us how beautiful you are. We want to see all of you. Take your clothes off." His voice is deep and it make me quiver. I've never felt more desired.

I slowly remove my tank top, followed by my bikini top, letting my breasts bounce free. My nipples are already hard, the feeling of six eyes transfixed on my body turning me on in a way nothing else ever has.

"Keep going," he growls, and the others nod, their eyes hungry to see the rest of me. I love the way their gazes all trail over my body like they each want to savor every inch. I know I want to savor every inch of them myself, so it's very much mutual.

I untie the drawstring of my shorts and yank them down, along with my panties. This isn't the time for a sensual striptease where I peel off every layer one by one. They want to see it all, to see all of me, right now. Their eyes darken with desire as I slowly turn around in front of them, giving them a glimpse of my every curve.

"Fuck, you're so gorgeous Aria," rasps Dimitri. "Look what you're doing to me. To all of us."

I can see his hardness straining against his shorts, and can't imagine they'll be staying on for long.

"Be our good little whore and show us how you like to be touched. We want to see how you like to do it, you filthy little slut. Spread your legs and show us your beautiful cunt and how hot you are for us." I adore it when they call me these words. If anyone else tried to call me these names, I'd punch them in the throat, at least twice. It would feel disrespectful, misogynistic. Degrading. But when these three call me these names, I know they're claiming me, praising me, and it makes little electric bolts tingle all over my body. Their words melt me to my core and make me want to please them, and to do anything they want. And they want to possess me.

I spread my thighs apart in front of them, exposing my bare pussy, which is growing wetter by the second.

"Look at how wet you are for us. You're soaking, aren't you?" Florian bites his bottom lip as his gaze narrows in on my pussy. "Show us how you like to rub your soaking cunt, and how it feels best for you."

I'm all too happy to stroke my clit while they all watch, using my arousal to wet my finger. I moan at my own touch, my senses elevated by having their eyes on me. They study the way I use my finger to rub against my clit, causing little zips of pleasure to ping through my body as the intensity builds in my core. I moan again.

"Stop," commands Josef as I start to get close.

I pull my finger away because he told me to and I would do anything he says. I really hope he lets me finish this time. I'm craving the release. Sometimes they let me get to the edge and then pull me back, over and over again and leave me like a sopping mess until the end of the day. But I'd never finish myself off without having their permission. Not only because I'm a little scared of what they might do if I did that, because it goes against our rules. But because it turns me on, letting them control my body like this. Letting them dictate if and when I get to feel the release of an orgasm, or if they just get to make me all worked up and then relinquish the privilege.

Some days, they don't let me come at all. They use my body however they see fit, plunging their gorgeous cocks inside my pussy, my mouth, my ass. They own every part of me, and they use me accordingly.

I know that if I obey them, at some point I'll experience pleasure like no other. They always make it up to me. But I'm also completely content serving them, making them feel good. Maybe my destiny is to make them feel so much pleasure, as and when they want it, that it makes them more powerful in some way.

"Should we let her have it, guys?" asks Dimitri, glancing at the other guys. "She's been such a good girl. I'm thinking maybe we should let her come after all. Maybe even more than once."

See, I called it correctly. I had a feeling that if I followed their commands today, they'd make sure I reaped the benefits.

"Okay, finish yourself off now. Rub your clit again," growls Florian. "And finger yourself while you do it. We're each going to spend some time with you later, by the way."

"I can't wait," I say as I return my finger to my clit, hungry to resume rubbing it until I feel the sweet release. I insert two fingers from my other hand into my pussy and fuck myself with them, soaking them in my arousal.

Dimitri and Florian have their cocks out, stroking themselves as they watch my solo performance.

I moan as the pressure continues to build within me until I can't take it anymore. Suddenly, pleasure tears throughout my body and my hips buck into the air. I continue to rub my clit through the orgasm, thrusting my fingers as deep inside myself as I can, feeling my pussy pulsating and clenching around them.

"Good girl," Josef rasps. "It would be a waste not to taste you right now, all that delicious cum gushing out of you." He glances at the other guys. "Do you mind?"

"No, as long as I get to taste her later," nods Dimitri. "Because I'm fucking starving."

Josef approaches me, dropping to his knees and dipping his head. My pussy is still sensitive from just coming, and he holds my hips down firmly, stopping me from thrashing around as he licks my swollen clit.

"Fucking hell, you taste amazing," he growls, his deep voice humming against my pussy. I moan as the vibrations trigger something deep within me, the coil in my core tightening as he lashes his tongue against me.

"Oh fuck," I squeal, and he yanks my pussy hard into his face. I'm barely unable to move, although my instinct is to buck my hips away. The coil continues to twist deep inside, pressure building until it has no outlet, and I scream as another orgasm peaks, sending shockwaves throughout my body. Electricity hums in my head as my legs shudder, and I wrap my thighs around Florian's head as he hungrily takes every last drop.

"That's our good girl. Our precious queen," growls Dimitri. "You did such a great job for us. And we've only just begun."

Chapter Twenty-Nine
Brick

We approach the check-in desk after waiting in line for what felt like hours. For such a nice resort, they could staff it up better, so people weren't impatient and frustrated the moment they got here. But then again, I've heard good help is hard to find these days, even outside of our criminal world.

"Ah yes, hi there. We're here to check in," I say, in what I hope sounds like the tone associated with an guest experienced at staying in upscale hotels. I've never stayed in a place like this before, and it's hard enough not to stand out with my burly physique. Even though I'm dressed in a designer polo and khaki shorts, I wonder if they can tell by the sight of me I feel more comfortable in the likes of a Motel 6. Sure, the guys and I live in a nice place now, and have access to money most people only dream of, but it hasn't always been that way for me and the scars of poverty in my early life are seared into my brain.

I'm not sure if my neural pathways will ever rewire and allow me to realize I'm no longer poor. Or to feel like everyone else can't see through me and just know my instinct is to panic about finding my next meal, despite the pantry and refrigerator in our gourmet kitchen perpetually overflowing with the best food money can buy.

The fact I'm vegan now strikes me with guilt. That I could be so picky about what I eat when I used to be desperate to find anything at all to fill my starving belly. That I get to embrace a philosophy about eating that some would say is reserved for the most privileged. It's actually a shock that I grew to be so physically big at all. Genetics, I guess.

The lady at the front desk smiles at me and nods at Rake. Her smile is genuine, from her straight white teeth to her warm brown eyes. Her uniform is immaculate, a suit pressed within an inch of its life and accessorized with delicate, understated jewelry. God, I'm glad I don't work in a job where I have to wear a uniform and be polite to people. I'd become homicidal in about five minutes.

"Ah, yes, Mr. and Mr. Slater. We've been expecting you! Congratulations!" She beams at each of us.

I eye Rake, who also furrows his brow and regards me curiously.

"I just need a credit card and an ID from each of you," she says.

I pull out the fake ID and credit card Aidan handed me on the way out. Not having taken the time to look at it, sure enough, I see Axle Slater embossed boldly on the credit card. The ID also matches.

Rake pulls his ID out as well and glances at it. He looks at me for a second with eyes wide but then quickly recovers, a beaming smile stretching across his face. "Ah yes. This is me, Alex Slater. That's us, Axle and Alex."

"I'm very impressed!" gushes the front desk agent, "at how quickly you've arranged an ID under your new last name! Usually people take a few months. That just shows your commitment to each other. How lovely! How was the wedding?"

I glance at Rake, who shrugs almost imperceptibly.

"It was...magical," I try to smile. "Everything we ever dreamed of? Isn't that right, uh... honey?"

Rake beams and puts his arm around me, while I try not to flinch. "Yes darling. It was everything we hoped it would be."

The front desk agent completes our check-in process and, still beaming, hands us each a room key. "Have a wonderful stay! We're so pleased you're choosing to spend your honeymoon with us!"

Through gritted teeth, I force out a smile. "Thank you. We're also so excited to be spending our honeymoon with you."

As we walk to our room, I lean over and whisper into Rake's ear. "Oh, there's going to be hell to pay for this when the other guys get here."

"I think it's hysterical," snorts Rake.

"You would," I growl.

"Hey. I didn't say there wouldn't be revenge."

"Now you're talking." I grin.

I use the keycard to unlock the hotel room door. Immediately, I notice towels have been twisted into two swans that together form a heart shape on the bed, which is also adorned with red rose petals. One bed. King-sized by the looks of it. I grab a card from the bedside table.

Congratulations, Mr. & Mr. Slater, on your recent nuptials!

We're so delighted that you're choosing to join us on your honeymoon as you embark on the rest of your new life together.

Please enjoy the complimentary champagne which we've placed on ice for your convenience.

- Hotel management

I groan while Rake cracks up in amusement.

"We're both way too big to share this bed. You're taking the couch," I growl, pointing to the foldout sofa in the corner.

I crack open the champagne and guzzle it straight from the bottle.

I think I'm going to kill whoever pulled this prank, even if it was a group idea.

Otherwise, we're never going to hear the end of this.

Chapter Thirty

Angel

"Do you think you'll ever miss him? Your father, I mean." I feel intrusive asking this question, but I can't stop thinking about what just happened with Devon and her father. "And if you tell me to fuck off because you don't want to talk about it, I completely understand."

I can almost see the cogs turning in her brain as she figures out how to respond. She fidgets, her fingers restless, and she chews on her bottom lip. "No, you're fine," she says. "I've wondered the same thing, you know. I think there will be moments where I miss who I hoped he would ultimately turn out to be. But that was just a ghost. He was never that person. I won't miss the person he really was. How could I?"

"That makes sense, and I'm sorry if my question came across as insensitive. I've just been thinking of you and all you've been through since you got to the islands."

"I could say the same for you," she says, pressing her mouth together and shaking her head.

"I know it's weird to say, but occasionally I miss my stalker," I confess. "Like, I don't miss him stalking me, or the rapes and the beatings, of course." A shiver runs down my spine at the thought. "But I just got so used to him being around, never being able to be free of him, that his absence has created some sort of weird void." I laugh, a hint of bitterness in my voice. "Man, that must make me really fucked up."

"Nah," says Devon, smiling at me with a tinge of sadness in her own voice. "I just think that makes you human."

We both sit in silence and gaze out over the water for a moment, in silent companionship. It feels comfortable despite the sad subject.

"Who ever imagined we'd be sitting here like this?" I say. "If you'd told me I'd be living on a tropical island with four men as my partners, trying to hunt down a dangerous criminal, I'd have told you that you were insane."

"Aren't we all a little insane?" She grins at me and gives me an exaggerated wink that makes her look more than a little unhinged.

We both laugh and lay back in our sun loungers.

If any of these tourists overheard us just now, they'd definitely think we were absolute psychos.

And they'd be right.

Chapter Thirty-One

Devon

On my way back to the room, I see a tall, shadowy figure. It's standing behind one of the large plants lining the pathway from the hotel lobby through to the guest room elevators. It's dark, but the person looks oddly familiar. Noticeably tall. Something I can't quite put my finger on. Although I don't think I know anyone who would wear a trench-coat and matching hat in hot weather like this.

Suddenly, it clicks.

"Rake? Rake, is that you?" I call after the shadow.

The figure turns and flees in the other direction, disappearing into the darkness before I get a closer look.

I return to the room and knock on the adjoining door. Angel calls out, "Come in!"

She's sitting cross-legged on her bed in comfortable-looking yoga pants and a tank top, tapping away on her laptop when I enter. She looks up at me, an eyebrow quirked. "What's up?"

"I know this sounds bizarre, but I think we're being followed."

"Oh shit," she says, clapping her laptop shut right away, her eyes wide with concern. "Tane's men? They're already on to us?"

I shrug and shake my head. "Well, I can't be sure, but I think the person I saw might have been Rake."

"Rake?! That's so weird, because I could have sworn I saw someone that looked a bit like Brick earlier. I figured I must be imagining things."

"Oh really? Did you try calling your guys?"

"Yeah, and they made it sound like everything was fine and everyone was still on the home island waiting for us to send over more information."

"Did you get to speak with Brick directly? Did you see him with the others on video?"

"No, actually. I asked to, but they said he was out on a job and wouldn't be back for a few hours. Which now that you mention it seems oddly convenient." She crosses her arms and furrows her brow. "You really think you saw Rake?"

"I mean, he has a certain gangly appearance about him. His height is hard to conceal. And the man was wearing a trench-coat."

"This is so weird."

"I know." I press my mouth together in a thin line. "What the hell are these guys up to?"

I pull out my phone and text the group chat:

Guys. You have some explaining to do.

Chapter Thirty-Two

Roman

"You did *what*?" Devon's voice is shrill.

"Why would you do that? You don't trust us?" Angel sounds furious.

I put my hand over the phone's microphone. "We're in trouble, guys."

"We can still hear you!" They both yell in unison. I sigh as I realize I should have used the mute button.

"Listen," says Zeke, his voice calm and measured. "We were just looking out for you. We put you in a risky position and so we wanted to make sure you had some protection in case anything went wrong."

"So you didn't trust us?" Angel fumes. "You don't think we're capable of the assignment that *you* gave us? Why wouldn't you just tell us?"

"Well, we didn't want you to be distracted," I try to explain.

"What? By Rake and Brick's dicks?" Devon's voice shakes with anger.

"Kind of. Yeah," I admit. "But more so, we thought it would be risky for you to be seen together, even just the four of you. And we know you find it hard to stay away from each other."

Nobody says anything for a moment. And the silence frankly is scarier than their audible rage.

"Wait. How did you even find out about this?" Aidan's voice breaks through the silence.

"As good as they usually are at being incognito, they went a little over-the-top at the hotel. They couldn't have picked worse disguises if they tried," Angel's tone is scathing, but perhaps with a hint of amusement. "Wearing trench coats and detective hats. Hiding behind pot plants that don't cover their massive bodies."

"Are you kidding me?" I roll my eyes and shake my head, and then rub my face with my hand. "What a fucking disaster."

"Well, you did send the two clowns of the group, so I don't know what you expected to happen."

"That's true. I bet they've been egging each other on."

There's another pause and then, after what feels like an uncomfortable eternity, Angel speaks up. "Well, this is ridiculous. And if it wasn't for the cover story of Rake and Brick being Mr. and Mr. Axle and Alex Slater, we wouldn't forgive you. But that is fucking hilarious. We just sent a congratulatory fruit basket to their room."

"Wait... You know about that, too?"

"It didn't take much detective work to figure out their fake names. We've built a rapport with the hotel staff here *like you asked us to,* and all we had to do was ask for the names of the guests matching their ridiculous descriptions. The gangly one in the trench-coat with a penchant for sequins and unicorns. The vegan lumberjack surfer who seems very uncomfortable in his surroundings. Hardly people that would blend into the crowd at a place like this."

"I guess we didn't think this through carefully enough," I say, beginning to realize how absurd it was that we sent Brick and Rake of all people. I put my face in my palm.

"It's okay," sighs Devon. "It gave us a laugh once we got over our initial rage."

"I'm glad you can see the humor in it," replies Zeke, sounding more than a little relieved.

"Please though, guys," says Angel, injecting a little more warmth into her voice. "Just be honest with us from now on. Your overprotectiveness ends up backfiring one thousand percent of the time. We're either in this with you fully or we're not. We're not the delicate flowers that sometimes you treat us as."

"You're right," Aidan responds, sounding more than a little sheepish. "You're two incredibly strong, fierce women. And we couldn't do this without you. We'll be honest with you from now on."

"So do you forgive us?" I ask, mentally crossing my fingers that they'll let this go.

There's a pause on the other end of the line, and I look at the other guys with trepidation.

"Very well," says Angel. "We have conferred and decided that we forgive you."

We all glance at each other, and a collective sigh of relief is audible from our end of the phone.

"We can still hear you." They both laugh.

Chapter Thirty-Three

Angel

Devon sets up the drone and presses a few buttons on the remote, resulting in some mysterious beeps.

"How do you even know how to fly one of these things?" I quirk a brow.

She shrugs. "I haven't done it before, actually. But I've spent enough time sitting down at the beach watching people act like idiots it wasn't too hard to figure it out."

"I guess we get to be those idiots now," I smirk.

Devon laughs. "But we're acting. It's for a purpose. I feel so ridiculous, but there's a reason we're doing this. Now pose!"

Against my better judgement, I run into the ocean. The water whips around my ankles as a wave cascades into shore.

"Jump! Jump!" yells Devon, as the drone buzzes into the air and hovers in front of me.

I feel myself blush as I do as she instructs, leaping as high as I can above the water and stretching my arms out wide above my head.

She uses the remote control to snap pictures. Ostensibly, they're of me flailing around like an influencer in the wild. But really, she's snapping pictures of the access points to the compound behind me. We're not alone here, as a bunch of others snap pictures in front of the incredible, palatial mansions that line the beachfront. But while they're trying to boost their followings on Instagram and other social media platforms, our photos will not end up online. We're going to figure out how to best breach Tane's compound, one drone picture at a time.

"I feel completely ridiculous, but it's for a good cause," I yell, striking another awkward pose.

Devon laughs.

When we're finally done with the photo shoot, we review the footage that we were able to collect.

"There's a gate that seems to be heavily manned on the south side." Devon purses her lips as she analyzes a few of the clearest pictures. "The guards are all visibly armed. They inspect each vehicle thoroughly as it comes in and again when it leaves. They have those angled mirrors on long sticks to look under vehicles, presumably to check for any explosives or other hidden items. There's an intercom that people seem to call when they arrive, with a watchtower overlooking that corner of the property."

"What about the north side? Any vulnerabilities?"

"Yes, that's where I think they might have a weak spot. Technically, the beach can't be considered private land. It's available to the public. So anybody can walk along there. And that means there are local guidelines where they can't create an eyesore that will scare families trying to have a beach picnic. Sure, there is still a huge fence topped with barbed wire along that side, but that looks a hell of a lot easier to breach than the front gate. But we need to verify because there might be cameras there we can't see."

"What are you thinking? We scale the fence? Blow it up?" I quirk a brow.

"I'm not sure yet. Maybe we need a diversion that will get people thinking we're trying to breach the front gate. While they're distracted, we'll breach the fence in the rear and enter the building on the northwest side, where there seems to be the least security."

I think for a moment and then tap my temple. "I think I know just the thing."

Chapter Thirty-Four

Rake

"Well, it seems like the girls have locked themselves away for a quiet night in tonight. So I was thinking we may as well take advantage of the amenities." This is a weird situation, and I'm trying to make the most of it. If there's a fun time to be had anywhere, I'm often the one to find it. Lemons out of lemonade and all that.

Brick arches a brow. "Oh yeah? What did you have in mind, Rake?"

"Well, apparently, restaurant management has booked us a celebratory dinner reservation. It's at the Italian restaurant off to the side of the lobby. And I think we should go for it."

Brick sighs and puts his face in his giant palm. "Oh god, do we really have to do this?"

I shrug. "Well, either we sit here cooped up together or we go out there and eat some pasta. I know what I'd prefer."

"Okay, I guess I could use some carbs as well," Brick nods. "And I do like food. But if you make any moves, I'm knocking you out, *husband*."

I smirk, and we quickly get ready before heading out the door.

This is not the trip I had planned. I was trying to scheme time with Devon, but that doesn't seem to be on the cards for the moment. Brick will just have to do.

CHAPTER THIRTY-FIVE

Angel

2 0 minutes later

"The gig is up, boys. Or should I say, Mr. and Mr. Slater? And we hear congratulations are in order." From the entrance to the restaurant, we call out to the guys, who are both seated at a table perusing menus.

"Oh shit! They're onto us!" Rake exclaims, and he and Brick stare at each other with large, guilty eyes before glancing around desperately for escape routes.

"There's no escaping us. We're blocking both the exits." Their faces are both pale and I try to keep my voice calm and serious, although it's incredibly difficult not to burst out laughing as we flank them on either side of their table. I can see Devon trying to keep a straight face, too. This is tough work.

"What are you going to do to us?" Brick asks, genuine fear in his eyes. These two large men can torture the most evil criminals, but they're clearly both afraid of us two women, who are much smaller than them, and whom they've come to protect without our knowledge.

"Oh, you'll find out soon enough. Enough with the questions, already." As if to emphasize her point, Devon raps the menu in her hand against her other palm as if she intends to smack them both with it. The men both visibly flinch, as if she's holding a metal baton and not a leather-bound menu.

"We can't believe you would do this to us. It's a real betrayal of our trust. And you know how we both feel about trust," I say, looking at each of them. I try to frown, but my mouth trembles in my struggle not to smile. Still, it has the desired effect and Rake's mouth drops open.

"She's right," says Devon, unblinking, her voice monotone. "You're going to be punished for what you did. This is unforgivable. You should both be deeply ashamed. Just wait until we're done with you." She smacks the menu in her palm again for emphasis.

Brick raises his hands in a defensive posture. "We were just trying to look out for you! To make sure you were okay! This assignment you're on isn't safe. The other guys agreed to it, too. And it was Zeke's idea!" Brick's voice is pleading as he throws Zeke under the bus, and Rake nods in enthusiastic agreement.

"Oh, we know," I say, my voice firm and my gaze as serious as I can make it.

"Yes, we know everything," adds Devon.

"You... do?" Brick's face riddles with confusion, and Rake quirks an eyebrow.

"Everything? Like everything everything?" Rake asks.

"Yes, everything," we say in unison.

"Mr. and Mr. Alex and Axle Slater, newlyweds on honeymoon," I add, causing the men to glance at each other and back to us and blush profusely. "Congratulations on your recent nuptials. We wish we could have been there to see the ceremony. We hope you enjoyed the fruit bowl"

Devon's face breaks into a smile, which immediately makes me laugh.

"You're laughing now?" Brick asks, confused.

"It's hard not to when you're both blushing so hard," says Devon.

"Actually, we're just giving you shit," I say. We both grin at them. "Do you mind if we join the married couple for dinner?" I point at the two spare seats at their table. "The pasta here is meant to be incredible."

Rake smacks himself in the head with a menu and closes his eyes, and then a smile slowly spreads across his face.

Brick flops back in his chair. "Oh my god, you had us so worried," he says. "You both looked so angry. And one of you being angry at a time is more than enough than any man could handle."

"That's why we each have four of you," I say, and everyone laughs.

Chapter Thirty-Six

Angel

I wake up to the feeling of a strong hand tracing its fingers ever so gently against my back as I lie on my side, facing away from the center of the bed. It leaves a line of delicate tingles in its wake, the gentle touch of someone who cares about me or is at least transfixed by the curves of my body.

A warm, muscular torso presses up behind me and I feel a soft breath in my ear. "Good morning, lover," he growls, his voice husky as he wraps a powerful arm around me.

"Good morning, baby," I say, turning my head slightly to nestle him into the crook of my neck.

God, I love waking up to this. I'm a lucky girl and I know it. My pussy knows, too, and it clenches as I feel his hardness pressing into my back.

"I thought you had instructions to stay away from me until you got the green light from the other guys?" I lean my head back and quirk an eyebrow at him.

"Well, it just so happens you're thoroughly irresistible and I couldn't stay away. It was agony having to keep my distance since we got here. Like literal agony. I had the bluest of balls."

"Well, in that case, I might just have to let you fix that. It doesn't seem fair to deprive you after all the effort you went to in order to get here."

His hand reaches down behind me, wandering its way to my pussy. "Oh Jesus," he groans. "You're so fucking wet."

"I woke up to a hot man snuggling against me and whispering in my ear. What do you expect?"

"That's my girl," he growls. "Seeing you're ready to go... how about a quick-ie?"

He quickly lines himself with my entrance. I cry out as he slides into me from behind in one thrust, his girth stinging me at first as he stretches my walls. I like that he makes no attempt at foreplay. He knows snuggling against me was enough to get me going, and to be more than ready for him.

I curve my body, tilting my hips against his pelvis to grant him greater access to my core.

"Oh god," he groans. "You feel amazing. I've missed you, baby."

"I've missed you too, Brick baby," I moan. "I'm so glad you're here."

This fuels his fire, and his pace intensifies. I cry out as he rails me, his cock slamming deep into my pussy with every thrust. His breath is ragged as he pounds into me fast and hard, his hard cock and its piercing dragging against my walls every time he sinks it deep inside me.

He lifts a leg to give himself greater leverage as he plows deep into my pussy and I cry out as I get full-body goosebumps. Pulling my hair back with a massive hand, he causes my back to arch and exposes my throat. He could crush me with his palm, but I know he never would.

His force causes my hips to buck, and I moan as I tilt my head back and my gaze meets his. His eyes are darker than usual, a combination of lust and adoration as he watches me from behind. "God, you look good, Angel. And you feel so fucking good," he growls in my ear. "I like watching you from this angle. But then I like watching you from every angle, my sweet Valkyrie."

He makes me feel beautiful, and wanted, and adored. And his cock makes me feel fucking fantastic. It's enough to send me over the edge, and I cry out as my pussy clenches around his cock as the orgasm tears through me.

"Oh yeah, come all over my massive cock, baby," he rasps, and my hips thrash around wildly as wave after wave of pleasure washes over me.

As my orgasm subsides, I feel his body tense, and he's also taken over the edge. His cock pulses within me as he releases, and he pulls me close until he couldn't be any deeper inside me. "Fuck," he pants. "You're everything I ever wanted and more. You're almost too much, but I also can't get enough. Fast or slow, day or night, you make me feel unstoppable."

"I feel the same way, baby," I say softly, turning my head again to kiss him softly on his gorgeous lips. His cock stays firmly ensconced in my soaking, very satisfied pussy. "I could never get enough of you."

Chapter Thirty-Seven
Devon

"Who is *that*?" We're reviewing more of the drone footage. Angel points at a woman who I can only describe as fiercely beautiful. Her strongly defined jawline balances her straight and proud nose, accentuating the angularity of her other features. But it's her eyes that are most captivating. Even through the slightly grainy video footage, you can tell they're piercing and intense, an icy shade of grey-green.

"That's Minka, one of Tane's chief officers. I recognize her from the files the guys put together before we left. But she goes by Beckett. She's intimidating, right?"

"You can say that again," says Angel, clearly mesmerized by the intriguing woman. "She's flawless. I'm not sure how I missed her, but there was quite a lot of info to go through."

I have to agree with Angel. Beckett's movements are rapid and deliberate, like a leopard calmly hunting its prey. Her head flits from side to side as she moves, simultaneously calm and hyper-alert, and it's clear she absorbs everything about her surroundings. It would be difficult for anyone to take her by surprise. "Apparently, she's quite the force of nature. Ex-military, I believe. Originally from Eastern Europe, but moved to the mainland when she was younger, and came to the island a few years ago. She's been by Tane's side ever since. Skilled in military strategy and torture techniques."

Angel nods, her eyes sparkling. "Based on her posture and the way she moves, I'd believe it. I know she works for a bad guy, but I'm like fan-girling over here."

I shiver. "I wonder when she's going to cross our path. I'm a bit scared, honestly."

"Hopefully after the rest of the guys are here. I think they're right. Tane keeps his best people closest to him, and she seems to be near the top of his list."

We continue to review the footage, making notes in an encrypted document shared with the guys. They made it clear that even the smallest details can be the difference between success and failure in this mission, and failure in this case more than likely equates to death. So we're as detail-oriented as possible, including anything that could potentially be useful when documenting times, places, locations and people.

By the time we're done, we've amassed a dense electronic file. "This *has* to be helpful. Somehow. We've managed to get much more info than I thought we would in that amount of time. I didn't realize he had such a large army, but I guess it makes sense."

"Yeah, and he might be based here, but his ties on the mainland are deep and strong." I shiver. "I'm surprised he hasn't figured we're out here yet."

"I really hope he hasn't, and this all isn't just a sick game to him," Angel frowns. "The last thing we need is to go walking into a trap. Especially a trap laid out by one of the most evil men in existence. Because if he is playing games, even the guys may not be able to protect us from that."

Chapter Thirty-Eight
Rake

It's not like my body doesn't have other scars. Scratches, nicks, markings... the things that come with living a life. Being an outdoorsy guy, getting into fights, being in the kind of line of work I am. All of these attributes come with the territory of being a little scuffed and rough around the edges. I'm hardly going to be asked to be a hand model anytime soon, my knuckles having been scraped raw several too many times.

But the biggest scar is the one I'm sensitive about. The one that stretches across most of my back, the gnarled and raised white flesh contrasting starkly with my deeply tanned skin.

Not many people are brave enough to ask about it, and I try not to look at it in the mirror because of the memories it brings back, so sometimes I have the luxury of being able to forget it's there. But now and then I'll glimpse it in my reflection, or someone will actually make a comment, and that forces me to remember. And on the darkest days, I force myself to look at it. To think about why it's there. It's a punishment in many ways, to make sure I never forget. Because I never deserve to forget what I did.

I loved my little brother more than anyone else in the world. More than any thing in the world. He was so cute, a little mini-me that followed me around and copied everything I said and did. He looked up to me, and it was my job to protect him.

But I failed, and now he's long dead, and it's all my fault. The scar will remind me of that always. I deserve to have that scar, that reminder.

My family didn't grow up with much in the way of financial riches, but our house was full of love. My parents doted on me and my siblings, valuing quality time and instilling in us a strong sense of family. We'd eat around the dinner table together every night, and Mom would put on game nights and other themed activities where we'd all dress up. We didn't need a lot to have fun, and she taught us to use our creativity instead of relying on money to buy the latest and greatest toys or games or clothing. It was a creative, fun house to live in. I think that's why I gravitated toward cooking as well, because that's something Mom and I would do together. We were like an original version of the TV show Chopped, where we'd find the ingredients that were on a manager's special or that the store was about to throw out, and get a basket of random food to take home. Then we'd have contests to see who could come up with the best creations. Our family would have a vote at the dinner table. Mom would usually win, but occasionally I'd come up with something so creative, so delicious, that my family would throw me a bone and do me the honor of awarding me that night's championship.

But those memories are bittersweet now. They're surreal, like a dream that starts out evoking pure joy. I'll cherish them, because they were such a precious, special part of my life, back when things were far more carefree. But now they're tinged with sadness, because I can never go back to those times. There's a darkness surrounding them, because none of us knew what was going to happen. Those times were special, but now they seem trivial, meaningless, even sad. Now, my family doesn't talk to me, and my brother is dead. There's no undoing either of those things at this point.

It was a regular day in the summer. Dad had been working on the commercial ferry like he always did in the warmer months, taking people back and forth *between the islands. His usual customers were a blend of locals who used the ferry to commute, and a sprinkling of tourists who wanted to visit places a bit further out and have a nice boat trip in the process.*

We spent a lot of our time out on the water back then, and I felt comfortable around boats.

But, like the Taurus I am, like the rambunctious and adventurous young boy I was, I felt invincible. I was always running round and bumping into things, tripping over, pushing and pulling at my siblings and friends with enthusiasm to get their attention and point things out. They all used to call me a bull in a china shop, and back then it was funny. My clumsy nature, people getting mad because I would accidentally break things. Back then, my quirks seemed innocent and harmless.

Through his job, Dad had made friends with a couple of his work colleagues who owned boats they liked to take out on their days off. One evening at dinner, when we were all gathered around the table, he was so excited to share his colleague had invited our entire family out on his boat the following week for some recreational fishing and a meal.

"You'll need to be on your best behavior," I remember him saying, half-joking. "We want to make sure we make a good impression, so he invites us out again. I've seen his boat, and it's really very nice. That includes you, Rake. Make sure you leave your clumsy self at home." Those words will ring in my ears forever. When dad said those words, I listened, and I really intended to do what he asked. I truly meant to make him proud by using my manners. I even made sure I wore my cleanest shorts and tank top and some lace-up shoes that day, so I'd look less grubby than usual. I'm not sure if Dad even noticed that, though. And my outfit is certainly not what anyone remembers that day for now. Things like outfit choices fade into inconsequence when you kill your brother, I suppose.

They told us not to run. The wind was picking up more rapidly than expected, and I think his workmate felt overly confident because he spent so much time on boats. Reflecting back, none of us should have been out there with the size of the swells. Unsecured kids careening around while the boat tilted about wildly wasn't a good idea. But I still made choices that resulted in the eventual outcome. If only I'd truly listened and stayed inside, sitting down and reading a book or something. But the wind whistling through the little gaps in the boat's construction, and the salty ocean spray whipping around us, was too enticing not to want to have a bit of fun. And it was fun to scare my brother, just a little. To see him look at me with his big eyes and figure out if I was teasing him or if I was for real.

I insisted on the game of tag that would have us running inside and outside. The adults were all too distracted trying to get things secured, the plates of food for our lunch and all the wine bottles careening around the dining area. As bottles smashed and silverware clattered and slid from one end of the boat to the other, an absentminded, "Children, go and sit in the living room area and hold on tight," was the most parenting we got. This left us free to play.

And play we did. I chased Ronnie outside and back inside, like a cat and mouse. He was thrilled, shrieking with excitement as I would repeatedly almost catch him and then, just as I was about to grab hold of him, I'd let him get away.

I didn't see the big swell coming, or the other boat that somehow had come loose from its moorings and was careening toward us from the other side of our vessel. I was just about to tag Ronnie, for real this time, when there was a loud cracking noise and our bodies flew sideways. I'll never forget the horrific sound of metal screeching uglily against metal, wood against wood, splinters flying through the air as one large boat rammed into another. Our boat groaned as the other pierced it from the side, and my already gangly frame careened sharply into Ronnie's tiny body.

As the boat rolled in response to the giant projectile hitting it, I grabbed for the railing with one hand while I also reached out for Ronnie. I think I heard him cry out, but I couldn't be sure because the noise of the collision drowned nearly everything else out. Time seemed to stop as I got hold of a bottom corner of his little yellow T-shirt, his favorite color. I felt a very brief sense of relief, but the floor wasn't level, the boat still rolling, and I tripped and missed the railing. My hand left Ronnie's T-shirt as I fought to steady myself, and that's when his tiny body tipped off the side of the boat. I clambered after him as the boat rolled again, and my own hands, slick with water and panicky sweat, slid right off the railing.

He knew how to swim, but the water was choppy and volatile. As I fell in after him, I glanced around wildly, but I couldn't see him, even with his bright yellow top. The water swirled and foamed around me, rightfully angry, as I fruitlessly tried to lay eyes on him.

It was only after I was pulled into the safety of a rescue boat that I felt the searing pain in my back and shoulder, where a jagged piece of metal had scraped its way down my back as I fell into the water.

For hours that day, the search and rescue team looked for Ronnie while my mother sobbed in the corner. I could feel eyes on me, and knew they were judging me for what I did. My dad helped with the rescue search, and after hours of unsuccessful searching, he returned, pale and haggard, like he'd aged twenty years in as many hours. I'd never seen him look weak before, and it was disarming.

I'd wanted to help with the search as well, but they wouldn't let me. I was too young, they said. But I know the real reason. It's because I was responsible for what happened, and nobody could bear to look at me.

They let me go to the funeral, but it was almost too much to bear. His tiny coffin, topped by his favorite teddy bear. Grown-ups sobbing loudly as my family took turns reading excerpts from Ronnie's favorite books and poems. I wasn't asked to speak. And again, I could feel those eyes on me.

My scar is ugly, just like me. Just like what I did. And now it serves as a permanent marker.

I hide my pain under humor and sarcasm, and pretend to be the funny guy. But that's just armor. A facade. I hate myself. I've almost given up so many times. Why did I have to run when the adults told me not to? Why did I insist on playing tag while they were all distracted? How could I abuse the trust that Ronnie placed in me? And how, more than anything, could I fail to protect him the way a big brother is meant to?

I'm the reason he died that day.

And I will never forgive myself.

Chapter Thirty-Nine

Devon

"I've been reflecting a *lot* on what we talked about. It's helped me to understand myself more," says Rake, his brow furrowed as his warm eyes gaze into mine. We're lying on the bed in my hotel room, enjoying each other's company in the cool of the air conditioning during the heat of the day.

Rake had previously alluded to pain from his past, but he hadn't been ready to open up and share his story with me until now. I think it was being here, having some alone time with him, that made him finally feel ready. And maybe, given my father's death, it just seemed like the right time. Either way, I'm honored and relieved that he trusts me enough to share something he's kept buried for so long, to share his scars both external and internal. I swipe a curly strand of hair out of his face. This man has so much depth. I couldn't possibly love him more.

"I've always had this overwhelming feeling that it should have been me who died that day. I would have swapped my life for my brother's in a heartbeat." He scrubs a hand over his face and squeezes his eyes tightly shut, like he's a living portrait of pain and regret and grief and irreparable guilt.

My heart melts seeing him like this. I gently rub his back and offer a sad smile. I'd do anything to alleviate the pain he carries constantly yet hides so well.

"I've never felt that I've deserved anything good that's come my way. If I find myself feeling happy—not just surface happy but actual happy—I instantly feel incredibly guilty. Because my little brother will never have a chance to feel happiness again, so why should I get that privilege?"

"That's a huge burden to bear, Rake. And I understand you think it was your fault, but it really wasn't. You were just a kid."

He frowns and shrugs. "That's not how it feels, though."

"How do you think it's impacted your life, other than the way it makes you feel about the incident?" I raise an eyebrow, compelled to understand how this one horrific incident has so indelibly shaped this man I love.

"I doubt myself when it comes to having any sort of responsibility. Like I'm doomed to fail, and like everyone expects me to. I feel like a joke."

"And that's why you make jokes all the time? To cover up how you really feel?"

"One hundred percent. If I can get people to laugh, to focus on something other than what I did, it's a win. I'm diverting them from the ugliness in me."

"And that's why you're so unafraid to put yourself out there and take risks that most people wouldn't?"

"Yeah, I suppose. It's almost like I put myself in situations where something bad was almost certain to happen. Because I felt like I deserved it. I like adventure and I don't want to give that up, but there are times I've been downright reckless and I'm lucky that I've walked away in one piece or with only minor injuries."

"Growing up, I couldn't help but think that even if I couldn't outright take Ronnie's place, it would just be easier for everyone if we'd both died that day. If I'd just flown over the railings and sunk into the water and never come back up. My parents never outright said it, but I used to think they would have preferred that, too. They could barely bring themselves to look at me after the accident. I know they still blame me. Everyone does. Hell, I blame myself."

"Do you think you would ever reach out and talk to them about it? Try to work through it together?"

"I'm just so afraid they'll continue to reject me. I don't think I could bear seeing them look at me like that ever again. Or rather, I couldn't bear them continuing to avoid looking at me."

"That's fair enough. And healing doesn't come on a fixed timeline." I gently caress his arm in an attempt to soothe him.

"I just thought I really knew why I act the way I do now," he continues, "and that I had it all figured out. But it's taken being with you, someone who really takes the time to see me, to get to really know that part of myself and understand how much more I still have to learn."

"Well, that sounds like progress to me," I say, smiling at him and resting my chin on his chest and running my palm over his torso. "How do you feel about it? Better at all? Did it help to talk about it?" I sense a little frustration from him, like maybe it was better when he thought he knew it all and now he's confronting his demons all over again. The demons he thought he'd vanquished but who were really just buried deep down causing him pain.

He glances down at me and smiles. "I'm trying to be frustrated, but you're just so fucking cute."

I smirk and my chest feels warm.

"But really," he clenches his jaw and I notice a sudden tightness around his eyes, "it's frustrating when you've checked something off the list and truly believe it's done. But then when you scratch under the surface, you find all these layers that still need a lot of work. Knowing I've just been applying a band-aid this whole time and that the damage is still very much in place in there, it's a little overwhelming, frankly." He pauses and takes a deep breath in, followed by a lengthy exhale. "But I know this is what will help me in the longer-run. It'll help all my relationships, including with the guys and, most importantly, with you. It'll remove some of the pain I've had buried deep inside for so long. I know that'll never fully go away, but recognizing it's there and why is a big part of the process."

"Well, I'm here if and when you decide you want to talk about it more." I smile at him and caress his jaw gently, enjoying the sensation of his stubble grazing against my fingers. It's not often that he's not cleanly shaven, so this is a novelty. He looks cute this way, but then again, I think he looks cute every way. My adorable, complex clown. So funny and light on the surface, with so much more brooding below, an intelligent intensity he only shares with those truly close to him.

He nods. "Thank you. I think I'm going to need to. I'm just still not quite ready. I'm getting there, though."

"We're all works in progress, Rake. None of us has everything fully figured out."

"Even you?" He dips his head and kisses me on the forehead, sending a little tingle through me.

"Especially me." I smile and boost myself up on my forearms. I need to get closer to this man's face so I can smother him in all the kisses he deserves.

Because he really does deserve them.

And he deserves me.

As well as all the good things that he never asked for because he felt so guilty about what happened.

"Please stop doing unnecessarily risky things by the way, babe. I mean, outside the realm of your naturally risky job. You have so many people that care deeply about you."

"Oh yeah? Does that include a certain pretty lady who's about to straddle me with her gorgeous thighs right now?" He wiggles his eyebrows in signature Rake style, and I can't help but snort before climbing on top of him as requested. Clearly Rake is over being vulnerable with me and his mind has switched to other things. Not that I mind. I've never felt closer to him, and he's never been hotter to me.

"Yes, it sure does," I wink at him.

"Mmm, I'm pleased to hear that. And I want to see just how deep you're talking about." I can feel his cock straining in his pants underneath me, and I can't help but grind myself against his hardness. Even through our clothes, his body is doing things to mine, and I know I'm getting wet.

"As deep as possible," I moan as my clit grazes against the clothing that's trapped between his hard cock and my pussy. "We're going to have to lose these clothes. I need you inside me to show you just how much I care."

Chapter Forty

Devon

"If you don't mind, we'll be needing this." Rake grins as he reaches out and grabs a soft rope from the middle of the table. I didn't know why he'd brought it over to my room, but I'm beginning to get an idea.

"Oh yeah? For what?" I ask innocently, although a grin starts spreading across my face at the thought of what he might have planned.

"You're about to find out," he grins. "I think you're going to find it quite exciting."

"Is it going to be like back in the old house when you all tied me up as a punishment?" It feels like ages ago when they held me captive in their house. So much has changed since then. For one, we're definitely lovers more than we are enemies now.

"Oh, this time is going to be way more fun. And you know I'll always make sure you get to enjoy yourself. Although I'm sure you already knew that. Besides..." he says, wiggling his eyebrows. "I've been practicing some new knots."

I laugh. He's always figuring out something new and fun, both in and out of the bedroom. I'm not at all surprised it's now extending to bondage.

Rake flips me off him and gets to work expertly securing the rope around me. My hands are strapped firmly behind my back, and the rope feels silky but strong. I like the sensation of being restrained and totally at his will. In this moment, I realize how much I've grown to trust him and the rest of these men. This is nothing like the first time they tied me up, when I was their captive, and they were merely trying to restrain me. This is something way more intimate and special.

"You doing okay?" he asks as he pulls the ropes a little tighter, rendering me further unable to move. There's a little pain where it particularly pulls on me and rubs in certain areas, but in a good way. To ask him to loosen anything at this point would be to deprive myself of riding that line. I twinge at the thought of completely letting myself go, and of being something he uses for his own pleasure, although I have no doubt he'll make sure I feel pleasure, too.

"Mmhmm," I reply. "I'm doing more than okay. I like doing whatever you want me to."

"Good girl," he growls in my ear. "You're doing such a good job."

He comes around to my front side and his gaze trails from my head to my toes. "Oh god," he rasps. "You look incredible. Want to see?"

I nod, and he snaps a picture on his phone. Another thing I could never have imagined letting anybody do before I met these men. He turns the phone to face me. The rope is tied in such a way that it zig-zags across my body, cupping my breasts. I have to admit, I look great. Sexy. I'm seeing why some people get so into this, and I'm glad I let him have his way.

"I do look hot like this." I smile. "And I clearly trust you."

"Well, you're going to have to. Because there's no way you're getting out of this rope without my help," he growls. "But first, I have plans for you. And I'm sharing this photo with the others. They're going to want to try it, too. I'm sure of that."

He bends me over, giving him full access to my pussy and my ass. He's right, there's no way I can free myself and I'm completely at his mercy. My pussy quivers at the thought. I don't normally consider myself a helpless person—in fact, quite the opposite—but in the bedroom, things are fair game and I'm more than happy to submit to his desires. "What are you going to do to me?" I ask, trying but failing to twist around to see Rake and get more of a sense of what he has planned.

"You'll find out soon enough," he growls, and I feel his hard cock pressing against my lower back.

"You look so beautiful at this angle," he groans, running his finger between my pussy and my ass. "Your pussy looks amazing, but I feel like I've been neglecting your ass lately. What do you think?"

His words give me butterflies. "Well, I'm completely at your mercy, so I don't have a lot of a say. But I'm down for you to fuck me in the ass, baby. It always feels so good when you do."

I can't see his face, but I know he's pleased by my response. He presses his cock more firmly against me. "Your hot little ass it is, then," he growls.

I hear the click of a lube bottle and shiver at the pleasant sensation of the clear gel being rubbed against the entrance to my ass. He works the tip of one of his long fingers in and I moan as he continues making his way further inside. My body is craving more, and even though I can barely move, I tilt myself so I'm pressing against his finger, driving him further inside me.

"How does that feel, baby? You like my finger working your little asshole?"

"Mmm, yeah I do," I moan. "Give me more."

He continues to stretch me out, adding a second finger and then a third. I shiver with pleasure as he works them into me.

"Are you ready for my cock in your gorgeous ass now, princess?" he grits out, and I feel him pressing his cock against my back entrance.

"Yes, please," I moan. "I need it now. Please."

"That's my good girl," he growls, and slides his long, thick cock into me. It's much bigger than his fingers, and it stings, but I take him eagerly. I love the way he makes me ride the line between pleasure and pain every time we're intimate. It's like he knows exactly how much I can take, and how much I want, and he likes to push the boundary ever so slightly. All four of the guys are like that, really. They know how to tease me and get me worked up, and how to leave me feeling them for days. They're collectively responsible for the best orgasms of my life. I realize how lucky I am being in a situation like this, and I'll never take any of them for granted.

"Fuck, your little ass feels so good," he rasps as he thrusts into me, working his entire cock inside. "You're so fucking tight. I love being in here."

"I know you do, baby. I love you being in there as well. You feel so fucking good."

The rope rubs against my wrists, reminding me that I'm bound and can't move my body in the way I usually do. I'm completely reliant on his thrusts and the way he moves his body.

He pulls on the rope, causing me to arch my back and giving him further leverage to enter me even deeper with his big cock. "Fuck," I cry out.

"Is that too much for you baby?" He growls in my ear. "Want me to stop?"

"No. Don't. Stop." I grit out. "Keep going. Please."

He groans. "God, you're so amazing. What a good job you're doing." Overcome by lust, he increases his pace and I cry out as his cock slides into me, right to his hilt. I cry out at the full feeling, enjoying him being so far inside me.

I don't usually come this way, but there's something about the angle and the way I'm tied up. Without warning, an orgasm rips through my body and my hips buck as much as they can within the constraints of the rope. I feel my ass contracting even more tightly around his cock and he groans, pulling on the rope even more tightly. It rubs harshly against my nipples and I cry out from the pleasure of my orgasm and the pain of the rope burn. He loves it when I cry out and combined with my orgasm, making my ass clench tightly around him, sets him off, and he releases deep inside me, pulling me to him by the rope.

"That's my girl," he growls in my ear as he slowly slides himself out of me, and I feel the pleasant sensation of his cum trickling from my back entrance. "That's my good fucking girl."

Chapter Forty-One

Rake

Later that evening

"What are we going to do now?" I raise an eyebrow. I feel extra giddy after my alone time with Devon earlier today, and I'm sure Brick suspects what we've been up to, but he doesn't say anything. He's far too preoccupied with whatever he's got on his mind.

Brick's eyes are wide and bright and his smile irrepressible. Clearly, he has something up his sleeve. "Well, I've always wanted to fuck some people up using the toxin from a poison dart frog. And I just love tattoos. What if, somehow, we could combine the two things?" He grins and dances from one foot to the other, barely able to contain himself.

"What are you thinking?"

"It just so happens that a few of Tane's men were at the local hardware store talking loudly about their plans to get tattoos from the local shop tomorrow. Which gave me this incredible idea."

"You mean...?" I quirk an eyebrow. This man is wild.

"Yep, I sure do! We're going to have a little fun at the tattoo studio."

I smirk and shrug, my arms out to the side. "Sure. Sounds like a good time to me."

The tattoo studio is easy to find, just off the main strip in the center of town. It's a standalone concrete building with a neon sign loudly advertising that it is in fact a tattoo shop, and the structure itself is painted mural-style with bright blues, greens and yellows that reflect the tropical island locale. The large windows proudly bear the shop's logo, which incorporates needles and tattoo designs.

Brick snorts when he sees a camera pointing at the front door. "It's one of those cheap decoys you can get online. I recognized it a mile away. I don't know why they bother."

I glance up at the camera and immediately see he's right. It doesn't even have a proper lens, just what looks like a cheap piece of plastic designed to deter the laziest of potential burglars.

Brick gets to work on the door, and it doesn't take long to gain access to the shop, despite the large metal chain that's wrapped around the entrance.

"How did you get so good at picking locks?" I ask, feeling a bit useless on this mission. I feel like I'm his sidekick, tagging along for the ride. But this is Brick's wheelhouse, and maybe I can learn something from him.

"My father taught me a lot of things. Picking locks was one of the more benign things he showed me how to do. And despite him being a total piece of shit, this skill comes in handy more frequently than you might think."

"Oh, I can imagine. Teach me sometime?"

"Totally. Consider it a date. I'll let you buy me dinner as long as you promise not to take advantage of me." He winks at me mock lasciviously.

"Oooh ah," I wiggle my eyebrows at him and grin. "No promises."

We enter through the glass door and a bell jingles overhead, but it's empty so there's nobody notified of our arrival. The studio is dark, but the streetlight outside illuminates it sufficiently for what we came here to do.

The interior of the tattoo shop is what I'd expect for a parlor in a touristy area. The walls are covered in artwork, documenting designs from the studio's resident and visiting artists. Behind the reception area lies the studio itself, replete with several faux leather reclining tables. There's a drawing area near the back with sketchpads, pens and pencils sitting on a large rectangular table.

Although it's dark, I can see this place is typically colorful and vibrant, and I imagine it teeming with clients and artists and buzzing with the sound of tattoo guns and music playing from the speakers overhead. It's eerie being here when it's empty, like an abandoned bus stop in the middle of the night.

Brick produces a box that he must have been concealing inside his leather jacket, which he's made sure to tell me is vegan leather several times. He removes the top and shows me its contents, revealing what looks to be about five small frogs.

"So why a poison dart frog? And I'm no frog expert, but these look kind of...weird?"

"Well, in some parts of South America, people will cover their blowgun darts in the frog's toxic secretions. This enables the toxin to be directly administered into their prey's bloodstream. Which is exactly what we're going to do here, but with tattoo needles."

I scratch my head. "Wait... aren't you a devout vegan? This doesn't seem... aligned with your beliefs?"

"Well, you're right that these frogs look funny. You see, they aren't real frogs. A few years back, a team of researchers at a university on the mainland found a way to synthesize the neurotoxin naturally found in poison dart frogs. It's called batrachotoxin and, when administered correctly, it messes with people's hearts and nervous systems. And you can buy it on the dark web now pretty easily, if you know where to look."

"What if someone else comes into the studio and they end up getting sick or worse? Like someone who's not one of our targets?" While I'm a lot more okay with murder and torture than I used to be, I still try to avoid harming innocent bystanders.

"Oh well, that's easy," shrugs Brick. "His guys fully booked the studio tomorrow and they won't be taking walk-ins. So the place is going to be teeming with our targets and only our targets."

I nod, truly impressed. This man might be quirky as fuck, but he thinks of everything. "You're a genius and a madman."

Brick grins at me, and I grin back.

I raise my hand to his in an enthusiastic fist bump. "To fuckery afoot," I say.

He nods, his eyes sparkling with excitement at what we're about to do. "To fuckery afoot."

Chapter Forty-Two

Angel

"I can't believe we found Tane Brown's holiday home," I say to Devon. We're both feeling quite giddy after stumbling on this piece of information.

"Do you think we've made the right call coming here without the guys, though? Or should we have waited until they're all here?" She crinkles her nose as if she's second-guessing herself.

"Listen, if Rake and Brick were around, I would have said something. But they went off to engage in some sort of mischief to do with Tane's men. So they can't have thought this was that risky. We're meant to be brave and relentless, remember?"

She nods. "You're right. We did say we would be. I'll stop being so worried. Besides, all we're doing is checking out an empty house. What harm could it really do?"

It's a palatial home, sleek and modern. And it's pretty close to what I expected Tane's home to look like. Top-of-the-line everything. Through the door's glass windows we can see a high-ceilinged foyer with large artworks and custom wallpaper adorning the walls, and a large, ornate staircase with intricately carved, curved wooden banisters. It reflects the tropical local environment, with just enough hint of heritage that comes across as respectful without crossing the line into kitschy.

We make it inside. Surprisingly, it wasn't that hard to get in. Brick has taught me well. And given Tane isn't staying here at the moment, preferring to instead reside in his high-security compound, his security detail has been diverted elsewhere. We're able to disable the alarm with relatively little effort, leaving us free to explore.

Out the back is an expansive yard, perfectly manicured, with a large infinity pool hanging over the side of a cliff with panoramic views of the valley and ocean below. The pool is the centerpiece of the yard, and stretches across the rear of the property, the back side mimicking the natural contours of a rock-encrusted lagoon. The pool is surrounded by a spacious sun deck boasting luxe loungers and large sun umbrellas, perfect for sunbathing and relaxation. A cascading waterfall gurgles to one side, adding a touch of tranquility and opulence.

Inside, the windows are floor-to-ceiling, and the sliding door leading out to the yard looks like it opens completely to create a luxurious indoor-outdoor experience. Beside the sparkling turquoise pool is a large outdoor kitchen with an expensive-looking grill, a massive kitchen island and a full bar.

The tropical landscape is meticulously maintained. Lush palm trees and vibrant flowers line the edges of the property, with an ornate gate as the only entrance and exit point aside from the house itself.

I wouldn't mind hanging out here if the house didn't belong to a murdering sadist. That's a pretty big buzzkill if you ask me.

I let out a low whistle. "How much do you think something like this would cost?"

"I'd think it would be in the tens of millions, judging by the location and the size."

"It's so tastefully decorated. Like it's over the top, but I was expecting something more garish."

Devon shrugs. "I'm sure he has an interior designer on the payroll. Maybe more than one. Easy to be stylish when you have a professional doing things for you."

"That's fair," I nod. "I would too if I was in his shoes." I shiver at the thought of being in Tane Brown's shoes. He literally orders hits on people and traffics women, weapons and drugs from the mainland and back. "His designer, murdering, raping shoes. Gross."

"Yeah, very gross," she agrees. "No manner of interior design tastefulness can make up for the evil things he's done. It's just depressing," she frowns. "Someone as horrible as he is having a place like this. It just doesn't seem fair."

I eye her skeptically. "I thought you would have worked out by now that life's not fair, Devon, especially with a father like yours."

She nods and shrugs, likely trying to avoid the sting of my words.

I continue. "I mean, people probably look at both of us and think it's not fair that we each have four incredibly hot guys who adore us and who would do anything for us."

"I suppose you're right," she agrees. "We are pretty lucky now that you mention it."

Unlike the sleek bright feel of the above-ground parts of the mansion, the basement is dark and menacing. But we feel compelled to explore it seeing we're here. Imagine if there was some detail down there that could lead us to exploiting Tane's weakness, but we didn't go because it was 'too scary.'

We look around for a light switch and locate one. After a moment, a light springs on above us and emits a dim orange glow and a disconcerting low hum. There's no way this guy can't afford proper wiring down here. This is all clearly for show, to add to the creepiness and horror of this bizarre area.

Devon walks ahead of me down the cold concrete pathway and gasps as she rounds the corner. "Jesus fuck!" She exclaims.

"What is it?" I run to catch up with her. "Oh shit! This is a whole goddamn torture chamber!"

Room after room bears a different horror, each more terrifying than the last. Bodies in all types of positions, the only commonality the way their eyes and mouths are frozen, contorted in terror at their fate.

"It's like he took every kind of torture you could think of and implemented it down here. The sick fuck! I've been to a museum that showed some of these things, but it was all make-believe. This is like... real people. And he's kept all the bodies which is just sick. They're full-sized human souvenirs."

A shiver runs down my spine and spreads through my limbs at Tane's bold depravity.

"What the hell?" I exclaim, pointing at a particularly heinous panorama of horrors. "Is that *bamboo* growing through a person? I have to google if this is an actual thing." I pull out my phone, and surprisingly there's reception down here, even though we're most definitely underground inside a concrete shell. "Oh my god, it is! This says that bamboo grows at the rate of around four centimeters per hour. Historically, captors would sharpen the bamboo and place their captive above it, and then let it grow into the victim where it would pierce their vital organs."

"That's brutal!" exclaims Devon. "And look over here. This person has their fingernails burned off!"

I find another room next door that's similarly bad, and resist the urge to hurl as my stomach roils at the sight. "This one has bamboo skewers placed under theirs." I find myself subconsciously squeezing my fingernails as if to make sure they're still intact. "What's this guy's hatred for fingernails, anyway?"

She smirks. "I'll make sure to ask him when we meet him in person."

An icy shiver runs down my spine. "Speaking of which, we really should get out of here. Clearly, we aren't meant to be seeing this. I'd hate for us to get trapped and become his next torture victims. This guy isn't playing around."

Devon nods and heads toward the door. "You're right. I've seen more than enough."

As we leave, closing the door behind us, I follow Devon down the pathway. But then a moving shadow catches my eye off to the side near dense foliage. I glance over, but as I do, I feel a sharp pain in the side of my head, and everything fades to black.

Chapter Forty-Three

Devon

I turn around at the sound of a loud cracking noise, just in time to see a shadowy figure knocking Angel to the ground and dragging her back into the house and shutting the door behind them. The person looks to be about a foot taller than her and at least a hundred pounds heavier than her, if not more.

Beside myself with panic and not wanting to lose any time, I race up to the front door and knock loudly, not that I expect anyone to answer and invite me in for a cup of tea. Then I see the video system to the side of the door. I have no doubt there are multiple cameras aimed directly at me, recording everything, but right now I just don't care. I have to get to Angel. I'd prefer not to die in the process, but I can't think about that right now.

Fuck! What were we thinking, trying to come here by ourselves? We were attempting to get information, but this was a reckless idea. Of course, the evil mastermind that runs the islands isn't going to leave his palatial holiday home completely unattended, whether he's here or not. He must have a small team that lives and works onsite year-round. I feel so fucking stupid for thinking we could do this alone. But now's not the time to critique our bad decisions. I need to get to Angel and fast. Whoever took her likely has plans for her.

My mind races as I try to remember how Angel got us into the home. There was a code and some type of disabling mechanism for the front door, but she had it inside her phone and I don't have a copy.

I strain my ear against the door, trying to get any sense of what might be happening inside, but the door is thick and I can't hear anything. I peer through the glass and see a shadow moving down the hallway away from me until it completely disappears from view.

I fumble for my phone and dial Rake.

He answers immediately.

"Well hello there, gorgeous! How are you doing? What are you wearing?"

"Rake! No time to talk. Please help. I need to speak to Brick right away."

"Well okay then. Nice to speak with you, too. He's sitting right next to me. Here you go."

I hear rustling, and then Brick's voice comes on the other end. "What's up, buttercup?"

"It's Angel. She's been taken. We're at Tane's holiday home. I need to get inside." My voice is raspy with panic and my heart is racing.

Brick's voice is calm even though I imagine he's freaking out on the inside at the thought of Angel being taken by one of Tane's men. "We can head there now. Where is it?"

"I'll text you the address, but I don't think there's time to wait for you guys. Someone dragged her back inside and there's a torture basement and... I don't think there's time. Help me get inside! Please!"

"I don't like the sound of this. But I'll help you while we're on our way."

Brick walks me through how to get into the home while I text him the address, and I follow along with his instructions as best as I can.

The door beeps, but then there's a red blinking light and nothing happens. "It's not working! Please help!" I plead. "My hands won't stop shaking. I have to get in there!"

"It's okay, Devon," Brick's voice is patient and reassuring despite his obvious concern for Angel's wellbeing. "You're doing great. You must just have entered the code wrong. Try to keep your hands still and give it another go."

A gunshot rings out from the other end of the home.

"Oh my god! No! Angel!"

Exasperated, I bang on the heavy door, but it's solid and I know nobody will be able to hear me. Trying to rescue her by myself seems futile, but I don't see any other option if I want to save my friend. Is she still alive? Is she already dead? I'm the only person who knows exactly where she is.

It's in this instant I realize that we really have grown to be friends. I flash back to the time she almost cracked me on the head with her surfboard, the clumsy bitch. And the first few meetings we had where we conspired to have the guys get their shit together and form a partnership. Suddenly, none of that animosity, that initial angst, matters anymore.

And frankly, maybe it never did.

From this vantage point, this snapshot in time, I can see that I was likely just projecting my own stress, and if I'm honest, maybe also insecurities, at everything that was going on in my own life at the time. It's hard not to have trust issues when your dad tried to sell you to a mafia boss to pay off his debt. And I was still learning to trust my guys back then. Everything was fresh and new and scary as fuck. I'm so glad that phase of my life is over, and things are so much different now.

Right now, all I care about is getting my friend back safely. My concern for her livelihood, and just wanting her to be okay, supersedes everything else.

Brick breathes heavily into the phone. It sounds like he and Rake are running for their car, and sure enough, I soon hear the beep of a car alarm and the sound of a car starting up. "We're on our way. Ten minutes away," he pants, his voice ragged.

I attempt the code one more time. This time, there's a green light and the sound of a lock releasing. I try the handle and it opens. "We did it!" I whisper loudly. "I'm going to get to her."

"Can you wait for us?" Rake calls out in the background.

"No, there's no time! I have to save her now!"

I run into the house, leaving the front door open, and head in the direction where I saw the shadow disappearing. This might be one of the most risky things I've ever done, and it may end in death, but I can't miss what might be the only chance I have to save Angel.

I find the door where I saw the figures retreating, and I rattle the handle. It doesn't budge.

Backing up, I run at it with all my might and smash into it. The door splinters near the lock and handle, but doesn't open. *Fuck!* I back up one more time. I let out a guttural howl as I run at it again and give it everything I've got, kicking the door as hard as I can. This time, the door smashes while the lock holds strong. The hole in the door is big enough for me to kick into a bigger gap. I'm then able to reach through and unlock the door from the inside. Miraculously, my hand isn't shot to pieces. I open the door and peek inside, scared at what I'm about to see.

To my surprise, instead of seeing an injured Angel, I see her standing there like a complete badass. She's standing in a strong stance, legs hip-width apart, and has a gun pointed at the slumped body that I recognize as the figure that dragged her away.

"Thought you'd never make it," she smirks, but her voice gives her away by wavering slightly.

I look at her in shock. "How did you disarm him? He was a big guy!"

"He might be big, but I was fucking angry. I'm so sick and tired of being kidnapped and there's no way I was leaving you out there all by yourself."

"Oh my god." A wave of relief washes over me and I run to her and grab her in a tight hug. "I thought you were dead."

"It takes more than one big, ugly guy to kill me. And I've had a lot of practice with people trying."

I smirk, but it morphs into a frown. "Brick and Rake are going to be here any second. But we're going to have to call the rest of the guys. They're going to be so pissed. Well, maybe concerned is a better word."

"That can wait. We can keep it between us four for now. There's no need to alarm them more than they already are. Everyone's safe. Well, except for this guy." She kicks at the guy's prone body with her foot and for the first time, I notice the scarlet dot between his eyes.

"Is he—?"

"Yep, he's dead as can be." She shrugs, just as Brick and Rake come hurtling through the door with guns drawn. Their eyes fly to us and then to the man lying on the floor.

"Jesus, Angel. You killed this guy?" Brick's eyes get a little googly as he looks at her and then back to the man again. "A kill shot to the forehead with his own gun, I'm assuming?"

"Maybe," she says with a gleam in her eye.

He swoons and a massive grin spreads across his face. "Be still my beating heart. I'm so proud of you."

Rake smirks and shakes his head, looking at me and Angel. "You two are something else," he says.

And he's right. We make quite the pair.

Chapter Forty-Four

Zeke

"Wait, wait. *What* did you see in his basement?" Aidan asks over the phone.

The girls excitedly describe the array of torture devices and methods they uncovered underground at Tane's holiday home. I shiver at the thought of what might be present in his actual compound if this is where he keeps things that are just for fun.

"I had to see this for myself." Brick's voice hums with excitement. "It sounds like he's somebody I could learn from."

"Just what we need." Slade rolls his eyes. "Brick doing an apprenticeship with Tane fucking Brown and his torture gang."

"Hey. 'A wise man can learn more from his enemies than a fool from his friends' is a real quote." Brick shrugs. "Don't knock it until you try it."

"I really don't like that you two went down there without us." Aidan runs his fingers through his hair. "That was far too risky. What if you got trapped in there? What if you became examples locked in two of those rooms? You should have waited until we could come with you."

"What kind of recon mission would it be if we didn't do any real recon?" I can tell from her voice that Angel is pouting.

"Okay, okay. Fair point," says Aidan in an attempt to placate her. "I'm just feeling very lucky that you got out of there without being injured or worse. From now on, please don't go do anything crazy like *entering Tane Brown's holiday home* without us. I can't believe I'm saying those words out loud."

"Just wait until you hear what really happened," blurts Brick, followed by an unmistakable "Ow!"

"What's going on? What are you keeping from us?" I ask, instantly even more concerned than before.

"Let's just say Angel made me really proud today," says Brick, in the unmistakable tone he uses when describing something gory. Murder or torture, specifically. "So did Devon, actually."

"Wait, what's going on?" Aidan sounds as furious as I feel. "Did Angel *kill* someone?"

"Look, we're safe and now you have more information than ever before," says Devon, her tone defensive. "I'd say mission accomplished. So instead of criticizing us and being so condescending, perhaps you could be more appreciative and thank us for a job well done."

I speak up. "You're right. You did a great job. Just please be safe. No more crazy adventures."

I can almost hear both Devon and Angel rolling their eyes through the phone.

"Yeah, yeah. Blah blah blah," says Angel.

"I'm serious, Angel." Aidan's tone is stern. "You belong to us. We care about you more than anything in the world, in this life or beyond. And none of us could live without you by our side."

"Same to you, Devon," says Skyler, his brow furrowed with concern. "So behave yourselves."

We hang up the call, and I turn to the other men, who are all unusually quiet.

"Oh god," I say. "What in the world have we created?"

"I don't know," says Roman. "But I think it's time for us to go to the other island."

The rest of the men nod.

It's time to pack.

CHAPTER FORTY-FIVE

Angel

Despite their better judgement, Brick and Rake allow us to drive back to the hotel in our own rental car. They'd wanted to split us up and have me ride with Brick and have Devon go with Rake, but we'd insisted on returning to the resort the way we came. After what happened earlier I'm hesitant to leave Devon's side, and she seems to feel the same way.

"Don't kill anyone else without us being there, okay?" Brick joked as we pulled away, but from the look on his face I can tell he means it, as if he has preemptive FOMO but also doesn't want us to get into further danger.

Devon takes the wheel this time, given my head is still feeling sore after the big guy smacked it earlier in the day. Luckily, though, I'm running on adrenalin after murdering the man, so I'm not feeling as bad as I otherwise would be.

As we drive through the lush green countryside, I notice a bright red shape off in the distance, glinting in the sunlight.

"What is that?" I ask, pointing toward it and squinting to try to make it out. Devon glances in the direction of my finger as we continue to drive toward it.

"I'm not sure. But it doesn't look like it's meant to be there. Let's go see."

A sick feeling swells in the pit of my stomach as we get closer to the unnatural shade of red. As we near it, I recognize the twisted red metal as being what was formerly a motorcycle. It's almost unrecognizable in its current form.

Then I see him.

A motorcyclist, still with a helmet on, appears to have been thrown off and is lying in the grass several feet away from the mangled bike.

Devon pulls the car to a screeching halt and we both tumble out of the car, rushing up to the injured motorcyclist. Although his arms are coated in blood, I immediately notice the distinctive spider tattoo on his right hand. He's moving so I know he's still alive, but his motions are sluggish.

"Diego!" The surly man from the butcher's shop is almost as unidentifiable as his bike. "Diego. We visited you at your shop. We're calling for help right now."

His helmet remains secured to his head, but one of his legs is at an odd angle. His chest is covered in blood, and more is trickling from within his helmet. I'm no doctor, but I know this isn't good.

"Tane's men...", the man's voice comes out as a rasp, and I have to lean in to hear him amongst the sound of vehicles in the distance and livestock rustling past on the other side of the wire fence.

"Diego, don't talk!" Devon pleads. "We have to get you an ambulance."

He tries futilely to lift up a hand and then lets it fall back down to the dirt and grass beneath him.

"No... it's too late," his voice is labored as he continues to grit out his words. "I need... to tell you.... something. The key... to this is the mass grave. It's by... the old church about two miles off the... main road. I should have ....told you before. Go to... to the... burial site."

"Burial site?"

"Mass grave.... so many bodies." His breath becomes more labored, but he seems to want to speak more.

"Thank you, Diego. But please, we need to get you help. Don't pressure yourself to talk."

"Please tell my girlfriend Desiree that I'm sorry... so sorry... for everything. And... most importantly... that I love her."

"I promise, Diego. We will tell her."

Blood continues to trickle from his mouth, followed by a gurgling sound that I am pretty sure is going to haunt my nightmares for the rest of my life.

I hold his bloody hand as the light fades from his eyes right in front of me, and he grows completely still.

My phone rings right as we return to our car. Devon calls an ambulance while I answer my phone.

"Why aren't you girls back yet? We've been back for a while now. Are you getting into more trouble?" It's Brick, and he sounds uncharacteristically concerned. While I know he's proud of how I handled myself earlier, I'm sure he's rattled because the outcome could have been very different.

"Wait. We need to go and fulfill a promise. We just saw something... and, well... we watched someone die."

"Someone else? Like a second person? Did you kill him too? Jesus. You're turning into a right serial killer lately."

"No," I explain. "It was Diego, the butcher who has strong ties to Tane and Denzo. We found him on the side of the road. He's given us some information. But for now, we have to go and deliver a message on his behalf. We made a promise, and it's the right thing to do."

"I'm coming with you," he insists. "It's non-negotiable."

"Okay, if you say so," I shrug. "But we're perfectly capable of handling it on our own." Truth be told, I'm still processing and clearly in shock. I can barely stop myself from trembling.

Today has been quite a day.

"I know you are, but I'm not taking any more risks. We've already put you in enough danger."

Brick and Rake come and meet us as fast as they can, and by the time they arrive, the ambulance is wheeling Diego away in a body bag. Firefighters are scraping up pieces of twisted metal and broken glass, and I blink back tears as the ambulance drives off.

"I—I've never seen the light go out of somebody's eyes before. Not like that."

"It's not something you ever get used to," he says softly. "I might enjoy the process, but that part always hits hard. Everybody has a soul, you know. No matter how bad they are." He turns around and pulls me close.

I can no longer hold back the tears that spring from my eyes, which sting like I've already been crying for hours.

We drive in silence, pulling up to a modest home in a suburb that skirts the main town. It's a simple weatherboard house with a tiled roof. Its tones are muted cream with brown accents, and it looks like most of the other houses on the street except for the large palm tree that rises tall in the center of the front yard. It didn't take long to find this place. It's pretty easy to find who you're looking for on islands like this, where everyone knows everyone's business.

I knock on the door with some trepidation, the others following along behind me with somber expressions. Knocking on doors used to be fun, because I was going to visit a friend or attend a party or something. But lately it seems to be because I'm delivering bad news, or am at risk of being kidnapped. I'm beginning to develop a fear of it.

I hear footsteps approaching, and can feel eyes on me through the head-height peephole. A nervous female voice sounds from the other side of the door. "Can I help you?"

"Is this Desiree?" I ask, my voice as gentle as possible.

"Ye-yess. Who is this, please? Why are you here?"

"My name is Angel, and these are some friends of mine. I—I have a message from Diego."

She opens the door, and she eyes me suspiciously. "He hasn't been home. Has he been fooling around on me again?" Her voice becomes shrill. She's a diminutive woman, but her eyes are blazing. I immediately notice that she's quite pretty, with large brown eyes that glow with a feisty intensity. Curly brown hair frames her face in soft layers. A subtle smattering of freckles cascades over her nose and cheeks. Based on her reaction to Diego's name, I can only imagine this woman has put up with some shit.

"Why is he sending you as his messenger? Why didn't he come home last night? I swear if he's running around on me again, I'll...". Her voice trails off, and tears begin to pool in her eyes.

"I—I can't speak to his past behavior. And I didn't know him very well. But he wanted me to pass on an important message."

"I'm sorry, what? Didn't know him? He's... dead?" Her voice drops to a low whisper. "Diego is dead?"

Fuck. She didn't know. I figured the cops would have come and knocked on her door by now. But maybe they have more pressing matters to take care of. Maybe this woman wasn't listed as his next of kin and nobody has bothered to tell her.

Well, great. I guess the duty is falling on me now. There's no going back. I can hardly lie to this woman.

My own voice is low, and I take one of her hands in both of mine. "Yes, I'm so sorry. He was in a motorcycle accident and he didn't make it."

Her free hand flies to her mouth. "Oh my god. I told him that piece of junk metal was going to be the death of him." Her tone is angry, but her words don't meet her actions, as her tears begin to flow freely now.

Not sure what to say, I continue to hold on to her hand while she absorbs the news.

After what feels like minutes, she stops crying. She glances at me again, and the suspicion in her eyes has returned. "You were there when he died? Did you... did you have something to do with it?"

I shake my head. "Yes, I was there. My friend here and I both were. And no, I promise I absolutely did not have anything to do with it. We just happened to be driving past and... well, we found him on the side of the road and recognized him immediately from his butcher shop."

She narrows her eyes at me and places one hand on her hip.

"Are you sure it was him? Not someone else who looked like him?"

"Yes. Positive. We recognized the spider tattoo and then we spoke with him while we waited for the ambulance."

She eyes us with suspicion, but her eyes water. I think she's beginning to realize we're telling the truth.

"Look, I know it sounds really strange. And I'm truly not here to upset you. But his last words were asking us to tell you that he's very sorry for everything. And that he loves you. We promised him we would. That's why we're here."

She lowers her gaze as tears break free, rolling down her cheeks. I reach out and touch her arm. "I'm so sorry for your loss."

I expect her to pull away, but instead she lunges forward and wraps her arms around me, clinging to me in a desperate, heartfelt hug.

"Thank you," she whispers, tears sliding down her face as she lifts her head to make eye contact. "Thank you so much."

Chapter Forty-Six

Brick

"So we're going to have our drone follow theirs," I explain. "It's going to monitor where theirs goes so it can get up close and personal with keypads and other security mechanisms."

"Like a stalker, but the drone version?" Angel eyes me skeptically.

"Exactly." I grin.

"Well, I'm plenty familiar with that general concept, sadly." She frowns. "Didn't we do a good enough job with our drone shots?"

"Oh, you did perfectly," I quickly say, because the information they gathered with their first drone outing has been invaluable. "The footage you captured, both photo and video, was more than enough. Very impressive, actually, given you haven't used one before." He shrugs. "But it takes a few sessions to get enough quality data. I've enhanced the images you captured, and we have an idea of access points that we might be able to breach. But now we need to go back and confirm things. The best way to do that is by following their drone with one of our own. They, of course, know theirs exists, so we send in a smaller one that's almost undetectable, and it follows theirs so closely that they don't notice."

"Won't they see there's a second one?" Angel quirks an eyebrow.

"It's almost undetectable by the human eye. The first one will capture most of their attention and it's not like most people sit there trying to find a second one. You would maybe be interested to know, my love, that the government is currently working on a stealth drone called the Valkyrie. I like to think it's named after you."

She smirks. "You're the only one who calls me that. And I can hardly imagine you working for the government, naming drones."

I shrug. "It's a coincidence, sure. But I'm a believer in happy coincidences and happy accidents. And, speaking of which," he says, glancing at his watch, "the other guys just arrived about half an hour ago. They should be here within about an hour, give or take."

"Oh really? They're all here on the island?" I squeal. Today has been a heart wrenching, stressful day, and I can imagine nothing better than being in all of their arms.

"Yes, baby, all six of the other guys have flown in. They had to take a few separate flights, but we're all here now."

It's the best news.

My men are all here. Just where I need them to be.

We're all about to be together again.

CHAPTER FORTY-SEVEN
Aria

I notice them in the bar before they notice me.

They stand out. Ten of them, looking as thick as thieves.

Dimitri sees them as well. "It looks like we might have some like-minded folks visiting the island," he gestures in the general direction of the group. "They could just be a large group of friends, but I reckon that one is with those four guys," he points at one of the woman, "and she's," pointing at the other one, "with the other four. They fit the description of the group we've heard about from the other island, except I heard the girls had brightly colored hair. It could be a disguise, though."

"They each have *four* men? It sounds like I need to find myself another boyfriend then!" I grin and wiggle my eyebrows.

All three of my men turn and frown at me.

"Rude! We're more than enough for you, if I do say so myself," pouts Josef, crossing his fingers firmly across his chest. "I refuse to share you with anyone else. These guys are quite enough."

"Yeah, I'd be too jealous to add a fourth," says Florian.

They're such a dichotomy. For whatever reason, maybe the bond they've built over the years, they're totally fine with each other being with me. But I even joke about adding another man into the mix and they lose their shit and become homicidal maniacs.

"Don't worry, guys," I say, smiling sweetly at each of them in turn. "You're the perfect amount of men for me. I was only teasing."

"Good, because if someone else even tries to touch you, we'll kill them and we'll make it hurt. No questions asked."

"Okay, that's very sweet of you," I say, having no doubt they wouldn't hesitate. "Dimitri, it sounds like it's time for us to make some introductions."

CHAPTER FORTY-EIGHT
Dimitri

Two hours later

We wait, watching and observing as the large group goes about their meal and enjoys a few drinks together. The longer we wait and watch, the more I'm convinced they're the group I thought they were.

Finally, I'm ready to approach and I walk over and extend my. Hand.

"Hey. I'm Dimitri. And this is Josef, Florian and Aria."

"You're...", the tall man shakes my hand and then gestures toward the four of us. But it's like he can't find the words and instead his fingers wiggle around between the four of us in a way that suggests we're somehow connected.

"Together? Yes." I nod. I don't really know how to describe what this whole situation is, either. But sometimes no words are required when you have something this good.

The man lets out a low whistle. "I never knew much about arrangements like this, but now we can't seem to keep stumbling over them everywhere we go."

I shrug. "Like attracts like, I guess."

The man grins. "It sure does. And we sure like our girls. I'm Rake by the way, and you'll probably never remember all these names, but this is Skyler, Zeke, Dom, Devon, Angel, Brick, Slade and Roman. Oh and Aidan," he grins at one of the muscular men with short, dark hair. "I knew I'd forgotten one."

"Gee thanks!" The man smirks.

"Anyway," I frown, "we've heard you've been asking around about Tane. A word to the wise, you don't want to attract his attention like that if you can help it."

"Oh, we're well aware he's a very dangerous man. We've had the displeasure of doing business with him over the years."

I smirk. "Ah yes, a common complaint around here. Anyway, that seems like something else we have in common. It sounds like we might have a shared interest in taking care of some loose ends with respect to Tane and his men."

Aidan frowns and runs his fingers through his hair. "No offense, but we're not looking for additional partners. In any sense of the word."

"Oh, neither are we," I scoff, looking at Josef, Florian and Aria, who all nod in agreement. "But realistically, it sounds like you might benefit from our help, at least on a temporary basis. A mutually beneficial business partnership of sorts."

"Tell us more." The burly man who I believe was introduced as Dom crosses his hands over his massive chest.

"Look, there might only be three... four of us, including Aria," I say, glancing at each of them. "But we know this island. We know the local dynamics here. We've been planning a takeover for a while now, but we just don't have the manpower that you do. We'd still be outnumbered, but with the fourteen of us combined, I think we might just stand a chance."

Aidan eyes me with suspicion. "How do we know we can trust you? That you're not just some lackeys for Tane and you're not going to just turn us over to him somehow or run off with any gains we make here?"

I shrug. "I guess you don't have a strong reason to trust us, and that's fair. We've only just met. But listen, sometimes you have to go with your gut. We're willing to partner with you without knowing you well. We've done some background research, and understand what you've been doing on the other island. We have respect for your work, and quite frankly, we need you. And we think you need us."

"It sounds like we need to have a longer conversation. I'm not excited about expanding our partnership, but I'm willing to hear you out. What do you think, guys?" Aidan looks around his group and there's nodding and shrugging, although the one called Slade remains scowling with his tattooed arms crossed tightly over his chest. He seems like a real charmer.

"Alright, we're open to at least listen. Tell us more."

"Absolutely," I reply. "But first, tell me about the poison frogs. I'm very impressed. I heard fourteen of Tane's men were taken out at the local tattoo parlor by some poison dart frog toxin that somehow made it into the men's ink. Apparently Tane is furious and running around like a madman trying to figure out who did it. You wouldn't happen to know anything about that, would you, by chance?"

I notice Rake and the guy in the leather jacket, Brick I believe, glance at each other with small smiles that really say it all. Brick smiles sweetly while the others look at him and Rake in shock. "I wouldn't know the first thing about that," he says. "But I agree it was a stroke of genius."

Chapter Forty-Nine

Brick

"So, we're going to fuck with his meat." I know it sounds dodgy the moment the words leave my mouth, but I like to say things in ways that make people uncomfortable. It's kind of my thing. And one of the many reasons why Angel and I get along so well.

Rake quirks an eyebrow at me, his mouth turning into an uncharacteristic scowl. "*Excuse me?* I don't know what sort of sick shit you and your boys are into, but I'm not touching another man's meat."

"One, don't be such a bigot. And two, I'm not talking about dicks, you moron." I roll my eyes. Of course, Rake would automatically jump to this being something sexual. "I'm talking about actual butcher meat. His guy, Diego, supplied all Tane's restaurants on the island, including his compound. And now that he's dead, and there's nobody to run his shop, we have a way to do whatever we want to his product before it gets where it needs to go. And if there's one thing about me, it's that I don't like meat, but I hate it going to waste even more."

"What should we do to it? More poison dart frog stuff?" Rake eyes me suspiciously.

"No, that's already been done. It's time for something else that's original. I think just enough to get people sick. Nobody needs to die over a ribeye. Hell, a cow shouldn't die over a ribeye."

"Speak for yourself, Brick. There's almost nothing I wouldn't do for a big juicy steak." Rake's eyes grow dreamy, a look of bliss spreading across his face.

I find myself just about drooling at the thought of a prime cut of beef, even though I haven't had one in years. "You're right. I miss a good steak now and then."

"Oh really? I thought you were vegan, bro."

"Oh, I definitely am. It doesn't mean a man can't dream even though I won't let my carnivorous thirst cloud my philosophical opinions. I have other ways to take care of that." I grin and wiggle my eyebrows. "Anyway, we need to concentrate. We'll need to find a way to get the tainted items into his supply chain, but that shouldn't be too hard. We just have to mess with the meat without any of Diego's employees knowing. They'll be so stricken with grief that they probably won't even notice."

"Well, what about the people that eat the tainted food? Like, innocent restaurant guests?"

"Our main target will be the compound, for sure. Tane's actual men are guaranteed to scarf the food down like rabid animals. But we do need to inflict some collateral damage. We need him to be distracted, for one. It sounds like he already is distracted over the frogs, so maybe that's not such a big issue." I shrug. "And we also need local law enforcement to be away from the compound, investigating why all the tourists are getting so sick here. It's their lifeblood, the tourism industry, and even though they would never admit it I bet you they run from serious crime the second a tourist claims someone took their snorkel equipment, let alone actually gets poisoned at a tourist trap restaurant."

We get to work for the next few hours, plotting and planning our next strike.

***

We enter the butcher shop, and it's just the way the girls described it to us. Carcasses hanging everywhere on sturdy metal hooks, and lots of blood and sharp tools everywhere. So basically, like my torture basement, just with animals instead of humans. For a moment, I have a flashback to my time with my father at the meat processing plant, where he taught me to dismember my first human body. I'd say it was a sad memory, but I'd be lying. Even though it was scary at the time, it's now one of my best ones. It's also why I'm vegan.

Our first stop is the office. It's locked, but it's not a sturdy device and I pick it within seconds using a credit card and a paper clip.

Looking around, Rake lets out a low whistle. "This place is a mess!"

He's right. The entire room looks like something out of *Hoarders*. It's stacked with invoices and receipts that must go back for years, and there's barely enough room for the two of us to squeeze through to the cluttered desk. But there, we find what we need. An order sheet that maps out what was meant to be delivered today. By the looks of it, there are about twelve restaurants awaiting their deliveries, as well as a familiar address. Tane's compound.

"This is perfect," I say to Rake. "Now we just need to dress the part."

He nods, and we squeeze our way back out of the cluttered room and down the narrow hallway.

In the back, we find the employee break room. It's a small space, and a couple of paper plates litter the small formica table in the center topped with half-eaten slices of pizza.

"Bingo!" Rake cries out, pointing at a hook on the back of the door that holds two white aprons.

"And here are the lockers." I point at the little metal squares at the back of the room. They're not locked, and sure enough inside are a couple of uniforms bearing the name of Diego's butcher shop. We don the shirts and caps that identify us as Diego's employees, just in case a bystander happens to casually walk by and wonder what we're doing in the dead man's business.

"So how are we going to fuck with the meat?" Rake eyes me curiously.

"Belladonna."

"Bella-what-what?" he asks, quirking an eyebrow.

"It's a homeopathic medicine. Official name atropa belladonna, otherwise known as deadly nightshade."

"Where the hell are we going to get a *deadly nightshade*? And who are you? Agatha Christie?"

I smirk. "No, man. It's a homeopathic medicine. I like to cure my ailments the natural way." I shrug.

"So, you just have some lying around so you can poison yourself whenever the mood takes you?"

"Nah, I use it regularly, actually. It's good for colds and hemorrhoids and some other stuff."

Rake shivers. "Don't tell me about your hemorrhoids, bro."

"I didn't. It's just one of the uses. It's not my fault you have a fucked-up imagination and can't help visualizing it."

Rake rolls his eyes. "Well, how does it help us, anyway? If it's safe enough for you to have around?"

"Well, technically, the entire deadly nightshade is a poisonous plant. But like I said, there are some uses for it in small doses that don't make people sick. However, with the right amount, it fucks up your nervous system, but not usually enough to kill someone."

"Oh yeah? What are we talking?"

"Well, it messes with saliva production. It can make you sweat, change your pupil size. Fuck with your urination and digestion. Mess with your heart rate and blood pressure."

"That sounds dangerous."

"Listen, we're not playing Go Fish here, man. We need people to be sick enough that it's an issue. And I have no problem killing someone who deserves it, but I won't take an innocent life. So, trust me when I say this is just what we need here and now."

"Won't it cook off when the meat is prepared?"

"We'll put it on the most prime of cuts. The ones that are likely to be the least cooked. Things that are more likely to be prepared raw or rare, like a carpaccio or a nice thick filet. That way, we have the best chance of fucking with the most people."

Rake lets out a low whistle. "Tane's going to be so pissed when people start reporting this. It sounds like he's already super pissed about Frog-gate."

"Precisely. And it's going to distract local law enforcement. They're going to be running all over the island trying to figure out what happened with Tane's precious meats. And that's exactly what we need to divert their attention."

"You're weird. But you really are also some kind of brilliant mastermind, you know that?"

I grin. "Oh, I'm well aware."

CHAPTER FIFTY
Slade

"I missed your cooking," says Angel, and her compliment makes me feel a little warm inside.

"You did? I thought you might leave me for one of the hotel chefs here," I grin. "I saw one walk past earlier and he was pretty cute."

"Never! Your food is genuinely a million times better. It's been nice trying some of the local fare, but nothing compares to the things you make."

To my embarrassment, I feel a flush creeping slowly up my neck and onto my face.

"Slade. Are you blushing?"

"No, of course not. I must have just caught some sun today."

"Suuure," she grins and winks at me, her hand playfully stroking my arm.

"Are you trying to get into my pants, Angel Benson?"

"Always," she winks at me, her eyes lowering to my crotch. "Did it work?"

I feel myself growing hard as she moves closer until her breasts are pressed against my chest.

"Mmm, I love it when you do that," I growl, my hands lowering to rest on the dip where her waist meets her hips.

"Let me show you how much I missed it," she purrs, tipping her head up to mine.

Our teeth clash together as she yanks her head down, and her lips meet mine in what can only be described as a violent kiss. We both want each other, and badly. I'm yearning for other parts of my body to clash against hers. Repeatedly. But I'm letting her take the lead for now. I have a feeling I won't have to wait long.

She yanks my pants down so forcefully that the top button comes off and clatters to the floor, skittering away off to the side.

"Easy, tiger," I growl. But I couldn't care less about the button and I don't want her to go easy at all. I just want her. I've missed her soft skin, the curvy angles of her body. The way she looks at me. Her scent. It's only been a few days since I last saw her, but it's been pure torture.

"Shut up and get ready to fuck me," she rasps back, her eyes ablaze with lust.

To think at one point, I despised this woman, even though it wasn't because of anything she did. It took me a while to get over myself and succumb to her beauty and her brains. It's painful to look back and confront the fact I was ever that stupid. What a waste, when I could have been with her even sooner.

She rips my shirt up and away from my torso, and I raise my arms up. The fabric pulls as she twists my shirt off me and I hear some stitching stretch. I'm going to need a new wardrobe by the time she's done with me at this rate, and I don't mind at all.

She's soaking wet, her arousal already beginning to trickle out of her. It glistens across her pussy and it's irresistible. I go to bury my face between her thighs, but she puts a hand out to stop me.

"No," she growls. "I'm going to ride your face."

"Yes please," I growl. I roll over onto my back and yank her on top of me.

She straddles my face, her smooth thighs wrapping around my head. I hold on to her hips and she mashes her soaking pussy down onto my mouth. I lap at her hungrily. She's the best thing I've ever tasted, and I'm a chef, so I know what I'm talking about.

She grinds herself rhythmically against my face, and her arousal smears across my mouth and nose and chin. But it only makes me harder. As soon as she's come, I'm going to pound the shit out of her gorgeous body.

She pants as she continues to ride my face, and by her ragged breaths and her increasingly jerky movements on top of me I can tell she's close. I can barely breathe due to the way her pussy is basically suffocating me, but breathing can wait. It seems non-essential. For now, my focus is on feasting on this goddess. On giving her pleasure. She comes first, literally and figuratively.

Her body bucks as a wave of pleasure crashes over her. I feel her hips and legs shake against me and she squeezes her thighs even tighter around my head. And I keep going. Licking at her clit furiously while her pussy pulsates against me.

"Fuck me. Now," she growls, clambering down my body and slamming her drenched cunt down onto my rock hard shaft. I moan at the sensation of her impaling herself on me.

"You're so fucking wet and tight, Angel," I growl.

"Shut up and fuck me," she grits out, her breath still rapid in the afterglow of her orgasm.

"Oh, you're feeling feisty today, are you?" I grin, and she puts her hand over my nose and mouth. I know she's only teasing and has no intention of choking me out completely.

But there's a very real intensity about her right now. Maybe she missed me as much as I did her.

And as much as I'm fine about sharing her with the other guys, there's something special about having our own one-on-one time to explore each other like this. If the others could see us now, they'd almost certainly jump in. But right now, I get the outright honor of Slade and Angel adult time. I'm so glad I offered to stay back and cook for the group. The food is ready for whenever they get back, so I just get to relish and enjoy my time with her.

The room is full of the sounds of our heavy breaths and moans, and our bodies mashing together as my cock pounds into Angel's wetness from underneath her. She slams her pussy down on my cock as hard as she can, over and over again, moaning each time she impales me to my hilt. I had every intention of fucking her, of taking the lead, but she's giving me a run for my money. It's like she's taking out all the stress and strain of the past few days on me and specifically my cock, and I'm here for it.

Soon, I feel my body tense and I smash her hips down as I release into her. "Jesus fuck, Angel. You feel so fucking good." I continue to thrust into her while my cock pulses and my orgasm gradually subsides.

"So do you, baby. So do you," she says, leaning down to give me a gentle kiss.

She is the most exquisite creature I've ever met. I live for moments just like this. And I'm never letting her go.

Chapter Fifty-One

Aidan

"So how has Tane gotten away with this for so long?" I ask. "Is it because everyone's just that scared of him?"

I'm meeting with Dimitri to find out more about how he and his group could help us. I almost canceled because my doubts have grown as I assessed the risks involved, because my instincts were of course to drop everything and run immediately to her side. My mind is swirling with all the potential implications of adding to our partnership, and it's taking all my effort to keep focused on what Dimitri is saying and to think of the right questions to ask.

"He was allowed to run things in the beginning because he helped us to take down Ren, the guy who came before him," Dimitri explains. "Everyone here really thought he was the lesser evil. That he was here to save us. And for a while, he did make things better on the island." He frowns, and his eyes darken. "But as time went on, we found out that we were deadly wrong. It seems strange to say it, but in hindsight, I think any of us would have Ren back over Tane in a heartbeat. He was brutal, but at least he had some sort of conscience. Tane seems to have no limits at all, and he's only getting worse"

"Why didn't people rise up against him and overthrow him like we're trying to?"

"By the time we realized what was going on, he'd become far too powerful. He has access to resources from the mainland that just don't exist here. He'd become an unstoppable force. Until you guys arrived and gave us hope again. But, no offense, others have tried and failed to take him down without our help. Knowledge of this island and the dynamics that support his business interests is critical. That's why we need to work together. Otherwise, we'll be letting Tane win. And for the good of all the islands, and our livelihoods, we can't let that happen."

On my way back to the hotel, I chew on Dimitri's words. He seemed to know what he was talking about, and his passion for solving the island's plight caused by Tane's rule seemed genuine enough. Still, I'm not a hundred percent sure we can trust the guy.

And my mind keeps ruminating on how we can keep the women safe from all of this.

When I get back to the hotel, I reach out to Zeke and ask him to meet me in the quiet lobby bar. I know Skyler is a joint leader with him, but I feel an affinity with Zeke as the most levelheaded member of the group. And right now, I need laser-focused calm and logic.

When I get there, he's already taken a seat in a dark corner, and ordered us a couple of drinks and a snack which the server brings over as soon as I sit down in an overstuffed leather chair.

I quickly download him on what I learned from Dimitri. He leans in as I speak, soaking in every word and taking care not to interrupt me. Once I'm done, he leans back and rubs his chin with his thumb and forefinger. "Clearly, we have to get him on the back foot. Make him think he's got one over on us."

"Yeah, but that's going to be easier said that done from what Dimitri shared." I run a hand through my hair. "He has too many guys on the ground, and he's going to figure things out quickly. There's unfortunately a chance he already has, but he just hasn't shown his cards."

"What do you think we should do about the girls?" Zeke asks. "We both want to keep them safe. I know that. But if we get them to stay back here, they'll be pissed and we'll be leaving them vulnerable. I'm not confident this hotel is truly secure, especially when it comes to the likes of Tane's guys. They'll stop at nothing to get what they want. Maybe we should bring them with us."

I quirk an eyebrow. "And put them in the line of fire? That seems like a terrible idea."

Zeke frowns. "So does leaving them defenseless while we go in there with guns blazing."

We're both silent for a moment, deep in thought. "What if we have a couple of us stay behind to protect them while the rest of us go after Tane?"

"And reduce our manpower when his team is already way bigger than ours?" Zeke sighs. "That will never work. We're already outnumbered and there's too big of a risk in diluting what we have to put up against him. Besides, look how it worked out, with Rake and Brick being sent on ahead. Angel started killing people and Brick got all obsessed with insane poisoning schemes."

I push the beer glass and the plate away in front of me. I need a clear head, and I don't have an appetite. There's too much to think about. "I don't know, man. None of these sound like good options. And are you sure we're going to be strong enough, even if all of us guys go?"

"I have to think we are. Otherwise, why are we even doing this?"

I catch myself running my fingers through my hair again. My head feels tight and I make a conscious effort to unknot my eyebrows, which feel like they're almost joined. "Should we consider pulling back and waiting until we're stronger? I hate to ask, but the risk could be too great right now."

Zeke frowns. "You know, I've thought about that, too. But it's a bit like having a kid, right? There's never going to be a 'right time'. Can't you see that? Each time we get stronger, so does Tane. He's like flesh-eating bacteria, spreading throughout the islands and destroying everything in his wake as he continues to multiply. And he's charismatic and powerful enough to keep luring more and more business partners in with the promise of wealth."

"That's a good point," I nod. "And from what Dimitri was saying, some key people on the island are starting to sour on Tane because his words aren't ringing true. Perhaps even people within his ranks that have historically been unquestioningly loyal."

"Right? And the truth is, this is the closest to Tane we've ever been, and quite possibly the closest we'll ever get. I think it's a case where we either take our chances now, or risk missing the opportunity forever. If we lose, well, we die now or we die later."

I nod again, but my mouth feels a little dry. I agree with what he's saying, but I'm also second-guessing myself because of the gravity of the consequences if this is the wrong decision. "Okay, I'm with you. We'll need to see what the others think, of course. And as for the girls, what option do you think we should go with? Do we bring them, leave them, or divide ourselves up?"

"I think we leave them. The hotel seems more safe and secure than bringing them to a criminal's compound. They should be okay there for a couple of hours."

I frown, and my chest tightens. "Well, if you're wrong, they'll almost certainly be dead. And I think you're feeling guilt about sending them on ahead here in the first place."

"Maybe you're right. Let's see what the group thinks. Regardless, what choice do we have? If this doesn't work out, we'll all be dead, anyway."

Chapter Fifty-Two

Zeke

We convene the group, all ten of us meeting in Devon's suite. The room is large, but the space feels small when packed with eight big guys and the two women.

Aidan and I share what we've discussed, and the relative risks we see associated with each option.

"So what do you think?" I ask. "Should we go for it? Form a partnership with Dimitri and his guys?" I look around the room.

"I don't like it. It seems too risky. I'm having second thoughts. The guy seemed trustworthy, but he's just new to us and… I don't know. I'm very concerned." Aidan runs his hand through his hair, which for once doesn't seem perfectly styled. It's unsettling seeing him feeling rattled and flip-flopping on the way forward. He's the Brixton who's always calm, just like me until the rare occasion when I'm given a reason to snap.

"I don't like it either," Skyler frowns. I'm a little surprised by this, because he's usually a little more willing to take risks than I am, and I'm intrigued by the idea.

"Look, I understand why you're suspicious. These guys popped up out of nowhere. And it seems a little convenient that they're all in the same type of relationship that we are. Think of the home court advantage, though. And if they really do understand us like that, we could make a powerful team. Fourteen of us rather than ten. There's safety in numbers."

"Yeah, but not when the extra people don't have a bond established with you," frowns Aidan. "What if they just turn on us and it ends up destroying everything we've worked for? People are unpredictable and opportunistic under this kind of pressure."

"Well, if it means taking down Tane Brown once and for all, I'm willing to take that chance. And you seemed to have a good gut feeling after meeting them, Aidan, although I know you're questioning that now. But I understand if you don't want us to take responsibility for such a big decision based on your instincts after only a couple of meetings."

Roman raises a hand, and everyone looks at him. "Question. How do we know that we'd be guaranteed top spot if we do take him down? Surely there are a bunch of other groups eyeing him, wanting his head on a pike. If we do the dirty work and get rid of him and his key men, there's no guarantee we'll be handed over the reins. It could be a bloodbath, with everyone vying for his power. Who's to say that's not precisely what Dimitri and the other guys are planning? Using our muscle and knowledge and then swanning in and taking things over."

Dom speaks up. "There are still ten of us and only four of them, and one's a girl."

"Hmmm." Two voices simultaneously clear their voices from the corner.

"Shit, sorry ladies," Dom looks sheepish. "I forgot you were there."

Devon and Angel roll their eyes.

"And here we were, beginning to think you weren't a group of complete misogynists." Angel folds her arms across her chest and Devon follows suit.

"No, no," I put my hands up in self-defense. "We don't think you're weak at all or anything like that. In fact, I think you're the two strongest ones here, mentally. You keep us in check and see angles that sometimes we miss. I think Dom just meant going by sheer physicality that it's more helpful having us guys in the room."

"Keep digging that hole deeper," smirks Angel.

"Okay, I give up! I take back what I said," says Dom, putting his hands up in mock defense. "The keys to our power, and being able to retain it, are the two of you. I don't think anyone would argue with that. Would you, guys?" He looks around the room and each of us nod with enthusiasm.

"The ladies have spoken." I shrug and glance from Angel to Devon. "What do you think we should do?"

"I think we give them a chance," says Angel.

"So do I," says Devon. "What do we have to lose?"

"Um, quite a lot," frowns Aidan, his brow furrowing.

"But a chance not taken is a chance lost," says Brick. "If this is the key to taking Tane down, I don't think we really have a choice, do we? And with the information we need to infiltrate Tane's secure compound, I think we're ready to put our plan into action. I get that it's nerve-racking, but using our drone to follow theirs around gave us all the rest of the information we need to make our plan a success. I think we're ready to go ahead."

I speak up. "I agree with the ladies and Brick. Let's expand our power, but make sure we trust but verify our new partners. They don't need to be with us when we go in, but they should at least be aware of the general plan so they can provide backup as needed."

Slade sighs. "Okay, I'm in".

"And if Slade is in, we're all in," smirks Aidan. "He's always the path of greatest resistance."

Slade scowls.

"And so what do we think we should do with the girls while we go off and do this?"

Devon clears her throat. "Guys, we're still here. Why don't you ask us what we think?"

"Right?" Angel frowns. "I think we should have a say in this."

I sigh. "Okay then. What say would you like to have?"

"Well, actually," she says, glancing at Devon, who nods in support. "We think we should be a fundamental part of the plan. We think you need us to take the lead in order to meet our goal of breaching the compound. And here's what we have in mind..."

CHAPTER FIFTY-THREE

Brick

The girls are both wearing discreet body cams outside Tane's compound, and I'm in a surveillance vehicle down the street with the rest of the guys.

The women are wearing the most colorful, outlandish outfits I've ever seen. Tight, bright shorts and tiny tank tops with push-up bras and plentiful jewelry. They're both also sporting long wigs and a lot of makeup, rendering them almost unrecognizable. Still very hot, but almost unrecognizable, that is. At my insistence, and out of an abundance of caution and practical thinking, they made a last minute decision to ditch their high-heeled strappy sandals, and so the only shred of normalcy about what they're wearing are their combat boots which have discreet steel toes, just the way I like them.

They strut up to the guard station at the front of the compound that's typically responsible for vetting and admitting guests.

A man's deep voice, official in tone, crackles in the speaker. "Can I help you?"

"Can you please help us?" Angel simpers. 'You see, our car broke down on the next street and we can't seem to get it running again." They both smile sweetly at the man. I smirk at them acting like helpless little damsels waiting for this big nice man to save them. Talented little actresses, both of them.

"This isn't AAA. This is a secure compound, ma'am." He frowns at them through the guard station window, but I see his gaze trail up and down each of their bodies, and he gets a little flustered. He's lucky I'm not standing there too, or I'd smash my fist through the station's window and snap his pudgy neck. Nobody looks at Angel like that.

"But please, can't you help us, sir?" Devon smiles coquettishly and flutters her eyelashes at the man. "We're new to this area and, well, we're scared about what will happen if we don't get our car back to our boss on time. He's going to be very mad and, well.. you see... that doesn't go well for us when he gets mad. You wouldn't want that to happen to us, would you, sir?"

He clears his throat and his face gets redder. "Ma'am, I'd love to help, but I'm not allowed to leave my post."

"Please, sir? I don't think it'll take very long," pleads Angel. "I'm sure it's nothing major and we just, well, need a big man like you to help us out. It will only take a moment. You just seem like a really nice man. And we won't tell a soul."

He shifts awkwardly in his seat. He'd better not be getting a boner or I swear I'll fucking kill him. Looking around the van I see each of the other guys is looking similarly irritated. "I'm not sure..." says the guard.

"Please, sir? We'll... make it worth your while." Angel adjusts her top, intentionally giving the guard a view of her cleavage, which looks extra perky and inviting with the assistance of a high-quality push-up bra.

A growl emanates from my throat. I don't like this at all, even though it needs to be done.

The man makes no attempt to avert his gaze. "Well, I guess I could help for just a second. That couldn't hurt, especially seeing things are quiet today and we're not expecting any visitors any time soon. I'll be right out."

He presses his burly figure up from his chair, leaving his post and moving out of our sightline. For a moment, I'm worried he's onto them. But then, there's an audible beep as the gate opens and he approaches the girls. The way he's looking at them is unmistakable, and my jaw clenches so hard I almost bust a tooth.

I can tell you one thing. If he's not dead by the end of the day, he will be by tomorrow.

Devon begins to root around in her oversized purse. "Let me just find my keys. They have to be in here somewhere!" Coins and other items jingle as she continues to scramble around. "Oh gosh! I'm such a clumsy girl!" Devon says as she tips the contents of her bag onto the ground. Money and makeup and tampons and various other items skitter all over the place. The guard looks on as Devon bends over to pick up the contents of her bag, taking the opportunity to sneak a peek at her cleavage before realizing he should probably help her. He grabs a couple of items from the ground, blushing at the sight of the tampons, and hands the items to her, taking the opportunity to brush his meaty hands against hers in an attempt at some type of awkward meet-cute.

Dom growls at the sight of the man ogling his woman and cracks his knuckles before making a move to get up from his vehicle seat and move toward the door. His nostrils flare and his chest rapidly rises and falls as his face reddens. "Fuck this. I'm going to get the fuck out of this van and—."

"Man, I feel you," Brick interrupts in a show of empathy and self-restraint. "But we can take care of this human trash pile later."

Dom growls again, but nods. "I don't like it. But you're right. We need to try to keep our cool right now or we risk putting them in further danger. Besides, I know they're just putting on an act to distract him."

In the distraction, the man doesn't notice Angel behind him as she pulls a taser out of her own purse. She pulls the trigger and zaps him with it. The metal prongs connected by a wire stick into his back and he cries out as the force takes him to the ground. He hits his head on the ground as he falls, and he convulses on the floor for a few moments before growing still. "Oops," says Angel. "We were just meant to incapacitate him, not kill the man."

"Oh, he's just going to have a headache when he wakes up," says Devon. "He'll be fine." She produces a rag soaked in chloroform from a Ziploc bag in her half-full purse and holds it over the man's nose, and keeps it there until he stops moving. They each take one of the man's legs and drag him across the ground, nudging his prone form into the shadows beneath a large bush underneath a palm tree. "Someone would really have to be looking for him to find him there. But we have to work quickly. He's not going to be out for long."

They unhook the man's ID and keycard from his pants, and head back to the now unmanned gate.

The women get into the compound using the code we identified during our drone surveillance, and silently slip into the guard booth using the keycard. The room is austere and impersonal, lined with screens featuring security camera footage. Passive aggressive memos are taped to one wall reminding people of key policies, and how to clock in and out for their shifts. A sandwich bag sits in the corner, presumably holding the guard's lunch which he won't be eating any time soon.

Angel taps at the security camera console, following the instructions Aidan gave her to put the camera feed on a loop. She's successful on her first try. Now, nobody looking at the footage would be any the wiser that the two women have snuck their way into the most secure compound in the island chain.

"Jesus, they're good." Rake lets out a low whistle as he scrutinizes the camera footage from our surveillance van.

Skyler smirks. "Nothing like a couple of hot women to lure a sleazy militia man away from his post."

"Doesn't mean I have to like it," I snarl, recalling the sleazy way the guard looked at them. He might be unconscious now, but that's not good enough for me. "If he doesn't die today at Tane's hand, he's definitely getting fired. And in that case, I'm going to kill him myself." I bare my teeth, and my blood feels like it is literally boiling within me. "Nobody looks at our women that way and gets away with it."

Next to me, Dom growls and cracks his knuckles. "I'm going to join you."

CHAPTER FIFTY-FOUR
Angel

"We made it!" Devon whispers. "That was easier than I thought!"

"Don't count your chickens before they're hatched, please," I whisper. "We still have to get the internal access codes from the other guard station. And there are bound to be more men inside."

We round a corner and almost bump into a tall, lean figure. *Fuck!*

I leap back, and realize it's *her*. The woman from the photo. Minka Beckett. The expert in strategy and torture. Just the person you don't want to run into when you're breaking into a madman's compound.

"Oh it's you," she says in a hushed whisper, her eyes scrutinizing us with fascination. "I've been monitoring you since your arrival, and I know exactly why you're here. Keep going. I'll pretend I never saw you." Her words seem as much of a surprise to her as they are to us. Devon and I glance at each other, confused, and back to her.

"But you're one of Tane's top people. Is this a trap? Why would you help us?"

"I can't believe I'm doing this. It goes against all my training, which causes me great internal turmoil, but I also know it's the right thing." I detect a slight accent, and her voice comes out as a husky purr just like I imagined when I first saw her photo.

"You're really going to let us go? Why?" I don't trust this woman for a second. She's perfection in human form, a coldhearted military killing machine, and it seems very weird she's stopping to help us. But something in her eyes makes me feel we should hear her out.

"Don't make me second-guess myself more than I am already." She narrows her eyes and looks down. "Don't ask questions. Just know that this is your one get out of jail free card. There will be no second chances. Take what you need and get out now."

"Why are you doing this?" I quirk a brow. "Is it because we're women? Is this some kind of trap? You're one of his top people."

"It's because you're not completely evil people, as evil as Tane anyway," she shrugs. "Flawed, perhaps. But aren't we all? The thing is, I've been studying you and I know why you're here. And I guess you could say I've seen the light after far too long. I've grown tired of Tane's complete lack of respect for the locals here. He takes and pillages and destroys. I don't have the tenacity or quite frankly the patience to take him down myself. But I believe you have a real chance here to do the right thing."

"And what about you? Where will you go? He's hardly going to let you get away with this without paying a steep price."

She frowns, and for a millisecond, I swear her beautiful mouth trembles. "Stop with the questions. I have enough connections on the mainland to safely get far, far away from here and make a new life for myself. But I've had enough of being complicit with his evil deeds. And I can't do it anymore. I guess my conscience finally caught up after many years of being a willing participant in his brutal regime. But I suggest you be very careful. I'm not the most dangerous person on this compound, and if you're caught, I can guarantee that nobody else will be this understanding."

She clenches her jaw, and again I detect a slight quiver before she hurries past us down the hall. Maybe she's not as fierce as she makes out to be. Or maybe she is, but everyone has a limit. It seems as if, after many years, like many people on this island, Tane has finally caused her to find hers.

We rush past her, too shocked to process what just happened. But this is our one chance and we don't want to give her a reason to change her mind. We hurtle around another corner, and I feel a hand reach out and grab me by my neck. A cold rag is pressed against my nose, bearing the familiar scent of chloroform. *For fuck's sake, not again.* My world gets fuzzy and then, once again, everything fades to black.

Chapter Fifty-Five

Angel

I wake up in a room which is poorly lit. It's fairly empty and the few items of furniture are covered in dust, including a few metal drying racks which look out of place in the industrial space.

My head is pounding, and I quickly realize I'm not alone.

A suited man stands in the corner of the room, casually pointing a gun at me. I turn toward the door and notice another large man standing behind me, his gun also aimed in my direction. Where the fuck did he come from? Who are these people?

"Wha—what's going on?" I ask. I mean, clearly I've been taken hostage *again*, but I have no idea where I am or who these guys are.

"It's really quite simple, you see," the suited man says in a calm tone, unbothered by the chaos unfolding around us. "We've been keeping tabs on you since the moment you got here. You think we weren't anticipating your arrival? I do have to give you kudos though... the two of you, being able to breach both the holiday home and the compound. No easy feat on either account."

I realize his appearance matches the description of Tane's second-in-charge. "You're—you're Denzo?"

He claps, long and slow, the connection of his slender hands creating an echo that reverberates around the room. "Well done, Angel Benson. Excellent detective work."

"I—I don't understand. How did you know where we were? You've known we were here all along?"

"We know everything that goes on around here. I can assure you of that. We've been surveilling you the entire time you've been on the island." His eyes gleam and a satisfied smile plays across his face like the cat that got the cream.

I don't even try to hide my scowl.

"Oh yes," he says, his mouth curled up in amusement at my shock. "You don't think we have connections at all airports here on the islands and the main routes back and forth from the mainland? You don't think we have thriving networks at all the major hotels and some of the minor ones? Nobody comes in or out without us knowing about it. We run this place."

"Then why did you let us move around freely all this time? Why did you wait until now to capture us?" I feel lightheaded as my heartbeat pounds in my chest, and my skin is crawling.

"It's simple, really. Our little game of cat and mouse was ready to come to an end. It was fun toying with you, making you feel like you had the upper hand. When we were really just waiting for you to feel like you had enough intel for your men to come and join you. And now, here you are. All ten of you. Easy prey. Much easier than trying to track everyone down in separate locations. Some might call us lazy, but I prefer to think of it as efficient."

Chapter Fifty-Six

Devon

I barely stifle a shriek as I fly into the room and come face to face with Denzo, Tane's second-in-charge for the past several years. But he's got company.

He has Angel, one of his arms wrapped tightly around her neck, and his other hand grips a revolver that's pointed directly at her temple.

The knife I hold in my hands suddenly doesn't seem as useful of a weapon as I'd envisaged when I tucked it away into my cleavage before we headed out.

"I see you've decided to join us after all," he says. His voice is polished but with an edge as cold as the steel of the revolver he's pointing at my friend. I have no doubt he's used a gun like this to kill people before, probably more times than he can count.

My mind flashes forward to the possibility of him pulling the trigger, of Angel's brain matter being splattered over the back wall, and I almost begin to retch.

"Please," I beg. "I'll do anything you ask. But let her go. Let us go."

He smirks. "Anything? As in you'd give up your men for your freedom?"

"Well—."

"Don't make promises you can't keep, Devon," he says. "That's the one thing we want, after all, you see. To eradicate the men you claim to love from the island chain once and for all. We don't need them anymore. There are enough groups out there more than willing to do our bidding for a fraction of your cut. And who make a hell of a lot less trouble than you and your men."

He glances at the knife in my hand and smirks again. I feel his gaze searing into my wrist and I try to still the tremble that threatens to betray my fear more than my voice has already.

"Drop your weapon, Devon," he says. "I'm not sure what you were planning to do with that, anyway. Hasn't anyone ever taught you not to bring a knife to a gunfight?" He narrows his eyes. "It's kind of insulting, actually."

"I— I—".

"Silence," he says, cutting me off, which is fine because I can't seem to find words, anyway.

"Please—," I plead, unsure of what I'm asking for.

"I suggest you follow my orders, or I might decide I only need one of you and that your friend here is disposable. Drop your weapon."

I frown and let the knife go. It clatters to the floor near my feet.

"Kick it away, to the side of the room," he gestures with the gun in his hand.

I frown.

"Do it," he orders.

I kick at the shiny blade and it skitters across the floor to the left side of the room, where it comes to rest against the painted cinderblock wall.

"Excellent," he says, pleased. "Now we're all here, we can get started."

"What the hell is that supposed to mean?" I grit out, furious that instead of saving Angel, I've just let myself get caught as well.

Denzo smirks. "Enough with the questions. But it's really quite simple. You're going to lead us to those men of yours. And when we find them, they're going to be killed. By you. And then you're going to kill yourselves. Our hands will be clean, and you won't be able to keep standing in our way as our power continues to grow."

"But you're already powerful. Tane's the most powerful man on the islands. I don't understand."

"Oh, you really don't, do you?" His mouth presses together in a thin line, and he frowns. "It's not just your men who keep devising ways to come for us. Once you have a certain amount of power, others will keep popping up to try to take it away from you. To keep on top, to keep relevant, you need to keep growing or you die."

He begins to pace around the room, waving his gun to punctuate his words.

"There are interests on the mainland vying for our power. They don't understand how the islands work, which is the only reason they haven't been able to take things over here. But they have men here now who are learning, absorbing. And pretty soon they're going to pose a significant threat to us. To all of us, including your men. We thought you were with us, that you would help us to fight off the advances of these competitors, but instead you're against us, trying to dilute our power. So we have no choice but to terminate our partnership."

"We could still help you," Angel pleads. "We don't want people like that trying to take over the islands, either."

"We gave you more power than you could have ever dreamed of, and you repay us by trying to kill us? To kill Tane? How naïve you must be to think we could ever trust you from here on out."

Angel's face falls. The man makes a good point. Our loyalty is completely out the window with this group, and who can really blame them?

This is beyond frustrating. We came so close to getting to Tane, and now his second-in-charge is about to kill us. We've been so careful while we've been here, gathering all the information we needed to get into the compound. But it's not enough. And now we're about to pay the price.

"Can't we just leave you alone? Remove us from your business and we can go back home?"

"That's not how things operate. You know that. Don't play dumb," he scowls. "You're problematic enough to distract us, and we can't have that keep happening. Look at the disruption you've already caused while you're here on the island."

I glance from Denzo to Angel. Her body is tense, her hands balled into fists, and I can almost see her brain turning as she figures out what to say next. And I know what she's thinking. The longer we can distract this man, and the other one with his gun pointed at us, the more time the guys have to find us. And as much as I hate relying on them to save us, we need them this time.

"In fact," he says, "I've found your presence here quite irritating. I was meant to be going on a family vacation, but instead I had to send my wife and children off without me while I stayed back to deal with the lot of you. It was going to be our first vacation in over two years. So, I'm going to have to let you both make up for it."

My stomach roils as I think through the many things he might have in mind. Torture. Rape. Murder. With this type of guy, anything is possible.

He glances between the two of us. "I'm intrigued, though. The last I'd heard, the two of you weren't on speaking terms. There appeared to be some type of rivalry between the groups. But now, here you are, making a nuisance of yourselves. And your men seem to be getting along as well. What changed?"

He's letting us know that he's been keeping tabs on us, gathering intel for far longer than we've been on this island. But there are clear gaps in his information. Maybe Tane's reach doesn't stretch quite as far or completely as he'd have us believe. It's not a giant secret on our home island that we've joined forces, and the fact Denzo is just getting up to speed is a bit of a shock.

Not that it matters now.

Because he has plans for us, and right now we have no way of escaping.

"As for you, Devon. I heard your father recently passed away. My sincere condolences." His mouth turns up in a small smile. It looks unnatural on him, like a child wearing his father's ill-fitting suit. I know his words are meant to hurt me, and they sting. He knows full well that Tane ordered the hit on my father, and that my guys were the ones who had no choice but to do it. And even though I knew it had to happen, it still hurts.

My stomach continues to churn, threatening to eject its contents as acid rises up within me, and my heart begins to thump in my chest. I feel my hands beginning to tremble, and my scalp crawls with the onset of an anxiety attack. *Not now, Devon.* I try to push the sensations away through sheer willpower, but to no avail.

"It must have been hard to forgive him for selling you to cover his debt, Devon," he says, seeming to enjoy playing with me in this way. Making me relive everything that happened. "And Tane was very disappointed when your men paid up. We had a variety of very interested buyers, you see." His mouth curves further upward, his cheeks pressing into the bags under his eyes and giving him a maniacal look.

"We had one gentleman who quite fancied the look of you. He had plans to keep you as his own sex slave. He's particularly into recreating his favorite snuff films, and he has quite a collection of those. He's had a few women sold to him before, but sadly, none of them seem to make it past the six-month mark. They just seem to... disappear one day. So that could have been your fate. Wouldn't that have been fun?"

Angel bares her teeth in a grimace. I can tell she wants to fly through the air and gouge his eyes out for the way he's talking to me.

"And then there was another bidder. He has quite the escort ring working yachts in international waters. Dealing with the filthy rich who have certain... appetites, shall we say... that are hard to fulfill on the mainland. Besides satisfying his many fastidious clients by catering to their every sexual whim, you would have had a role in grooming the younger members of his team. And when I say young...". He pauses, placing his hand about three feet off the floor.

Bile rises in my throat. I take a deep breath and swallow to try to keep it down.

"Do you want me to go on?" He raises an eyebrow. "Oh, I'm so sorry, Devon. I can see that I'm upsetting you. But before I stop, just indulge me with one more. The third bidder wanted to make you a star. You were going to be featured in a movie. Where you would be the subject of a gang bang, after which the men would flay you alive and perform sexual acts on your corpse before consuming you."

His words are too much, and I can't keep it in any longer. I heave and retch, the contents of my stomach ejecting onto the cold concrete floor.

Denzo looks disgusted. "My, my. How rude of you to come in here to my facilities and make a mess." He tsks, waving his gun in the direction of my vomit. "You're going to need to clean that up."

My eyes water and my throat stings. My hands are shaking more now. I feel helpless, frustrated at having no choice but to stand here and listen to this man's evil words.

And Angel, standing beside him with his gun trained on her, looking just as helpless.

"You're sick," I spit.

"Twisted," says Angel.

"Maybe I am," he shrugs, unbothered by the accusations.

"Why are you telling me all of this?"

"Just merely pointing out Tane's and my own disappointment at not being able to see any of those scenarios play out. Part of the deal with the bidders is that we claim video footage as part of the package. But in your case, we, of course, didn't get any of that."

I glare at him, the sick fuck clearly enjoying indulging me with all the what-might-have-beens.

"Anyhow, I heard your father shrieked just like a pig when he was killed. Did you know that pigs are capable of making noises at one-hundred-and-fifteen decibels, which is higher than the frequency of a supersonic Concorde? Although from what I understand, you were too weak to stay and watch him die. Do I have that right, Devon?"

I refuse to answer, my mouth pressed firmly shut. My nostrils flare, my breath ragged as my pulse continues to throb in my head.

"I don't know," he says, looking up to the ceiling as if deep in thought. "If I were in your shoes, I might have stayed just for the closure. I imagine it wasn't easy, sitting there in some other room, just waiting to hear that it had been done. Or did you find that easier, having the ability to make up some scenario in your head where he just died peacefully in his sleep? Rather than his entire facial structure being broken down while he was alive, right before his body was dismembered and buried in the jungle?"

I lose control, vomiting again. The guys tried to protect me from the gory details, but this despicable human is delighting in telling me everything. In bubbling up all my memories to the surface and combining them with horrors I didn't yet know.

"Shut the fuck up. Stop tormenting her!" Angel cries out. Her voice is deeper than usual, the way it gets only when she's outraged.

"But I'm enjoying this," says Denzo calmly, amused by the emotion he's elicited from her.

"You came here to kill Tane and me. So why would I stop to exchange pleasantries? Why would I allow anything at all to be on your terms?" He scoffs, his eyes glancing down at the knife near the wall, and I feel myself blush. "And the insulting way in which you intended to do it. No, there will be no leniency toward either of you. Or to your men. Many people are going to die tonight. But none of them will be me."

"Just let her go. I'll help you." Angel's voice is low now, her uncharacteristically brown hair gleaming softly in the dingy light. She'd be almost unrecognizable without her vibrant purple locks, without the fierce intensity of her flashing eyes. They're a dead giveaway.

What the fuck is she doing? Trying to spare me, I suppose. It's a far cry from the show of animosity the first time we met. To think our friendship has come this far, only to end in death at the hands of Tane's second-in-charge. We didn't even make it to the big boss.

"Why would I do that?" He quirks an eyebrow.

"She's already been through enough," Angel shrugs, her mouth set in a frown. "You said it for yourself. Let her grieve her father properly."

"If she wanted to grieve, she should have stayed back on the other island and worn a black suit or something, not come over here gallivanting around in her Vineyard Vines or J. Crew or whatever... that... is," he says, gesturing at my resort wear. I grimace at him, baring my teeth. He's planning to kill us but takes the time to insult my clothing choices?

"And besides, if I let her go, she'll presumably run straight back to the men and they'll come rushing here trying to rescue you... which, now that I say it out loud, isn't a bad idea." He pauses, as if chewing on his words. "No, no," he shakes his head. "She knows too much. Locations, how well we're armed. She'll give them information that won't be beneficial to us. She stays. You both stay."

Angel scowls.

"Frown at me all you want. In fact, I prefer it that way," Denzo says. "In fact, you've got me thinking. I don't really need either of you two to be alive at all in order to get the guys to come running here. In fact, it's easier if neither of you are here. All I need to do is get them to think you're here."

My blood turns to ice and my body tenses. I was counting on him needing us in order to buy some time.

"Ah yes, brilliant. Thank you for inspiring me and making me realize the flaw in my prior plan, Angel." He beams at her, his eerily white veneers giving way to inflamed red gums.

She's seething, her chest rising and falling at a rapid pace, her pupils tiny black dots searing into him.

"And now you're both going to make up for my lost vacation." He laughs softly, and it echoes against the concrete, creating a creepy effect like there are multiple versions of him in the room. "I'm going to have some fun with this. Davidson, get the stool." He gestures to the large man, who I'd just about forgotten was in the room with us, even though his gun has been pointed at us the whole time.

The man shuffles to the side of the room, gun still aimed in our direction, and uses one of his meaty arms to collect and bring back a rickety looking three-legged stool.

"I'll let you decide who goes first," he says, glancing back at us. "And I'm aware you both familiarized yourself with Tane's underground torture museum. And I'm feeling benevolent today, so I'll let you pick the way you want to go." He looks from me to Angel. "So, who will it be?"

"I'll go first," I blurt.

Angel gasps. "No! I will."

"Seriously, I will," I insist.

"Well, isn't this a show of politeness and pleasantry? Both of you are so willing to volunteer to die for the other. Not that it matters. Seeing both of you are going to die tonight, anyway." He gestures at the stool. "Seeing you volunteered first, Devon, why don't you come and sit here?"

I take a deep breath and slowly walk over to the stool. It bends and flexes under my weight as I sit on it.

"Devon," Angel rasps, her voice wavering with a fear that I've never heard from her. It's hard to see her like this, such a fierce warrior begging and pleading with a psychopath. I can barely look at her face, the terror painted on her only serving to fuel my own.

"Now, Angel. You can choose how Devon dies. How long it will take, and how much pain she will feel. It's all up to you. And it will be at your hand."

"No," she whispers."

"Oh, it's not a choice. It's an order. And I'd have Devon return the favor, but of course she won't be available, so I'll need to take care of you myself."

"No!" This time I do look over at Angel, the rage in her voice startling me out of my stupor. So do Denzo and Davidson. She springs at Denzo, her sharp nails clawing at his previously immaculate face.

In shock, he lets go of his gun, and it clatters to the floor. She and Davidson both leap to their knees, scrambling for it.

But she's too late. There's a loud crack and Angel grunts, toppling onto her side and rolling onto her back. She grimaces and clutches at her side, growing pale as she lifts her blood-coated fingers up into the dingy light. She gasps as the thick scarlet liquid drips from her hand.

Denzo smirks. "Sad. You're trying to take away my only fun for the day. But we won't let you off that easy."

Angel grimaces as blood continues to trickle from her wound, adjusting her body in an attempt to make herself more comfortable. She clamps her hand down tightly over her bullet wound, trying to staunch the flow.

"I guess she's not going to be much use after all," he says. "It's a shame. I'm going to have to do this myself. But you still have a choice. What will it be? Bamboo growing through your vital organs? A matching gut shot so you can lie next to your little Angel friend and die beside her? Something else you saw that you'd prefer?"

"You're fucking insane," I growl, rage bubbling within me like a simmering cauldron that's about to boil over. *Keep it together, Devon. Angel needs you.*

Angel moans and I glance back at her. Blood is still flowing, forming a large puddle beneath her prone frame. Her skin is deathly pale, and the normally animated woman is eerily still. It's like she's trapped inside a hell she can't get out of, and her only option is to look on as her life fades from her.

"Let me make sure she's okay. Please," I beg. "She's dying. She needs medical attention."

Denzo smirks. "Well, she shouldn't have been so fickle trying to attack me. She's scratched my face, and that's just impolite." He lifts a hand and runs his fingers over the raised red lines on his face as if fascinated by them. She narrowly missed one of his eyes, and he winces as his finger travels near it and his smirk becomes a scowl. "I admire her tenacity, but there's no way I can allow her to get away with doing this to my face."

We're like an amusement to him, and he wants to have his fun before snuffing us out. And before he has the guys come rushing into a deadly trap. We're dispensable pawns in his power game.

He'll let her bleed out right here and now if I don't do something.

My head pounds as my mind scrambles for an appropriate distraction. *Think, Devon, think.* My hands ball into fists and I feel a knuckle crack. We've come so far, and I can't let this brave woman bleed out on the floor while an unhinged madman looks on with amusement. It wouldn't be right for her to die this way, here and now, and I could never face the guys.

I glance around wildly, but nothing comes to mind. *Please hurry*, I silently beg the guys. *I can't do this without you. I need you. We both need you.* Then it clicks. Thank goodness we're both wearing body cams, and Denzo hasn't seemed to notice.

Chapter Fifty-Seven

Brick

I have the choice to turn left or right, and I feel the inexplicable pull to go right. It's like someone is calling to me, even though the only noises are my footsteps and my racing heart which threatens to burst out of my chest.

I fly to the right and instantly hear noises coming from behind the second door. Without hesitation, I burst through. This isn't the time for logic or the caution that Aidan or Zeke would have probably preferred. I need to act now, and fast. Both of the girls' lives are at stake. I just hope nothing has happened to them yet.

I burst through the door and immediately assess my surroundings.

A dark-haired man in a suit fitting the description of Denzo stands directly beside Devon, holding a gun. Another larger man who looks more like one of Tane's stereotypical goons stands further away, his gun drawn and pointing at her.

And then I see her. My Angel. My Valkyrie. She's lying on the floor, and by the pallor of her skin and the large crimson puddle rapidly growing below her, I can tell she's close to death.

I must save her. She's everything I've ever cared about, wrapped up in one gorgeous package. Angel is my hope, my trust. And she's my salvation. Without her, I'd have nothing to live for.

Everyone freezes as I enter the room, momentarily startled by my arrival. It's all I need.

As the suited man moves to raise his weapon, I shoot him in the arm, immediately disarming him. His mouth drops open, and he cries out as his gun clatters to the floor, and he grabs his wounded arm with his other hand. I had the opportunity for a kill shot, but this man has answers that we desperately need, so I'm taking my chances by keeping him alive. For now.

In the commotion, Devon leaps to her feet.

The larger man starts to move his aim from the women to me, and I shoot him straight through the forehead, a hole appearing right between his eyes. If he's this close to Tane, he's not the type of guy that would miss. He crumples to the floor and blood begins to pour from his head, forming a puddle on the ground.

The man, who I assume is Denzo, smirks at me. "You're not going to shoot me in the head?"

"Oh, I'd more than love to, believe me," I growl. "But there are two reasons I'm not going to do that. Not yet anyway. One, you have information that I'm going to delight in extracting from you. And two, you hurt my girl. I'm going to make you pay for that. But first, I need to make sure that she's going to be okay. That means you're going to take a nap."

I rush at him and grab the stool, raising it high above my head and bring it crashing down over Denzo's head. He thuds to the floor, his prone figure stripped of its usual elegance. "Your designer suit's not going to save you now," I smirk.

But as much as I'm going to enjoy making this man feel inordinate amounts of pain, my current priority is Angel. I have to get her out of here.

"How long has she been like this?" I drop to the floor beside her, not caring that my pants are immediately saturated by her blood.

"Maybe ten minutes before you got here," Devon replies, her voice ragged with fear. "She was trying to save us and there was a scuffle and the gun went off."

I'm trying to stay calm like I'm normally able to do in high-stress situations, but this is life or death for Angel. My breath feels unusually quick and shallow, and I feel like I'm about to pass out. But I need to be level-headed and think on my feet. I don't have time to lose my shit and get all hysterical. Angel needs me.

As I figure out what to do, Rake and Roman come bursting into the room. They take one look at Angel's ashen face and their own faces grow pale.

"We could take her to the local hospital, but there will be too many questions," says Rake.

"I have a guy on speed dial," says Roman, whipping his phone out of his pocket and frantically pressing the touch screen. "He's probably helped treat Tane's men before, but from what I know, he's a neutral guy and can be trusted. His focus is on medicine, not politics or crime."

"Well, that sounds like the best option we have right now. As long as he can save Angel, that's all I care about." I glance at Devon. "You can stay here and help me, or you can go with them. It's up to you."

"Oh, I'm staying. I want to see this through to the bitter end." Raw emotion flashes in her eyes, a fiery combination of rage and pain that only one thing can fix. Murderous revenge.

"You like ramen?" I ask Devon.

"Huh?" She furrows her brow, clearly confused by my seemingly random question. "I don't understand."

I shrug. "Like the noodles."

"Brick, I know what ramen is," she sighs and clenches her jaw, frustration emanating from her. She needs to calm down. You can't rush genius.

"Oh, all will become clear. I'm a big fan myself. Took to studying the art of noodle making at home. Sometimes Slade lets me help with dinner, and it's my go-to. It's a fine art in Japan, actually. There are families who have passed their secret recipes down through their ancestors. What a lot of people don't realize is that the first iteration of ramen actually originated in China and made its way to the Yokohama district in the early 20th century."

"Brick, this is all very interesting, but I don't see what it has to do with… this…". I gesture at Denzo, who is now sitting up against the wall. His legs are tucked into his body, held closely by his hands. His mouth bears a smear of blood, and his head lolls to the side like he can't quite keep it up.

"Hand me those drying racks, will you?" He points at the racks that lay against the far wall. They're metal and cheap, the kind you can find at some dollar stores. But we're not here to do laundry. "For the first time in his life, Denzo is about to be strung out."

Chapter Fifty-Eight

Devon

"The biggest problem I've encountered with making noodles at home is finding the place to put them," Brick explains as I hand him the metal racks, still completely confused about why he's picking now of all times to prattle on about noodles. "So what people tend to do is repurpose things that noodles can be strewn across. Like these, for instance." He props one of the drying racks up, hooking the metal around itself so it stands up in an A-frame shape. I follow his lead, and soon we have six drying racks neatly set up in a row in the middle of the room.

"I still don't understand what this has to do with Denzo."

At the mention of his name, the man rouses. He glances at us, and then over at the drying racks, clearly as confused as I am. The tendons in his neck are taut, and his pulse is visible.

Brick expertly binds the man's hands behind his back. The rope is tight against his wrists, and there's no way he could wiggle his way out. Clearly, Brick has done this before and many times.

Then he really gets to work. He produces a scalpel from his pocket and begins to score a hole in Renzo's abdomen directly through his suit jacket and shirt. The scalpel is so sharp that it takes a moment for the incisions to begin to bleed, but then the blood begins to really flow.

Denzo's eyes bulge, and he squeezes them shut for a moment before they fly open again. His chin trembles and his nostrils flare.

Brick begins to unravel the man's intestines, slowly pulling them out of his abdomen.

"The large and small intestines are collectively around fifteen feet in length," he says casually as he continues to unravel the sausage-like strings from Denzo's stomach cavity. "And we're going to see that for ourselves shortly."

Denzo moans and whimpers, and he appears to be conflicted about whether to keep his eyes firmly clamped shut or to watch as Brick carefully disembowels him.

Brick is methodical, and although it's very clear he wants this man dead, he refuses to rush. His self-control is impressive as he continues to pull the bulging spaghetti-like tube from Denzo's abdomen and carefully string it up on the drying racks, weaving it neatly from rung to rung.

"You're lucky, you know," he says to Denzo. The man glances up at him as if to say 'are you fucking kidding me?' but his mouth remains slack and agape as blood continues to pour from him. "You know why?" Brick continues. "There's such a thing as transanal evisceration. If I decided to go that route, I'd be pulling your intestines out through your asshole. So be grateful I'm gathering them directly from your stomach."

My own stomach roils at the thought, but I'm also intrigued by what's going on. There's a certain joy in watching an evil man suffer. And this man deserves everything he's getting, especially after what he and his goon did to Angel. I hope she's okay. I hope the guys got her help in time.

"Do you have any last words? Would you like to make a final phone call to your wife?"

Denzo blinks, and his breath comes out in a husky rasp. "My wife...".

Brick grabs the phone, which is sticking out of the man's trousers. He places it by Denzo's face, which enables facial recognition to unlock it and scrolls through his contacts. "Wifey, I take it?" he asks, and Denzo nods.

Brick hits call and places it on speakerphone, and soon the room is filled with the echoes of a ringing phone.

"Denzo?" A nasal voice with a New Jersey accent reverberates off the cool concrete walls. "Denzo, I've told you a million times that I've had enough. You're constantly letting us down. You're not here for me and the children like you promised you would be. So now, I'm having my own vacation. And I've brought my boyfriend, Sal. That's right, I have a boyfriend. And I don't care anymore if you know or not. He takes care of me. He pays attention to me and buys me all the nice things I ask for. Unlike you."

"Hon—honey, I—." He tries to speak, but it comes out as an almost-silent whimper.

"Enough, Denzo. We're done. My divorce lawyer will be in touch in the morning. And he's the best that money can buy."

"I—." Denzo helplessly reaches a hand out in the direction of the phone, but he's nowhere close. The call is ended.

"So you see," says Brick, "your wife is going to be just fine with, uh... Sal, was his name? So you literally have nobody who cares about you. Was your unquestioning loyalty to Tane worth it? Perhaps, if you base your life's worth on finances. But from the way she was sounding, she's going to take you to the cleaners. So you have nothing to lose anymore. You should just tell us how to get to Tane."

Denzo presses his lips together as he glances up at Brick, but then he shakes his head.

"Loyal to the end, are you? Some would say that's impressive, but I just think you're an idiot. Let me do you a favor." He makes a move toward Denzo, but then stops and glances at me. "Or actually, I think we might turn this into a team sport."

Chapter Fifty-Nine

Brick

I'm seeing a side to Devon that I haven't noticed before. Or maybe it's a whole new side she's just learning about herself. It's fascinating what rage and trauma can do to a person.

"Do you want to do the honors?" I ask.

"Yes I do," she says, narrowing her eyes at the man. "You hurt my friend. She's like a sister to me, and one of the best people I know. And you know what? That's the difference between her and someone like you. People care about her. Your wife is probably off fucking anyone that looks at her on the little vacation you were supposed to go on. In addition to her boyfriend... Sal, was it?" Denzo frowns at her, because in his current state, that's the most he can do.

"Your kids probably despise you and don't know who you are except that you have money to put them through private school and to dress them in fancy outfits. The truth is, you're a sick and sad little man. You're going to die now, and nobody is going to miss you. Most people probably won't even notice you're gone." She's never met him, but it's like she sees right through him.

She spits on Denzo, and his eyes dull with the resignation of what's about to happen.

She brings her foot down hard and stomps on his face. His bones crunch, and as she raises her foot back up I see his previously delicate, slightly upturned nose is now bent to the side and smashed beyond recognition. She raises her foot up again and again, continuing to stomp at him over and over again. Soon, his face is completely pulverized and each stomp causes blood to splatter all over the three of us. But she keeps stomping, working herself into more and more of a murderous frenzy as she continues smashing his skull into the cold concrete floor.

I can't help but wonder if this is partly cathartic to her because of what just took place with her father, finally giving her the opportunity to take out her rage at yet another evil men.

"Devon... Devon....". A voice rings out of the near-darkness. It's Skyler, and he takes her by the arm. "Devon, that's enough."

"I don't want to stop!" She screams. "I'm tired of stopping! Of being polite. This monster tried to kill Angel! He has to pay!" She continues to stomp at the man, her body shaking with unbridled fury.

"He's dead, Devon. And he won't be coming back."

Finally, she stops. Skyler wraps her in his muscular arms, and she leans into his chest, panting from exertion. "It's okay, baby. I've got you," he whispers.

But it doesn't stop there, because I'm not done yet.

"You take a break," I tell Devon, meeting Skyler's gaze. "Sky, you two hang out over there while I take care of this."

Skyler nods, and looks on with curiosity as I get to work.

Removing his bloodied and torn shirt and jacket, I use my favorite scalpel to flay Denzo's torso. I pay meticulous attention to preserving his tattoos as I split his flesh from his body in one large sheet. It's easier said than done, and I tear the flesh in a few places, but overall I do a decent job and I nod to myself once the flesh is finally completely separate.

Devon gags at several points, but she can't seem to look away as I peel the corpse's flesh away from bone and tissue and slide it over his head like I'm removing a wife beater. I produce a trash bag from my jacket pocket and place the flesh singlet inside it. I like to be prepared, because you never know what you might need in the moment in the line of business we're in.

"What are you going to do with that?" Devon asks, her eyes large.

"Tane's been so hospitable with us here on the island. I'm going to send him a little thank you gift."

She gasps and her eyes widen even further. "What do you mean? You're going to send him Denzo's flayed flesh?"

"Well, it's actually a little more involved than that. See, you know I like a good faux leather jacket," I say, gesturing at my own signature outfit. "Once I've had a chance to tan it, Tane's going to receive his own version, and given the distinctive tattoos Denzo had all over his body, he will have no question in his mind where it came from. And his will not be vegan. It'll be from an animal of the human variety."

Skyler's jaw drops open and he blinks rapidly. "Bro..." he says, suddenly speechless.

Devon's hand flies over her mouth, but she keeps her eyes locked on Denzo's prone corpse which now looks like a slab of meat from Diego's butcher shop. "How did you even think to do something like that?"

"Well," I explain, "I was inspired by a university library on the East Coast of the mainland. You see, it was confirmed a few years back that four of their books are what are considered anthropodermic, which means they're bound in human skin. Technically, the binding could be from a closely related primate. So I learned more about the process because that is clearly fascinating, and thought 'what if this extended to clothing?'. And here we are! I finally get to put my new skills to use. I can't wait to see how it turns out." I can't help but grin.

Skyler nods slightly and a grin spreads across his face as my words sink in. "Dude, you're one sick fuck," he says. "But that's kind of amazing."

Chapter Sixty

Devon

"You were pretty good back there," says Brick, once I get a chance to regain my breath and perhaps a shred of my sanity. His eyes are bright and glossy as he squeezes my shoulder.

I'm still shaking. "I don't know what got into me. I've never killed anyone before. Not like that." I pause, apprehensive about saying the next part, even though I need to. "But I kind of see why you like it." I reflect on the satisfying sound of Denzo's bones crunching under my feet. Watching him transform from a sophisticated man in a suit to an unrecognizable mish-mash of bones and blood and ripped flesh. Let alone what I witnessed Brick do to the man's body afterward. It was horrific and repulsive and also technically skillful. And I couldn't look away.

"Be careful," he warns. "It's addictive."

And I worry that he's right. Because the feeling that washed over me back there was pure rage. I enjoyed hurting Denzo. It was intoxicating, hearing his whimpers and shrieks. Reducing him to a pulverized puddle of twisted gore. Having that power over another human. Relishing in causing him incredible amounts of pain and suffering. Being the one to cause the light to go out of his eyes.

Once I got going, I was consumed by bloodlust and I couldn't stop. Skyler almost had to pull me off the guy. I was so engrossed in what I was doing that I had tunnel vision. All I could see was Denzo, and all I could think about was ending him. Of removing him from this earth and rendering him less than human in the process. And I relished every second of it.

I'm scared for myself.

I'm scared of myself.

Chapter Sixty-One
Brick

The doctor is a serious-looking man in a white coat with closely cropped salt-and-pepper hair. He's accompanied by a couple of assistants who carry in his medical equipment. The man gets straight to work assessing Angel's condition before hooking her up to a fresh supply of blood and a fluid IV.

"This was a close call," he says, frowning as he watches the beeping monitor beside her bed. "A few more minutes and...".

"Don't say it," I plead. "I can't bear to think about losing her."

I look down at her fragile form. She's still very pale, but a small amount of color seems to be making its way back into her cheeks. She looks so vulnerable lying there while the portable machines beep around her. If anything had happened to her, I wouldn't have been able to live with myself.

She looks up at me, her eyes glazed by the painkillers that course through her body. She's groggy and disoriented, but she's still the most beautiful woman I've ever laid eyes on.

"Did I do okay?" Her voice is labored, like it's taking every ounce of her remaining energy to get out just a few words.

I brush a lock of hair away from her face, which is still more pale than her usual olive tone. "Oh Angel, you were absolutely perfect."

"Is he dead?" She attempts to prop herself up on her elbows, but winces and lies back down.

"Don't exert yourself. You're injured. And you can ask Devon all about what happened with Denzo when you're feeling better. But yes, he's been taken care of."

She frowns. "Sorry to slow you down."

"What do you mean? You tried to save Devon and yourself, and a gun went off in the struggle. You're a fucking hero."

She glances down at her bandaged abdomen and glances over at the beeping equipment. "I don't feel like one right now."

"Well, you are," I shrug. "Everyone thinks so."

She rolls her eyes. "You sound like a super fan. Are you an Angel stan, Brick?"

"My Angel, my precious Valkyrie. I would follow you into hell if that's what it would take to be with you for eternity. Our souls are intertwined, and that doesn't end in death. And for as long as we walk this earth, I'll do everything in my power to destroy anybody who ever causes you pain."

"You really mean that?"

"Yes. Completely. If someone cuts in front of you at the grocery store, I will slice and dice them. If somebody gives your salon a bad review, not that they would have reason to, I'm coming for them. If someone so much blinks at you the wrong way, they're dead."

She gives a wry smile. "Some of that sounds like overkill."

"Nothing is too much for you, my Angel. You're mine. Ours. And that means I will spend every day for the rest of my life proving it to you."

Chapter Sixty-Two

Devon

After Denzo's grisly demise and Angel's shooting, we left the compound and returned to the hotel to meet the others. It wasn't what we had planned, but it was really our only option. Our intention was to regroup and plan our next moves, and we knew we had to act quickly because clearly Tane would be onto us after the day's events. But we were surprised to receive a message from Tane insisting we meet him in person to discuss what had happened. It's almost certainly some type of trap. But what choice do we have? If we flee the island, he'll just catch up to us.

So we're meeting him at a high-end sushi restaurant. It's not a place that he owns, but instead it's ostensibly neutral. He no doubt has connections here, but at least the place doesn't belong to him. And it's a public space, so we're hoping there's less chance of an all-out shootout. Despite Tane's depravity, he seems to want to portray a sense of decorum. Which is easier when you have an army of loyal followers to do your dark bidding.

Upon arrival, the guys stake out the building. It's a fusion of sleek, contemporary construction and traditional Japanese design including bamboo and teak wood elements. Tane is subtle enough not to have lined up his goons in a row outside the door, but we're sure they're around. We enter through large bamboo doors and find ourselves in a dimly lit lounge with a peaceful atmosphere. Candles flicker on each table, and Japanese antiques and bonsai line the room. We walk across a clear plexiglass walkway framed by large rocks. Plump koi swim underfoot as water features trickle on either side giving the space a serene ambience.

A hostess greets us with a warm smile and leads us past the restaurant's centerpiece, a sushi bar where a famous master sushi chef expertly slices the finest seafood the island has to offer. I glance over as he plates sashimi and elaborate, delicate garnishes onto handmade ceramic dishes featuring traditional Japanese designs. I make a mental note to return some day, but we're not here for sushi. Servers dressed in starched uniforms unobtrusively shuttle plates and sake back and forth between diners, the kitchen, the bar and the sushi counter as if they're performing in an elaborate orchestra. We're guided past the main dining area into a private dining room featuring high-back leather chairs surrounding an enormous, dark wood table. The room oozes authority and power, just as I'd expect from a man like Tane.

He stands to the rear center of the room, flanked by two giant men carrying large firearms. It's funny to think I've never seen Tane in the flesh before, given how much time we spend thinking and talking about him. And given what he tried to do to me because of my father. Sure, I've known what he looks like from various news articles where he's been snapped at charity events with a variety of women much younger than him dangling from his arm. But there's an energy about him in person that a photograph could never capture.

From his appearance, I'd guess he's in his early fifties. His coiffed salt-and-pepper hair gives him a distinguished and mature appearance. He seems sophisticated and mature, and exudes an air of confidence, charisma and authority. His face bears a few subtle scars and weathered lines, a reference to his earlier life lived working his way up into the heart of the criminal underworld.

His eyes are sharp and penetrating. It's like they can see right through me, into my soul. And he's one of those men who rocks a perpetual five o'clock shadow, which only adds to his rugged charm. He's dressed immaculately in a custom-tailored charcoal gray suit, accessorized with cufflinks, a wristwatch and a silk tie. I think he might be the best-dressed man I've ever seen, if you're into suits.

I'm a little aroused at the sight of him, honestly, despite all the horrible things he's done. He's elegant and ruthless, and he's got me a bit flustered just being in his presence. I can't let the guys know how hot and bothered he's made me, or I'll never hear the end of it. There's something intoxicating about a very powerful man, even if he's an evil piece of shit. Okay, I'll admit it. I'm fucked in the head, and clearly in need of further intensive therapy. Daddy issues. All I want to do is mouth 'oh my God' to Angel, but she's still back at the hotel fighting to survive, although the doctor has offered a positive prognosis.

From the way he holds himself, so calm and composed, I imagine Tane rarely yells. He'd only need to say the word, and one of his loyal goons would do whatever he asked. It's powerful, his insane amount of self-control even in the most stressful situations. Clearly, Tane is keenly intelligent and calculated. It's no coincidence that he's grown to such power over the islands and beyond. All of his actions appear deliberate, and no detail goes unnoticed. I'm sure he expects the same from the many men and women that work for him.

He removes his designer sunglasses and stares at us one by one with his penetrating eyes, as if he wants us to know he can see right through us. "Ah, the Brixtons and... what do you call yourselves again? The snakeheads or something like that?" His speech is measured and deliberate and his voice is deep and commanding, demanding attention. But I don't get the sense that anyone ever questions him. He's the big boss for a reason. Seeing him in the flesh and feeling his palpable energy, I don't know if we've properly thought through what we've put ourselves up against.

Skyler frowns and rolls his eyes. "We don't. I'm Skyler, and this is—."

Tane raises his hand calmly to cut him off. "Oh, I know exactly who each and every one of you is. And I know why you're here, but you see, your little plan isn't going to work. Your Brixton woman—Angel—is in the hands of my men as we speak. It was naïve of you to leave her back at the hotel. Especially in the hands of a doctor who has worked for me for many years. If you're very lucky, I will release her and you can all run back to your island with your tails between your legs. And you can believe I'll be reallocating your share of my enterprise the moment you return. If you try to pull something like this again, next time you won't be so lucky."

"You're bluffing," Aidan frowns and despite his words, his face is stricken with concern. "There's no way you have her."

"Oh, I don't bluff, Mr. Brixton." He purses his lips. "It doesn't serve anyone. Believe me on this. And now we're going to take Devon as extra collateral."

I gasp as one of the large, armed men rushes over to me and grabs me roughly by my arm, pulling me back to the other side of the room. Struggling against his grip, I wince as his large hand only wraps more tightly around my bicep.

Dom makes a move to rush toward me, but the other armed man points a gun directly at my head, and Dom puts his hands up in surrender.

Suddenly there are noises outside, and some kind of disturbance in the previously tranquil dining room. The armed man who isn't holding Devon skirts around us and rushes outside to investigate.

"Why are you being so tolerant, then? Why don't you just kill her now to send us a message?" Skyler blurts at the elegant man, who allows a slight smirk to pass across his face as he eyes him back.

I glare at Skyler, my mouth dropping to the floor. What the fuck has gotten into him?

"What the fuck, bro?" Dom growls, cracking his knuckles and looking like he's about to charge at Skyler, and I share the same sentiment.

"Are you asking me to change my approach?" Tane asks. "Because if you really insist, I'd be happy to oblige." He smirks at me and I narrow my eyes at him. But my limbs are shaky and my heart feels like it's going to explode. I've never felt closer to death.

"No!" Says Aidan, a little forcefully, a strange expression on his face. "I believe Skyler was just trying to understand your thinking. Leave them both alone. Look, we appreciate the generosity of this gesture, of bringing us here today to let us know your stance on what has taken place. As for the business side of things, please don't cut us out completely. We enjoy working with you, and this has all been a huge misunderstanding." His voice is pleading and it's almost pitiful.

The other guys stare at Aidan like he's lost his mind, and I wonder what's gotten into him as well. There's no way Tane's going to want to continue doing business with us after we proved our disloyalty. What a strange question to ask and what an unusual moment to do it.

"Very well, I'll let you go," shrugs Tane. "You've made the right decision. But there's no way in hell you will retain your business interests. I don't work with people who cross me. Now get out of here and off this island, and don't come back. We will return Angel and Devon safely once we're satisfied the rest of you have left the island. Take her." Tane nods at the guard, who still grips my arm tightly. I know I'm going to have bruises. That is, if I survive the night.

The burly man nods and begins to shove me toward the door of the private dining room. The commotion outside suddenly grows louder, and gunshots ring out, followed by screams from dining patrons. Loud noises that sound like fireworks start banging outside. The guard roughly shoves me toward Skyler and runs out the door, and Skyler and I both almost topple over from the momentum. He manages to regain his balance and grab me before I fall, and he clings to me.

Tane backs up, pressing a discreet button that opens a door behind him, and he dives through it. It pings shut behind him. Dom runs to the door and inspects the panel, but can't seem to be able to work out how the man gained access.

"Fuck!" He yells, kicking the panel in frustration.

"Are you okay?" Skyler asks, turning me to face him and giving me a once-over, deep concern in his eyes. "Are you hurt?"

"I think I'm fine," I say, but my shaky voice gives me away.

I'm confused. I'm mentally hurt. I'm incredibly shaken. And I'm deathly scared for Angel.

Chapter Sixty-Three

Skyler

"Why the fuck did you pull back? And what the hell was that, Skyler?" Dom growls, all of the men eyeing Aidan and me with astonishment.

"It was a setup," Aidan explains. "Dimitri texted me right as we were about to go in. I was able to fill Skyler in on our way in here, but we had to act on the fly. Tane was luring us into a trap. He had guys lined up outside, ready to take us out as soon as we exited the restaurant. Dimitri and his guys set up a diversion and were able to distract his sniper team just long enough for us to get out. If we didn't have them backing us up from outside, we would have been dead for sure."

"And I'm sorry I said what I did, Devon," I frown. "You have to know of course I didn't mean it, and that I was calling Tane's bluff. I could hear the noises outside and I knew I needed to say something outrageous to distract him and his men from what was going on. It was our only chance to save you even though it was pretty extreme."

I make eye contact with Devon, silently begging her to forgive me.

After a moment considering my words, she takes my hand and squeezes it. A surge of relief meets the adrenalin already coursing through my body.

"And what about Angel? Do Tane's men really have her?" Roman looks like he's going to jump out of his own skin with worry.

"They tried," says Aidan. "They shot the doctor and took her from the hotel room. But Dimitri and his guys were able to secure her and rush her to safety in their compound. We owe them. They've saved Angel's life."

"How did Dimitri and his guys manage to be in two places at once and effectively save both of the girls?" Roman ask, his brow furrowed in confusion. "There are only three of them, plus their girl."

"That's a fair question," says Aidan. "But their loyalty runs deep around here. They may be a small group, but they have deep relationships that they can call on when they need it. And they've been instigating the souring sentiment about Tane. They were able to gather allies who were only too happy to help us out today."

"I can't even bear to imagine what would have happened if...". Dom trails off. His eyes water and he rubs at his face.

"Come on, man," Brick squeezes his shoulder. "We can't go there right now. Stay focused."

"I get where he's coming from. We've just almost lost them so many times," says Dom. "And it's always because of our actions." He frowns. "We dragged both of them into this life, and now it's like they're addicted to it."

Devon narrows her eyes at Dom and then juts out her jaw.

He continues. "So if something happens to either of them, we have to take responsibility. I'm so sorry, Devon."

She frowns and then takes his hand in hers, squeezing it as well.

"Dom, you always take responsibility for things way out of your control," I say. "Devon's father's debt? Not your fault. Angel's psycho stalker of more than a decade? Definitely not your fault, either."

Dom looks skeptical. "I guess. But this Tane part... Come on man. We knew it had to be a trap. Bringing Devon here, leaving Angel there. What the hell were we thinking?"

"Yeah," Zeke says, frowning. "I guess that was all on us. And me in particular. It was my idea in the first place sending the girls over here early. I take responsibility for that. Today just seems to have been a series of poor decisions."

"Well, at least they're safe now. There's no sense dwelling on the what if's or we'd all be fucked, right?" I look around the group, meeting everyone's gaze one by one. "But we're all here, alive. So let's go get Angel back and figure out where to go from here."

The rest of us nod and we file into our vehicles, driving off as quickly as we can without drawing raised eyebrows from neighbors in the surrounding community. Although I'm sure we're not the strangest sight they've seen, given how close they live to Tane Brown and his goons.

I guess the question about whether a partnership is the right thing to do has been answered for us. Anyone who saves our women's lives is a friend of ours. And now we owe them.

"Let's get Angel and get the fuck off this island," I say, and the others nod.

We need to regroup, and fast.

A target now has been placed on us. We're no longer under the radar, although maybe we never were.

There's never been more on the line. But at the same time, we have new friends who have proved more than useful.

There's no going back from here.

Chapter Sixty-Four

Angel

My recovery is quicker than anticipated. Aside from the blood loss, the gunshot managed to avoid all my vital organs. The doctor told me I was very lucky. I was so sad to hear he was shot by Tane's men.

Of course, I'm a little disappointed I didn't get to meet Tane in person, especially after Devon told me what he was like, but I guess almost dying is a good reason to have missed the excitement. And I have a feeling I'm going to get another chance to meet him some time soon.

"How are you feeling about everything?" Aidan asks, gently tracing his strong hand down my jawline. He's sitting beside me on the corner of the living room couch. As beautiful and exciting as the other island was, it's amazing to be home.

I exhale and shake my head as I recall the events that took place. "That day was... scary. And also exhilarating."

"Yeah, my adrenalin was certainly pumping. And I wasn't even in the room when it happened. I'm just so relieved that nothing worse happened to you, baby."

"He's right," smiles Brick, his voice more gentle than normal. "We're really proud of how you handled yourself, not just that day but the entire trip. We never could have done this without you. We're so proud you're our girl."

His words almost make me melt as the other men nod in agreement. There's not a fraction of condescension in his voice, just pure admiration. And, well, love.

I take his jaw gently in one hand and turn his face to mine and kiss him deeply. He returns the kiss, his teeth clashing with mine as we give in to our hunger.

I hop up from the couch and grab his hand, tugging him to stand, and head toward the door. "Come on," I beckon to the other guys. "Come with us."

Requiring little convincing, they all leap to their feet and follow us toward the largest of the bedrooms. I notice Roman and Brick's cocks already straining in their pants as they follow us down the hallway and into the spacious room.

I jump onto the bed, pulling Aidan with me into the center where I jump on top of him, straddling him with my thighs. Through our clothes, I feel him straining against my core, eager to get out. My pussy clenches and I feel my arousal building as the other men surround us.

I grind my hips gently against Aidan as Roman approaches me from behind and kisses my neck and shoulder, sending shivery tingles down my spine. Brick and Slade flank me, caressing my arms, my back, my ass.

Brick grabs my hair in his large fist and pulls my head forcefully to one side, giving Roman better access as his lips trail along my throat.

Roman nips playfully at my neck. "Our beautiful, brave girl," he growls. "You belong to us."

I've never felt more wanted. More beautiful. Sure, we've done this before, but the events on the other island have brought us even closer together. No matter where I am, as long as I'm with these four men I feel like I'm home. And there's no better feeling than being part of something bigger, something that you believe in. And having the adoration of four hot men who'd do anything for you isn't so bad, either.

Temporarily breaking away from Aidan's kiss, I turn my head to Slade. He groans as my mouth meets his, our lips and teeth hungrily clashing. Our tongues explore each other greedily as I continue to grind down on Aidan.

Roman lifts my shirt up from behind and I lift my hands so he can pull it over my head. The cool of the air conditioning combined with the heat of the four men causes my nipples to harden instantly. Aidan gazes down appreciatively at the silver bars that catch the moonlight streaking in through the window. He's the most conservative of the four men, but for some reason I think he might love my piercings almost as much as Brick.

Four sets of hands caress me now, cupping my breasts. Two hands reach out and tug on my nipple bars. The two hands feel different, and I'm not sure which two guys they belong to, but they're in sync as they caress me, tugging just hard enough to ride the line between pleasure and pain. I moan as Roman once again nips at my neck from behind.

Turning to face Brick, we meet in our own deep kiss, our tongues wrestling. My pussy clenches at the thought of what he can do with his tongue in other parts of my body. This big, burly man devoted to killing people in the gnarliest of ways, deriving his own pleasure from torturing and maiming others, but also from bringing me some of the most spectacular pleasure I've ever felt in my life. My tender giant. My loving psycho.

I reach down and Aidan groans as I rub his hardness through his pants. "Why don't you let the others go first this time?" He grins, being selfless as usual, his eyes dark with lust but always willing to share with his brothers.

I jump off him and turn to my right, unbuckling Slade's belt and unbuttoning his pants, which are straining at the crotch. His cock springs free and erect, and I turn to Brick and undo his fly. His girthy hardness makes my pussy clench hard. I take it in my hand and dip my head toward Slade, taking him into my mouth. He groans as I tease him at first, swirling my tongue just around the tip, my hand firmly at the base of his shaft. I take him into my mouth more fully and suck his cock as I swirl my tongue around his hardness. He gently rocks his hips, allowing me to take in more of his length as I continue to lick and suck.

Aidan unzips his own pants, releasing his cock and stroking himself as he watches. I feel Roman's hands cup and caress my ass, my kneeling over Slade's cock giving him a generous view of my ass and pussy from behind.

I continue to stroke Slade while I turn to face Brick, once again dipping my head so I can take him into my mouth this time. I ignore the clicking of my jaw as I accommodate his girth, managing to wrap my lips around him. I bob my head up and down on his rock hard cock, swirling my tongue. Pulling back slightly, he groans as I pay attention just to the tip. "Oh fuck, Angel," he rasps.

Roman's hands are exploring now, dipping inside my panties and I feel his fingers as they caress my wetness, my arousal beginning to trickle out of my entrance and over my entire slit. He inserts two fingers, and then a third, and slides them in and out of me and I moan, creating a humming sensation around Brick's cock.

Roman slowly slides his fingers out of my pussy and trails them up to my asshole, which he then circles, wetting it with my arousal. I gasp as he slowly works one finger in, my pussy clenching firmly in anticipation of what's coming. He adds a second finger, and my body tingles at the sensation of having my back entrance breached by his big, strong fingers. I crave more of him inside me. As if reading my mind, I gasp as he yanks my panties down. I hear the flick of a blade and then feel cold metal against my hip, and then a brief sting as the elastic of my underwear is cut free. The material is roughly yanked away, and Roman's fingers return to my asshole. This time he's less gentle, sliding two fingers right into me. I gasp at the slight resistance and then again at the feeling as he fingers my ass more quickly this time. It stings, but in a good way, and still I crave more.

I remove my mouth from Brick's cock, continuing to stroke at his shaft. Aidan's own hardness is right in front of me and he kneels to meet me as I continue to stroke at Brick and Slade while Roman fingers my asshole. Without hands, I dip my head and this time take Aidan's cock into my mouth. My breath is fast, my heart pounding in my chest, and this time I don't make any attempts to tease. He groans as I take as much of him into my mouth as possible on the first attempt, feeling his hardness deep in my throat, my head bobbing on his cock with an insatiable greed.

We work like a synchronized team, hips bucking and fingers pulsing in rhythm as we enjoy each other. The room is filled with the sounds of soft moans and the slurping noises of me giving Aidan what from his reaction seems to be the best blowjob of his life.

There's power in the way we operate as a group. The simultaneous roughness and tenderness with which they treat me. Taking me, claiming me as their own. But also giving me the power to have a say in my role within the group, including in the bedroom.

"You're perfect, you know that, Angel?" pants Slade as he bucks his hips in rhythm with my hand as I continue to slide it up and down his hard shaft. His hand caresses my breast and tugs at my nipple, and I recognize it as one of the hands from before from its roughness. The hands of a chef, used to grabbing hot pots and pans and plates and working with fire, now focus solely on exploring my body.

Roman removes his fingers from my ass and I cry out as he replaces them with his tongue. He flicks it against my rear entrance and I moan against Aidan's cock as Roman rims my asshole, lapping at it, devouring me. Little tingles rush through my body and it's hard to keep track of all the shivers of pleasure. I don't need to think about what I'm doing, even though I have four men in my hands, in my mouth, one of their mouths on me. It just works somehow, like we all instinctively know what to do.

From the way Aidan's body is tensing, he seems close, but before I know what's happening, I'm being flipped over onto my back. My legs are lifted into the air and my thighs spread wide apart by two pairs of strong hands. I gasp as Roman resumes licking my asshole while Brick dips his head and licks my pussy from the side. He dips his head and slides his tongue right into my hole, his head only inches from Aidan's, and tongue fucks me with abandon. Aidan does the same with my ass, and the sensation of being double penetrated by two tongues is almost too much. "Jesus, fuck!" I cry out. One of my hands is still wrapped firmly around Slade's cock and he groans as my palm involuntarily clenches against it.

Aidan leans forward and kisses me deeply, his tongue swirling around mine. Saliva spills from our mouths and across my cheek and neither of us care. We're so wrapped up in this bliss. He comes around to the side and slides his cock into my mouth once again, and I take it in eagerly as he thrusts into me. He reaches a hand to the back of my head, forcing more of himself inside me and I instinctively gag, but then relax my throat as he rocks his hips back and forth. Slade moans as I continue to stroke his shaft, dipping his head to take one of my nipples into his mouth and tugging on the bar with his teeth until I cry out, my moan vibrating against Aidan's cock.

My breath grows ragged as I continue to take Aidan in my mouth, heat building within my core and spreading throughout my body as my heart races with desire. My coil tightens and I grab onto Brick's ponytail with my free hand, crushing his face further into my pussy as he continues to lap at me from my pussy up to my clit. He flattens his tongue against me, the bundle of nerves swollen with desire and pulsating at his touch.

My orgasm hits me with force, stars popping in my periphery as Brick and Roman lap at me while my hips buck wildly against their mouths. My pussy throbs and my whole body shudders as they continue to devour me, Brick lapping up the arousal that pours forth from my entrance. I gasp against Aidan's cock and he groans, not letting up as he keeps thrusting his cock in and out of my mouth. My hand continues to work Slade's cock, my movements jerky at the distraction of the orgasm that slams through me, but he doesn't seem to mind and instead takes my hand in his and continues to stroke.

Finally, my orgasm subsides, leaving my pussy buzzing with satisfaction. Brick and Roman both move back and kneel, and Aidan removes his still-hard cock from my mouth.

Brick swipes a tendril of hair away from my face. "That's our girl," he growls. "Look at the way you come for us. You did so good." I might have just came, but his words have my pussy clenching and ready to go again. But this time I want more. I want them inside of me, all four of them. I need to feel them claiming me from the inside. Showing me how much they need me, just as I need them.

I feel the cool, smooth sensation of silk as a blindfold is tied around my head.

"Wha—what's happening?" I pant?

"You're going to do what we say now," growls a voice at my side. It's hard to pick out who's who now.

"Get on top," rasps another voice, or maybe it's the same one. It's too hard to tell. I think it's Slade, but I can't be sure with all the sensations as hands continue to caress me. Blood throbs through my temples, but this time in a pleasant, exhilarating way, making it hard to differentiate tones and touches.

I reach out and touch large, muscular thighs covered in a manly sprinkling of hair, and I obediently climb up, straddling the figure and finding myself pressing firmly against a very hard erection. I reach out and grab it, immediately confirming by its length and girth that it is Slade. My pussy throbs in anticipation, and I line him up with my entrance. I slide my soaking pussy down onto him. "Good girl. You know this is our pussy. That you're all ours."

"Mmmhmm," I rasp as I slide myself up and down on his cock. Two sets of hands reach out, each grabbing one of my forearms and raising my hands up to my sides. They guide me as I bob my pussy up and down on Slade's cock, and he groans.

"Fuck, Angel. You're so fucking tight."

"And you're so fucking big, Slade," I moan.

"You know it's me?" He asks, sounding slightly surprised but also pleased.

"I'd recognize that cock anywhere, babe," I reply, a grin spreading over my face.

"Good girl," whispers a voice I think is Roman. He follows up by nipping at my ear and trailing kisses down my neck in a way that confirms it's him.

"Lean over," says a gruffer voice, and there's no question it's Brick. Complying, I lean forward so my tits press into Slade, my body squished against his while I continue to glide up and down on his cock. I feel a hand on my ass and then a cock pressed against my back entrance. Sure enough, Brick's identity is confirmed when the girthiest of the men pokes his tip inside me and I feel the smooth metal of his piercing. "Oh fuck, Angel," he cries out alongside my gasps as he works his way into my ass. My body tingles, zips of electricity running from my core to my extremities at the feeling of having two men inside me.

Roman moves forward, placing his cock inside my mouth and I take it eagerly, swirling my tongue around the tip and then the shaft. He's uncharacteristically forceful, overtaken by lust as he thrusts his hips and fucks my face. My saliva washes over his cock and he pulls it out briefly, causing the liquid to gush from my mouth, over his cock and onto the bed, strings of it attached from my mouth to his cock, causing him to groan.

"Oh fuck," he growls, and out of the corner of my eye, I see Aidan's eyes transfixed at the sight as he strokes himself.

"You're so fucking beautiful," growls Aidan as his hand works itself up and down his length. "You're the most perfect thing I've ever seen. And you're all ours. Look at all of them inside you at once."

He's right, and my body is so riddled with the sensations of each of them in me and on me and touching me in all kinds of ways that the coil snaps within my core and I come hard, arousal gushing from me as the orgasm slams through me so intensely I feel like I might pass out. My legs shudder as my pussy and ass clench around Slade and Brick.

"Your turn," I growl. I turn around, Aidan still kneeling on the bed behind me and I straddle him, facing away. I slam myself down onto his cock, sliding down with no resistance despite his size. I'm soaking from my own arousal, his precum and everything else. He moans as I bounce up and down, impaling myself on his rock hard cock with my soaked pussy. He reaches around and cups my breasts, tugging on my nipples as he rolls them between his thumbs and forefingers while the other guys watch. He's so patient, letting the other guys come first, even though I know he wants me just as much. Sometimes I think he might want me even more than I do, but he is never greedy. He knows he'll get his chance. That's one of the many things I love about him. And they're all like that to some degree. It just manifests in different ways.

I feel lightheaded. This session has been going on for a while now. I've come so many times and my body is becoming exhausted. But it's still tingling at the touch of these men, and I have no intention of stopping until we're all completely satisfied. I continue to bob up and down on Aidan's cock as he caresses my breasts. The other men look on, in various stages of hardness, but still all at least partially aroused. I know it's getting them off, watching me ride Aidan in this kneeling reverse cowgirl position, my back arching, which makes my breasts stick out as they bounce around wildly in Aidan's large hands.

And then it happens again. Without warning, the coil within me snaps as yet another orgasm rips through my body at lightning speed. I shriek as pleasure threatens to tear my body apart, my legs trembling uncontrollably. Aidan groans as my pussy clenches firmly around his cock and he comes as well. I feel his cock pulsing inside me as he unloads while the other guys look on, cocks in hand.

Finally, we're both done and we lie there with our limbs entangled while we regain our breath.

Slade strokes himself to completion, and I moan as his warm ejaculate coats my thigh and ass. I never used to think I was someone who liked to be jizzed on, but I've come to realize how much I enjoy it when these guys do it.

"Before we visited the island I didn't realize they made beds big enough for four big guys and a woman who's as hot as fuck. I'm so glad we got one of our own." Aidan smiles at me lazily.

"I know, right? It's a sound investment. Because I'm expecting many repeats of what happened tonight." Roman eyes me hungrily and licks his lips. "Not that I want to assume anything, of course."

"Oh, I'd love that," I wink at him and grin.

Because there's one thing I'm certain of.

I could never go back to not having this.

This is my new normal. It might not seem normal to other people. But I don't care what other people think. I never have.

This is my life, and I'm never going back.

Chapter Sixty-Five

Devon

"Tane gave you a boner, didn't he?" Rake smirks at me, his eyes twinkling with amusement.

I roll my eyes. "Listen. One, *way* too soon. And two, he's a criminal mastermind, not a male model."

"Just admit it, Dev. He turned you on." He grins and tries to tickle me and I pull away, flustered.

"I don't know what you're talking about!"

"Hey, it's totally fine," Rake wiggles his eyebrows. If I'm honest, he had the same effect on me. So much power, just radiating from his every pore. It was a turn-on."

I quirk an eyebrow at the ridiculousness of this man. "Oh yeah? What in particular?"

"He's just such a master of negotiation and manipulation. He's developed the most complex alliances and cultivated rivalries amongst his enemies. And he's done it all with such finesse. And his code of honor... the people that work for him have had such respect and loyalty toward him over the years. They'd never have double-crossed him. It's been the key to his success." Rakes eyes take on a dreamy appearance, and a lazy smile spreads across his face. "And he's smart about other stuff, too. You should have heard the way he spoke about literature, art and history in a recent podcast I listened to. He's incredibly well-read and cultured despite being raised in the criminal underworld." He pauses. "Although, to be fair, it sounds like that sentiment is changing quickly, on that island at least. And it was a bit pathetic of him when he ran away through that secret door."

I snort at the thought of Rake having a paradoxical man-crush on the biggest mafia boss of the islands. "You're so weird."

Rake shrugs. "I never claimed to be anything close to normal."

Chapter Sixty-Six

Devon

Angel was looking flushed this morning. She had a glow about her that I couldn't quite put my finger on at first. But by the way her eyes sparkled when she described getting some alone time with her guys, it didn't take much to figure out how the five of them had spent the night.

I felt a bit jealous at first, but my guys volunteered to help Dimitri and his men tie up some loose ends from yesterday and I know that needed to take priority. Knowing they were doing their part helped to put things in perspective. And now I have a plan of my own. It'll be my turn to be glowing just as soon as they've had a chance to rest. And I have quite the thing in mind. Something we've never tried before.

When they returned, I let them shower and rest for a moment, knowing they'd need their energy. But when they wake, I'm sitting naked on the side of the bed, and they waste no time figuring out what I want.

"Jesus, Devon," says Zeke, running his strong hand over my back. "You're so gorgeous." He kisses the small of my back and continues his way up my spine until he's breathing in my ear. He bites my ear lobe and my core clenches, my chest quivering at his touch.

The other guys quickly follow his lead. Soon, we're all naked, and I have so many hands on me that I can't work out who is doing what. All I know is that it feels incredibly good. Fuck, I'm lucky.

"Wow, we've sure come a long way from when we used to be together but keep things very one-on-one, haven't we?"

"What do you mean?"

"Well, each of you would fuck me, and sometimes some of you would watch. It could be one after the other, even. But the way we are now... the way we can all be involved at the same time... I never imagined it could be this way. It's exhilarating. Like our bodies are all working together, seeking the same thing. That you crave me and need me at the same time. And we've found ways for my body to reciprocate. To take all of you at once."

"Well, you most certainly have," smiles Skyler, gently swiping a lock of hair off my face and tucking it behind my ear. His eyes are soft and gentle and full of admiration. "You're our good girl, always figuring out how to please us. We're so proud of you."

"Well, I have something in mind to take things to the next level." I bite my lower lip. "I've been thinking about this a lot."

"What's that?" asks Skyler.

I feel a lightness in my chest, and my pulse quickens as I get ready to tell them what I have planned. Although, knowing them so well, I'm pretty sure they're going to be down with this idea.

I take a deep breath. "I want two of your cocks inside me at the same time. Well, all four, actually. But two *inside* the same part of me."

Rake clears his throat, and his eyes grow large. I've clearly got his attention. "We're talking in your pussy? Two of us?"

"Why not?" I grin and shrug, my pussy clenching at the thought. It's liberating being able to talk about something I've been thinking about for some time. It felt so forbidden when it was tucked away in my mind, just a nascent thought. But now that I've uttered the words out loud, it feels like I've freed a butterfly from its cocoon. It's still a little wobbly, but with a few stretches and a little practice, it's going to be ready to soar.

Just like me when it comes to saying what I want.

Angel has been a good influence for me in that regard, I think. And so has the closure from my dad.

"But you don't mean sword-crossing, right? You don't expect us to start touching each other," says Rake. "Even though I guess clearly two of our cocks are going to be right up against each other. But only for you."

"Not that there would be anything wrong with that," Zeke adds quickly. "But we've made it clear that it's just not something we do. Our attention is on you. Everything we do sexually is with *you*. Not with each other."

"Oh yeah, definitely," I reply. "This would be all about me."

"We're not small, though," says Dom. "You'd be taking a lot inside of you at one time. There's a risk we'll straight up split you in half."

I sneak a glance down at his crotch, knowing he knows full well he has the most girth. He's right, though. They're all large guys.

"Oh, I'm counting on it. I've been thinking about it a lot. And I'm ready for you."

Dom raises my arms above my head, using his large hands to grip my wrists together. I'm helpless, but I don't want to be helped.

"You really want this?" he rasps. "For such a good girl, you can be very bad."

"Mmm, I want this," I moan. "Please. I need all of you. Just, please...".

"Are you begging for our cocks, my little Devo?"

"Yes... I want all of your cocks. I need you right now."

"Beg for more if that's what you want," Dom growls.

"I'm... begging... you. Please. I need it."

There are so many hands everywhere. On my breasts, caressing my clit, cupping my ass. At one point, a large hand grabs hold of my hair and yanks it roughly to the side, exposing my neck. Someone nips at my throat and it sends shivers up my spine. I feel two mouths on me now, the breath from both somehow both hot and cool at the same time as they pant from their own exertion.

I don't know where to look. I close my eyes for a moment, relishing the multitude of sensations rushing through my body, coursing through every nerve ending. I feel full, and I can barely move, so I just let my body ride along with the rhythm of Dom and Zeke's hips that gently roll mine back and forth.

A large, rough hand tips my chin upward. "Eyes on me," Dom's deep voice commands. I immediately open my eyes and obey, his gaze meeting mine. His eyes are like midnight, consumed by lust. His teeth gnash against mine and I taste blood on my lips, and it only adds to the sensory overload I'm experiencing.

I moan, a low guttural sound forming in the base of my belly and humming into Dom's mouth.

"Do you see that? Look down," he growls, grabbing my hair in his hand and yanking my face downward this time so I can join him in watching as his and Zeke's cocks simultaneously plow my pussy.

"Oh my fucking god," I grit, my breath ragged as I watch the two men rhythmically pulsing in and out of me. It may be the hottest thing I've ever seen.

"Describe how it feels. Tell us how it feels to have two cocks inside you at once."

"I—," I pant, barely able to get the words out as the most electrifying sensations zap throughout my body. "I feel full, like you're stretching my pussy in the best way."

"You love being our little slut, don't you? Taking our cocks all at once. Aren't you a greedy girl?"

"I'm your greedy girl," I moan, and I mean it. I'm theirs.

"Can you feel how deep we both are inside you right now?"

"Yes," I groan. "So deep. I can't—". And I can't take it anymore. My body reacts to the pleasure of having two massive cocks inside me at once, and the orgasm hits me in rapid waves. My legs shudder forcefully and the clenching of my pussy almost pushes the two men out of me but they hold on tight, managing to stay inside as I ride it out.

"Fucking hell!" Dom grunts, and I feel him and then Zeke releasing inside of me in rapid succession, their cocks pulsating within me.

"Holy fuck!" I scream, and it almost sends me over the edge again. "I don't know how to describe that feeling but I want it again," I pant as they gently slide back out of me leaving me sticky and very satisfied.

Skyler brings over a damp washcloth and gently cleans me up. "There's nobody in this world like you, Devon baby," he says, leaning down to kiss me on my lips. "We're yours for life."

All I can do is lay there and smile while I regain my breath. "And what a life it is," I say softly. "I wouldn't change it for anything."

"You really mean that?" Rake asks, leaning down to kiss my forehead. "Because I guess I always thought I was here to save you. But now I find myself the one being saved."

I smile at him fondly. "And I thought you were the one that needed to be fixed. But then I realized it was me all along. Not that anything was fundamentally broken as such... although some would argue that was the case. But there was something missing. A void deep inside of me that I could never quite put a finger on. Until you came along, that is. For some, it would take one person to fix that gap. In my case, all four of you are my missing pieces. Some might call that greedy or weird. But it is what it is. Each of you fix me in a way that nobody else could. And between each of you, the void has gone. I'm complete. Your darkness has helped me to truly embrace my own for the first time. And in the darkness, you have shown me light."

Chapter Sixty-Seven

Aidan

"We need more time to plan before we're certain we'll get the upper hand. I don't want to delay this either, but we're firmly on his radar as a group and he's going to hit back stronger than ever. The good thing is, we've gathered enough intel to be able to hit him where it really hurts. And now we're fourteen strong instead of ten, with deep connections where he lives."

"You're so goddamn sensible, Aidan," growls Brick. "I was looking forward to inflicting pain on Tane and his men."

"Oh, you'll definitely be able to. It just won't be today. And don't act like you didn't get to inflict any violence while you were there. How many men did you torture, poison, and so on? So many. Including Denzo, who's been Tane's best guy since as long as anybody can remember. You especially had fun with him, too. You made his skin into a leather jacket and posted it to Tane, for goodness' sake."

A slow smile spreads across Brick's face, his eyes dreamy. "So many," he says. "Their screams were wonderful. Denzo's in particular. So I guess you're right. We just have to be a bit patient. I can do that."

"You sure you can wait? You're not going to go off on you own and do anything crazier than you have already? It could compromise everything for us just because you have the urge to inflict more violence before we're ready. No more poison dart frogs, and no more contaminated meat. And definitely no more leather jackets. At least not in Tane's direct world."

Brick lips his lips, scraping his bottom lip with his teeth as he glances in Angel's direction. "I guess I'll have to channel my obsession toward other pursuits in the meantime," he says, his gaze trailing across her body. "Find other, more constructive ways to inflict pain and derive my own pleasure."

Angel gazes back at him, her eyes locked on his from underneath her long, dark eyelashes. She smiles. "I'll do whatever I can to help you with that, baby."

"Oh you," he says, playfully batting at her arm and grinning. "It's so nice to know I can always count on you. And I'll be patient because I want to check out the mass grave the girls told us about."

I laugh and shake my head.

Brick really does always have an angle when it comes to Angel.

But really, don't we all?

Any chance to be with her.

To get to know her better.

To bond more closely with her than we already have.

Give her pleasure. Receive her pleasure.

To be inside of her. To devour her.

We want it all.

And she wants it all just as much as we do.

God, I love this woman.

And so it begins. Another chapter. It's an ongoing journey. Sometimes I wonder if I'll ever long for its ending, but that's always just a fleeting thought before I realize that, in many ways, I hope it never does.

ABOUT THE AUTHOR

Heidi Stark is an indie dark romance author who grew up in New Zealand and now resides in the US.

She is inspired by the locations she visits on her travels, and the people she meets along the way.

When she's not writing, you can usually find her voraciously reading dark romance, listening to podcasts, dreaming about her next book, or indulging her reality TV obsession.

Learn more about Heidi Stark at her website. Sign up for exclusive content and her newsletter here.

You can also find out more about Heidi and her upcoming books on social media:

Facebook Page

Facebook Group

Instagram

TikTok

Also By

Standalones

- Ruthless Choices

Blood and Sand (Dark Reverse Harem Mafia Romance)

- Sea of Snakes(Book 1)

- Sea of Sinners(Book 2)

- Sea of Rage (Book 3)

- Sea of Pain(Book 4)

- Sinners, Rage & Pain: The Brixton Trilogy(Books 2, 3 and 4)

- Sea of Demons(Book 5)

Billionaire's Takeover Collection

- Irreversible Decision

- Compelling Proposal

- Love Merger

- The Billionaire's Takeover Collection (all 3 of the above!)

Novellas

- Love in a Seedy Motel Room

Sign up for my newsletter herefor the latest on new releases, promos, giveaways and events!

Join me on social media:

Facebook: @heidistarkauthor

Instagram: @heiditstarkauthor

TikTok: @heidistark_author

Twitter: @heidistarkauthr

Websitehttps://heidistarkauthor.com